5.95

Gabrielle Roy's prominent role in the literature of Canada was established with the publication of her first novel in 1945. That book, *The Tin Flute* (or *Bonheur d'occasion*, as it was titled in the original French), was awarded the Prix Fémina, thus becoming the first Canadian work to win a major French literary prize. It also earned a Governor General's Award.

In 1947 Miss Roy was elected to the Royal Society of Canada. She won a second Governor General's Award in 1957, this time for *Street of Riches*, which also won the Prix Duvernay. In 1971 the Quebec government awarded her the Prix David for her entire body of work, which includes ten novels.

The youngest of eleven children, the author was born in St. Boniface, Manitoba, and was educated there and at the Winnipeg Normal School. After teaching for some years in rural Manitoba, she travelled to England and France where she studied drama and began to write. At the outbreak of World War II, she returned to Canada and made her home in Montreal.

In 1947 she married Dr. Marcel Carbotte. Since 1950, Gabrielle Roy and her husband have lived in Quebec City.

Gabrielle Roy

Garden
in the Wind

Translated by Alan Brown

Enchanted Summer

Translated by Joyce Marshall

General Editor: Malcolm Ross

New Canadian Library No. 155

McClelland and Stewart

The Canadian Publishers
McClelland and Stewart Limited
25 Hollinger Road, Toronto

Manufactured in Canada by Webcom Limited

Books by Gabrielle Roy

The Tin Flute
The Cashier
Where Nests the Water Hen
Street of Riches
The Road Past Altamont
The Hidden Mountain
Windflower
Enchanted Summer
Garden in the Wind
Children of My Heart

Garden in the Wind

Contents

*F*ar be it from me to propose an interpretation of my writings or characters to those kind enough to be my readers. I would much prefer to know what they think about these things.

For once, however, I think it may be useful to give some explanation of the short stories in this book. Two of them, published elsewhere, appear here in reworked form. The first, *A Tramp at the Door*, was rewritten more than twenty years after its first version. It is a dangerous undertaking to try to tighten the meaning of an old text without losing the candour or the original lyricism that gave birth to it. If I persisted in taking up this story again it is because it represents rather well, I think, the slightly medieval or "holy-image" aspect under which, far out on the plains, when I was a child, Quebec appeared to us, through the medium of our parents' stories on the subject. They were immigrants to Manitoba, but they had never, in their hearts, left their Lower Canada behind, and they embroidered, they embroidered. . . . If ever Quebec held an irresistible attraction for its scattered children

9

it was surely at that time, through the magic of tales told around the old Majestic stove.

More or less for the same reason I dug out again the story *Hoodoo Valley*, a fairly just account, I thought, of the chimerical dreams that guided so many immigrants of Eastern and Central Europe in their settlement in the lands of the Canadian West: poor people who, because they had tried to follow their star, ended in the most total disillusionment. These unlucky dreams I learned of through the recollections of my father who, as an officer of the federal government, had the responsibility for settling many colonies of Slavic origin, and particularly a group of Doukhobors, "people as gentle," he said, "as they were impossible to convince."

The two other stories in this volume were not previously published. *Where Will You Go, Sam Lee Wong?* was left for a long time at the stage of a first sketch, abandoned, as it were, along the road, and would no doubt have stayed there had it not been for the persistent way in which this Chinese came back to haunt me, reminding me that I might be the only one who had imagined his life and, as a result, was able to give it reality. What power such a summons has over a writer's heart, coming out of God knows what limbo from a character begging to be given life!

In the same way, *Garden in the Wind* was born of the passing vision I had one day of a garden filled with flowers at the very outer limit of cultivated territory, and of a woman working there, in the wind, a kerchief on her head, who looked up and followed me with a long, perplexed and supplicating gaze which never left my memory and never ceased to demand – for years and years – the thing we are all asking for, from the very depths of our silence: Tell about my life.

G.R.

A Tramp
at the Door

A Tramp
at the Door

My mother was expecting something or other. She kept going to the door, drawing back from the windowpane the white curtain hemmed in red linen and staring long and vaguely out at the drenched countryside. Suddenly she gave a start, one hand going up to her forehead.

"Somebody's coming," she announced, and went on, her voice filled with surprise: "Coming here, it looks like!"

Rain was rattling on the roof. On either side of the house we could hear water from the spouts splashing down from the overflowing rain barrels. Evening was falling. From the ditches, filled to their banks, a white steam went up. Beyond the slope of the rye field you could see no more than a few blackened, bare treetops emerging soaked from the mist. For two days we hadn't seen a living soul pass by. "Not a cat, not even a beggar," my mother had sighed.

The man pushed the gate open. We could see him tip back his head and try to smile as he saw the two gable windows of the house and perhaps the smoke from the chimney. With every step he had to fight the wind, pulling his dark coat tight around him. The garden shrubs near him were twisted and

13

tousled by the wind. Because of the shadow that already lay dark beneath the hedge, the man was on top of Farouche's kennel before he saw our German shepherd about to spring.

My mother stifled a cry.

Almost at once we saw Farouche wagging his tail, wiggling his body and crouching in front of this man whose strangely gentle, coaxing tone we in the house could catch between the gusts of the storm.

My mother breathed a great sigh, even more astonished than she was relieved.

"Well," she said, "that's the first time I ever saw Farouche make friends that fast!"

The man straightened up and seemed to be surveying all the ways of entering the house. Finally, overcoming his hesitation, he made a half-turn and came rapping on the back door which looked out on the farmyard.

My father, sitting by the fire, was in the grip of the unbearable boredom he suffered with each return of the wet season to our country of the plains. The whole day long he hadn't said a word. You wondered if he really felt he belonged there with the rest of us. Buried in his thoughts, he hadn't seen the stranger coming, and even the sound of our voices had most likely not come through to him.

"It's somebody who doesn't know his way around here." This was my mother again as she gestured to me to open the door.

As soon as autumn came we lived in the big room. The small lean-to that served as a kitchen in the summertime now turned into a kind of storage space where we could pile furniture and tools no longer needed. I went through this freezing space and with difficulty lifted the rusty latch. A wallop of rain took me in the face. The man's head appeared, feebly lit by a vestige of light coming from the big puddles around the

14

pump. All in all, it was a rather nice tramp's face, the kind that isn't any particular age and asks for a bowl of soup and will go on his way right afterwards if he isn't offered an attic for the night. We didn't see those people often in our out-of-the-way parts, maybe one or two a year, if that. But this one seemed to have a certain dignity and wasn't in a hurry to beg. A short, reddish, frizzy beard, pearled with great raindrops, invaded half his cheeks; the peak of his cap threw a clean line of shadow on his forehead. His eyes, very gentle and smiling, almost tender, sparkled under the wet fringe of his lashes.

"Well! My little cousin!" he cried in a voice that was as soft and flexible and unsettling as his gaze. "You must be my little cousin Alice!" he went on, laughing.

I shook my head.

"No? Must be Agnes, then!"

"No," I said, irritated. "I'm Ghislaine."

"Of course, just what I thought! Of course you're Ghislaine. I should have known it, even if I never saw you."

As he spoke, his hands made as if they were drying each other, and he laughed behind his beard and his foot cleverly pushed at the door I was holding slightly open.

Somehow he was inside.

"This is the Rondeaus' house, I guess?" he asked, and his incredible, friendly smile swept around the interior of the damp, cold shed as if he found it welcoming and filled with people.

"No," I said, "we're the Trudeaus."

"Why, sure, just as I was going to say," he went on coolly. "Rondeau, Trudeau, names as like as peas. Right, cousin?"

He gave me a little nudge, and I saw his eyes shining with satisfaction.

"Now, little girl, you just go and tell your father there's a cousin here from the land of Quebec."

I went before him into the big room – he was right on my heels – and blurted out to my father, as if in mocking reproach: "He says he's a cousin from Quebec."

My father stood up and made an odd gesture, as if to take the stranger in his arms, but the impulse failed him. Yet his handsome, aging, peaceful face betrayed not so much a withdrawal as the vagueness of someone suddenly awakened from a dream.

"Well, now! What part of Quebec? Saint-Alphonse?"

"Saint-Alphonse," said the man.

He approached the stove. His clothes were starting to steam. My mother brought the Aladdin lamp. She lifted it a little above the stranger and you could see great rips in his clothing, some held together by bits of string, others gaping to reveal glimpses of his red shirt.

But the man directed at my mother a gaze so filled with friendship that she set down the lamp and busied herself elsewhere without speaking. We could see that she was excited from the way she opened all the drawers of the sideboard without finding what she wanted.

For a moment the man stood alone in the middle of the room, trying to catch our eyes, which fled his. He drew up a chair by the stove, sat down and breathed a great sigh of well-being.

Then in the silence, two or three times, we could hear his soft, rather drawling voice: "Saint-Alphonse, yes sir. That's where I come from. Saint-Alphonse. . . ."

My father took out his tobacco pouch. He was about to fill his pipe when the stranger held out a hand and, unabashed, helped himself to the tobacco. Then, after lighting a short clay pipe, he settled back in his chair and murmured distinctly: "Thank you. Much obliged."

The two men smoked. My mother fussed among her pots

16

with an unusual amount of noise. And sometimes her lips opened as if she were about to say some wounding word. The stranger looked around at us children sitting in the corners, observing one after the other, and smiled out of his beard. He made little jabs with his chin, winked at each of us, then started the rounds again. A badger that we had tamed, still highly suspicious of strangers, actually slipped under the man's chair. He took it by the scruff of its neck and laid it in his lap. The little animal, far from protesting, licked his wet beard and, its claws retracted, allowed itself to be rocked like a baby. As wild and speechless as our only friends – our animals – we were astounded to see that two of them had taken up with this stranger. Even my mother seemed impressed, and that must have aggravated her ill humour. Little by little we slid off our chairs to come nearer. The strange man gave us signs of encouragement in the manner of the magician our parents had once taken us to see at the rodeo in the next village.

My father had stood up. He was pacing to and fro in the room, his hands behind his back. Then, planting himself in front of the vagabond, he asked: "But whose boy would you be then?"

"Me?" said the man. "Why, the one that disappeared."

A glimmer of interest showed beneath my father's lowered eyelids.

"Gustave?"

"Yep. Gustave."

"But they thought he was dead!"

"He wasn't dead. He went to the States. I'm his boy."

"Oh!" said my father. "You're his boy!"

"I'm his boy," the stranger repeated in a voice that was soft and stubborn.

And he turned his smiling face to where my mother was

beating her pancake batter. He seemed determined to drag from her a look, a smile, a word. But she was speeding up her supper preparations so as to stay out of the conversation. It wasn't long before the first spoonful of batter dropped into the hot frying pan. A pleasant odour filled the room. Outside, darkness spread over the desolate, naked landscape. All that could still be seen through the windowpanes was the vague glimmer of water accumulated in great pools between the patches of brush, in the hollows of the plain or running in streams. The man stretched out his legs. He took time to look around the room, low-ceilinged, large, furnished with an oak sideboard and old, modest but solid pieces so well-polished and softened by use that they reflected a long contentment. Then, without moving, he began smiling at nothing again, to himself.

"But what put you onto our trail?" my father asked suddenly.

The stranger raised his blue eyes, which shone in the direct rays of the lamp.

"In Saint-Alphonse."

"Oh!"

My father gave a long sigh.

"It's been a mighty long time since I saw hide or hair of any of them from Saint-Alphonse."

It was his turn to look toward my mother, so tiny, so much younger than he. A big apron tied around her waist, she was leaning attentively above her pan and the flame at times leapt perilously close to her face.

"How long is it now, Albertine, since I was in those parts?"

And indeed it was she who was charged with refreshing his memory on events he had described to her about people she had never seen.

She took a little while to reflect, mentally juggling dates, her pretty eyebrows arched high and her mouth a little open.

"You told me you were fourteen when you left home and you hadn't set foot there since. You figure it out. About fifty years, if you were telling the truth."

She always ended up with that reservation, as if to throw back the error, if error there was, solely upon my father.

Then, sulking a little, and because the stranger's presence doubtless irritated her, she added: "What's more, you haven't written the folks at home for fifteen years. It's a real shame!"

"Yes," said my father, ignoring his wife's last remark. "It'll be fifty years. I wouldn't even know them back there anymore."

He looked down, his face lit up by distant, melancholy memories.

My mother placed her fists on her hips. Quickly, without looking at the stranger, she said: "It's ready! Come on, children. Come and eat, Arthur."

The tramp too stood up gaily. He chose a seat by the wall, slid in, pulling his wretched jacket tight around him, and, once established, seized his fork.

"Yes," my father mused, "there's a lot of things back there I never heard a word about."

The man speared a large slice of bread with his fork. He bit the bread in the middle, then, smiling, his mouth full, he promised: "I'll tell you all about it after."

II

After supper he actually did begin to tell us about the relatives, helped along by my father who would situate things in time by his questions: "Marcelline, now, you must have found she'd aged? And I suppose Eustache took over the farm. . . ."

We knew very little about my father's people. He'd never told us at one time how many brothers and sisters he had. On occasion, and as his reveries would have it, he would let a name drop: Marcelline, Philomène, Aristide. His tone changed, too, according to his mood.

One day, for example, when the soup was too salty, he had grumbled: "Albertine, are you going to start making salty soup like Philomène?"

"Who is Philomène?" we asked.

My father seemed more disconcerted at having provoked the question than by our breathless curiosity. Philomène, he finally admitted, was his father's second wife. A sign from my mother at that moment advised us not to push our researches any further. So it was that my father managed to keep the shades of his childhood for himself alone. At times, though, he himself renewed this singular aura of mystery attached to our uncles and aunts in Quebec. He spoke of ill-defined figures and always in the past tense, as if they had ceased to exist. That's why we were surprised that evening to hear him say, "Marcelline, now, she must have aged?"

Marcelline had made her entry into our family one evening when my father, seeing my mother patching old clothes, protested: "Now don't you start going on like that penny-pincher Marcelline!" The moment his sister's name had slipped out he walled himself in silence.

Others popped up, as faceless as Marcelline. They seemed incredibly far away yet, like that Marcelline, they would suddenly become attached to our lives through their penchant for patching old rags or because of a dreamy warmth that would spread at twilight through the house. And we never knew how many shadowy beings would rise up at our next question, behind Philomène or Marcelline, or if they'd be revealed thanks to some irritation of my father's or in a moment of more tender feeling. One thing we did know: you had to wait for these confidences, never push.

Well, that evening my father sat close to our strange visitor and, behold, names were flying from his lips, those associated with his ill humour as well as the ones we heard on feast days – and others we had never heard at all: Uncle France, Aunt Eléonore, Cousin Brault. You'd have thought a dike that had stood too long against the past had given under the flood of hurrying memories. The visitor gave little signs of approval. His eyes followed my father with an attentiveness that was ingratiating, sustained and encouraging, an attentiveness I have in later life observed in very few human beings. Truly, we might have imagined that it was my father who had just arrived from his travels and that the other one was there only to corroborate the facts or testify to them.

At last, when my father gave the other his turn, our visitor started in with his own stories. He spoke in a restful voice that he seldom raised. He dipped into his memories as into a heap of thick and rustling leaves, fallen at the trees' roots, in autumn.

We, the Trudeaus, were, according to him, a family out of the ordinary. The old couple, alas! had died working, on land that was richer in stones than pasture. But they had left behind them solid testimonials to their ingenuity, a thousand things well done, well carried out, if it was no more than a fence, a barn door or a delicately sculptured weathercock on the roof of that same barn. Whereas nowadays. . . .

Several times he stopped to make sure that my father was listening with pleasure. In fact, my father seemed to have changed, to have emerged from a kind of penumbra as he renewed touch, so to speak, with his family, divided and scattered to all corners of the country by obscure misfortunes or obstinacies. In one swift glance our visitor would seize the trace of an emotion; then, sure of his trail, he would take off again without more emphasis but as if animated by a great desire to please.

What began to strike us then about this singular creature was that from the depths of his solitude he accused no one but seemed rather to assume all faults himself.

On the subject of family, however, it can't be said that he gave us many important details that first evening. Apart from that, he described minutely Christmas parties, New Years' parties, winter-evening parties, wedding parties, and suddenly Montreal, the great city, and suddenly Joliette, the small city, where the people of Saint-Alphonse went shopping. Then he'd comment on pioneer days, only to drift unexpectedly to meals of buckwheat cakes and wild honey or memories of square dances in the kitchen; and we'd see my father tapping lightly on the floor with toe and heel.

But already, through our visitor's account, these vague, far-off relatives of ours all seemed to have changed their characters – even Marcelline, who was no longer grasping, only provident. Eustache had inherited the paternal land and made it bear fruit; he raised his children courageously. Anais, now, there was nobody like her for spinning the local wool and filling the cupboard with bolts of homespun. Devout she was, too, never missed her week-day mass. Uncle France had made it to a hundred, and they'd had a fine Christian birthday for him with all the children and grandchildren, of whom two were attending the seminary and three had taken vows. Family was something sacred: nothing could be as touching as the members of a single family knowing each other by their voices and opening their arms. Alas, people sometimes rejected their own flesh and blood when it turned up from afar, especially if it wasn't very clean or a particularly shining case.

This was said in a tone of resignation that made us all hang our heads, except my mother who, on the contrary, raised hers defiantly. She was sewing, a little off to one side, sticking her needle so impatiently into the cloth that she often pricked herself. Then we could hear her groan softly as she put her lips to the finger where a drop of blood was forming.

In the middle of a silence my father asked: "Marcelline, now . . . did she ever mention me, sometimes?"

The man assured him warmly: "Oh, for sure! She often talked about her brother. . ."

"Arthur." My father completed the sentence.

"That's it, Arthur."

My father pulled up his chair until his foot almost touched the stranger's muddy boots. He lit his pipe for the fourth time and asked a question that astonished us greatly.

"Did they know back there that I'd been appointed justice of the peace?"

"They knew it," affirmed the vagabond. "Marcelline was very proud."

A happy silence followed, broken by my mother's noisy sigh.

The man turned in her direction: "What about you, cousin, which parish are you from? Maybe I know your people too. . . ."

My mother rose up, all round and little and trembling at this mode of address, as if the stranger's hand had touched her.

"She's from the prairies," my father hastened to explain. "I married her out here."

"What of it?" the man insisted. "I've drifted around every which way at harvest times. Maybe I knew her folks."

No one took him up on it. The man seemed hurt. A little later his pale-blue gaze grew fixed and we could see that he was close to sleep. For a second his eyelids would drop, his eyes would glaze, and before they closed you could see in them a vague smile of apology and a slightly crestfallen expression.

It had just struck eleven. But my mother was acting as if the evening had just begun. My father, for his part, kept looking at the clock, pulling out his watch and comparing the two. The stranger dozed in his chair for minutes at a time, then awoke with a start, trying to cover up by winking at each of us in turn and changing posture.

My father said suddenly: "Hey, children! It's bedtime!" Then, without waiting for my mother's approval, he suggested: "Maybe you could make up a bed, Albertine. . ." He hesitated, then concluded: ". . .for our cousin. . . ."

"Gustave. After my father," explained the stranger,

yawning. "Gustave, that's me."

My mother stood up without a word, took the lamp and left us in shadows and then in darkness as she went up the steps leading to the attic. We could hear her moving a cot around, opening trunks. Through the half-open trap door a cold draught swept down on our shoulders, soon bearing with it the odour of fresh linen.

Later, having awakened, I could hear my mother speaking in a low voice to my father: "You always told me your brother Gustave was built like a giant, tall and broad, the strongest one in the family. This one's a puny runt. . . ."

"Far as that goes," my father replied, "you take any family around here. The big men don't always have the big sons. Maybe he takes after his mother," he added after a pause.

"That may be, but couldn't you see he was at a loss for an answer when you asked him for news of Marcelline and Philomène?"

"That's only natural. He's been on the road a lot. It couldn't all come back at once."

"Oh, that's the excuse, is it?" exclaimed my mother in a hostile, discouraged tone.

In the next room to theirs the man was snoring peacefully. Once he mumbled a few words in his sleep. Then I thought I heard, at the end of a jovial little laugh: "Good day! Good day, dear cousin!"

III

He stayed at our house three weeks. My mother gave him some clothes left by a former hired man, and they were about Gustave's size. Early in the morning, he used to wash in the kitchen sink, and comb his beard, and turn out quite presentable.

During the day he tried to make himself useful and took special pains to anticipate my mother's wishes. He'd bring in wood; run to the well as soon as the pail was dry, repair the traps. One day when she complained there'd been no mail for a week because of the roads, he went off on foot to the village. He came back at day's end with a letter which he held out to her in the hope, no doubt, of getting a friendly word.

In spite of everything we couldn't get used to the idea that he was supposed to be our cousin. We ordered him around like a farm hand. "Better get the wood in before the rain soaks it." In the daytime we called him "you" or "the man" or "him." My mother, above all, because she was afraid of having him with us all winter, would say each morning, looking out at the road unwinding toward the dark, dank woods:

"There's going to be a big snowstorm before long. A person won't even be able to get out of here."

The man seemed not to hear. In the daytime we paid little attention to him. But in the evening, as soon as the lighted lamp stood on the table, this strange creature, through what kind of spell we didn't know, became indispensable to us. Every evening he again turned into "Cousin Gustave."

He appeared sensitive to this kind of disgrace, of which we absolved him every evening. Silent the whole day long, he regained the use of words as soon as our eyes, grown softer, consented to look at him again. Then, in his quiet, unchanging voice, he would once more tell the story of Marcelline's second wedding, or Uncle France's hundredth birthday, but always adding fresh details. "Hey, you didn't mention that last time!" my father would cry. And Gustave would look at him with a vague reproach in his eyes, as if he wanted to say: The things I know are too vast, too many-sided. You can't get all that out at once.

"Well, go on," my father would hurry him.

Gustave, cut adrift from his vision, would set off again, but on a new tack.

His stories proceeded by short stages, often interrupted at the most touching or fascinating part, so that we were always inclined to give him another day of hospitality in order to hear the end. And finally we had to admit it to ourselves: if Gustave's story the previous night had been a good one, we were polite and well disposed toward him the following day. But when he'd disappointed us, we had ways, unconsciously but cruelly, of showing him.

Well, this fellow Gustave grew very skilful. He spun his stories out. He cut them into little slices in a way that later became familiar to us through the radio. Everything was used to stretch them out. The landscape would be painstakingly described. The village teacher, the notary and the doctor had their parts to play. Jumping from one family to the next, it might happen that he got into events that barely concerned us but livened up his story immeasurably. There was one about the son of Magloire the blacksmith who hanged himself in the barn with his own belt; and the one about Fortunat who, at the age of twenty, married a rich widow of fifty.

One evening, when I pointed out that all this had nothing to do with us, he turned toward me a look that was courageous and untamed: "Come now! Who's related to who? There's a question: where it starts, where it stops, who knows?"

Then, as if he realized that our suspicions could be nourished by this odd remark, he gave a little strangled laugh and went patiently back to the tale that especially pleased my father, about Marcelline's second wedding. Little by little he grew lively again, and treated us to the fiddler who had made Marcelline, at fifty-five, dance for the first time in her life.

"What! She got up and danced?" asked my father.

"Yes, sir, she danced!" Gustave affirmed.

And in his eyes as pale as water we thought we saw Marcelline's cotton lustre skirt whirl and pass by.

"So she got up and danced!" repeated my father, delighted.

One night my father mentioned two of his brothers who had also settled out West, Uncle Alfred in Saskatchewan and Uncle Edouard in Alberta. In a sentimental mood, he admitted his regret that he had failed to keep in touch at least with these two.

Gustave let my father go on for some time, then he promised, in that spell-binding voice which sometimes sang through our house like the winds of the wide world: "Who knows, maybe I'll drop in and see them one of these days! You just give me the right address and if the good Lord wills, I'll give them your regards."

That was all that was said about our western uncles, whom we had seen only once, Alfred when he had started off from Montreal and stopped to see us on the way, and Edouard when he had arrived from Quebec with his family and almost settled nearby.

As Gustave could give us no news of these two, my father asked for more news from Quebec, in particular about a charlatan he had known in his youth and who, it seemed, had made a fortune.

"Oh, yes! Ephrem Brabant!" said Gustave.

And that evening he began a story that lasted almost a week.

This charlatan, Ephrem Brabant by name, had started off by handing out samples of his cough syrup to the congregation as they left the chilly church on Sunday mornings. But the remedy that someone had taken for his cold had miraculously cured him of another much more serious illness. Thanks to an early spring, the news of the cure spread rapidly around the countryside. It was at once attributed to Ephrem, who was a "seventh son."

Now Ephrem wasn't about to belittle the powers and properties of his remedy any more than he denied the supernatural gifts attributed to him. A pious man, gentle and charitable, he was quite ready to admit that faith helped medicine along. So, as he enjoined his customers to prayer, he sold them more and more little bottles. The same herbal product with different labels and in different containers brought relief to stomach cramps, asthma and rheumatic pains.

Ephrem's renown spread beyond the limits of the village. Soon he had a little covered cart and a horse as black as night, and he went from farm to farm leaving brown bottles wherever he stopped. People in perfect health tried his remedy and declared they felt none the worse, which added to Ephrem Brabant's prestige as much as the cures themselves. He had grown a beard, which he trimmed to a point, and wore a black, wide-rimmed hat. His photo appeared on the bottles of syrup. Everyone in the area called him Dr. Brabant. It was at this time that he had the notion of writing and distributing an almanac to publicize the testimonials of people cured by his attentions. It was to contain, as well, practical advice for people of various ages, the interpretation of dreams and all the known signs of good or inclement weather. The fellow could neither read nor write, but he had immense practical knowledge based on direct observation of rural life. For the spelling and fine phrases he depended on a son he had sent to school. He moved to Montreal, to a luxurious house, and despite being hauled to court, he accumulated a tidy fortune.

This was the story Gustave told us. Or, rather, this was the version we created with the passage of time and according to our desire to draw our own conclusions. Gustave must have told it more simply, and perhaps with more indulgence. For he blamed no one, judged no one. Almost every creature found mercy before him. If some really bad ones turned up, Gustave had them die off quickly, which in the end appeased my mother.

IV

Now that I think of it, it's true he talked very little about the members of our own family, apart from saying they were fine people. The unforgettable ones he managed to dig up elsewhere. After the story of Brabant, he told us about Roma Poirier who murdered her husband by putting ground glass in his soup day after day. Oh, the strange, cruel and fascinating beings he brought to our place in the evenings, when the pails swung and rattled on the fence posts outside and from the woodland's edge coyotes yapped incessantly.

Long after he had left, as unexpectedly as he had come, long after his features had blurred in our memories, or his gentle way of smiling as he talked of the most sinister events, it would happen that those characters – the charlatan, the murderess, the old man of a hundred and I don't know how many more – would turn up in our thoughts. A whole unconnected cohort, the friends of Gustave the tramp, who revealed them to us perhaps less through his words than through a certain slow way of pulling back his coat as he reflected on their lives, or by an occasional amused smile at the troop of them.

He knew the great wickedness of the world quite well but he neither judged it nor renounced it. Nor the great distress of the world. Of that he sometimes gave us a glimpse beneath his heavy eyelids, as he stared at a windowpane whipped by rain and branches.

But, above all, it was the great piety of the world that he had seen and recognized.

And through this, in the end, he found grace even in my mother's eyes.

One night he was telling about the pilgrims flocking to the sanctuary of Sainte-Anne-de-Beaupré. The nave appeared before us, filled with votive offerings, with longboats and schooners for lamps. Thousands of crutches hung between the stations of the Cross, as if the lame, on their march toward God, had recovered their agility and taken off for heaven through the pale openings of the stained-glass windows. A pious murmur rose in the shadows; our house was too small to contain the piety of the pilgrims, their thanksgiving, their wild hope. Gustave led us beyond all the paths we knew. We followed his blue gaze, a pool of water in the night, toward a dim region through which he led us to the sound of chants and organs.

There was always someone who sighed loudly when Gustave's voice fell silent and we came back to the reality of our house.

Of course he mixed up times and persons, but which of us, living on the prairie, far from the beaten path, could have told true from false in his accounts?

He had quickly seen that the mistress of the house appeared to listen only when he talked of miracles and pilgrimages. From that moment we could get him to speak of nothing else. He carried us to the places of prayer up and down the length of the St. Lawrence. At the very words "St. Lawrence," we were captured at once, for he had given us such a gripping vision of the river. He talked of it as a living creature, a tumultuous force, and yet at times so kind that its flow made no more than a murmur. He had described it as having its source in the Niagara cataracts (he was a little careless about geographical accuracy). Then he showed us how it fled toward the sea, encircling a great island whose name we loved: Anticosti.

Then one evening he ran out of places of prayer on the St. Lawrence. And he began to describe St. Joseph's Oratory, built stone after stone with the people's offerings. My mother (she had a special devotion for Brother André) stopped sewing and for the first time spoke directly to Gustave. She normally addressed him through the mediation of one of the children. "Ask him," she'd say, "if he's seen the hammer"; or, "Was he the one that took the shovel? See if you can find out. . . ." For in the process of making himself useful he mislaid things, and my mother, who would have had scruples about accusing him directly, didn't hesitate to burden him with a latent guilt.

But this time she looked him in the eye and said: "Tell me, did you ever see him? Brother André?"

Perhaps Gustave felt the full risk of a careless answer. My mother, depending on her mood, would give him a heaping plateful at dinner, or nothing but the less tasty scraps. Did he understand the thirst for spiritual adventure that lived in this serious little woman, sentimental and deprived of the joys of church? Could he conceive of her longing for "back home," she who had been born out here in the plains? And maybe, after all, he *had* seen Brother André, for had he not assured us that he'd seen the Prince of Wales and Sarah Bernhardt? In any case, he described him to us so faithfully that much later, when we received a calendar from Quebec

33

bearing a lithograph of the saintly Brother, we all exclaimed, "That was him, sure enough!"

For greater effect he assured us at the end, after his accumulation of evidence: "I saw him the way I see you now...Madame!"

He no longer dared to say "Cousin" to her, but could not pronounce "Madame" without a perceptible hesitation and a note of regret.

From that moment on he grew in my mother's esteem. Henceforth, she gave him an attention which if not always benevolent was at least sustained.

V

But this state of affairs didn't last long. This little devil of a man, who could down plates of porridge in the early morning and fried pork piled up on his plate at other meals without putting on a pound, this "puny runt," as my mother called him, for she still doubted at times whether he had really seen the faces of saints and sanctuaries, this tranquil old soul, perhaps he was waiting for nothing more than to tame my mother, and then away he'd go, leaving the fireside, the set table and the lamp that shone in the window on rainy nights.

One morning we caught him at the door, staring at the scrubby copses that cut the horizon beyond the swollen coulee. The rain was still falling. Soon it was mixed with snow, and before the day's end the prairie, under its puffy vestment, seemed quite round. Only once did we see him at the door. But we knew he wanted to be on his way, as we had known three weeks before, just from seeing him sit down and sniff the smells of the house, that he wanted to stay. He was just like a big, skinny dog we'd had when we were small, who would beg to come in when the weather was bad and beg to go out when it was worse.

It was no use, my father's going back to the stories of Marcelline and France and Cousin Brault the fiddler, who left by himself for Montreal with his violin and played in orchestras there to the great shame of the family: Gustave's face had darkened. He looked at the door, nothing but the door, the one through which he had made such a joyous entrance. He looked nowhere else and seemed to be pining away each day. For we were witnesses to a strange phenomenon: the clothes my mother had given him seemed to be his own as long as he was happy to stay among us, but then we saw them collapse, hang loose about his shoulders, getting in his way. And what about the stories, the wonderful stories forever extinguished in his eyes! As the sky of our prairies is empty when all the wings have flown south, so Gustave's eyes grew bleak and, as it were, uninhabited. That was perhaps what we held against him most: not having any stories in reserve behind the farther mists of his pale smile.

One evening my father went so far as to offer him a little pay if he wanted to work. My mother showed no offence. Gustave's eyes were grateful, but he gave no other reply.

Next day he was gone. He must have slipped off at night, raising the latches cautiously. Farouche hadn't barked.

My mother flew into a rage. She ran to the silver drawer, to the relic box, to the crockery pot where the change was kept; nothing was missing anywhere. She counted the knives, the spoons, the candlesticks, but had to admit they were all there. Then she was even more humiliated.

"What did we do to make him leave like that?"

My father, for his part, inspected the barn, the granaries, the sheds. He came back discomfitted. The shadows on his mute face revealed a regret that did not fade away. From time

36

to time he sighed. At last one evening we heard him complaining, or accusing us: "We didn't receive him the way he deserved. He showed us: he went away."

But we had news of him the following year. In the mail one evening, along with the catalogue from the store in town and the weekly newspaper, was an envelope covered with an unknown handwriting, awkward and blotted with ink spots. My mother opened it at once. Leaning over her shoulder we read along with her. From the wet smell of the paper I cried out before reading a word: "It's from Gustave!"

A skip to the laborious and childish signature confirmed it. It was Gustave's.

He'd made it to Uncle Alfred's place in Saskatchewan and said he'd been asked to send regards. He said very kind things about the three girls, Emilie, Alma and Céline, whom my father, by the way, had described as hard to marry off: "Too fancy." From the lines a certain gaiety emanated. You could feel that Gustave was happy. No doubt he was telling his funniest stories in the evenings. A thin smell of tobacco clung to the paper. Crosses at the bottom were meant for kisses.

A little daring, this last familiarity! My mother didn't fail to be offended. My father grew cheerier and we often heard him prophesy in a satisfied tone: "You'll see, he'll be back one of these days."

The following year Gustave was in Alberta. He told us about it in a letter written at Uncle Edouard's place. Uncle Ed and Aunt Honora were working three-quarters of a section with their son. Gustave had helped with the harvest, which had been a good one. They had had him driving the truck, and he'd delivered the grain to the village. One girl was getting married this fall (he didn't say which one, and this unsettled point was the subject of many discussions among us). Another was taking orders. (My mother, to shut us up, said that could only be Paule, because of an old photo that showed her as rather scrawny, her eyes turned heavenward.) Anyway, all were well, including Gustave, except Honora who had stomach trouble. But he was sending for some of Ephrem Brabant's remedy to cure her. He didn't know yet if he'd spend the winter with the "relatives" or go and see a brother of Honora's who'd settled "across the big mountains."

My mother made a few objections, not so much to shake our convictions as to put her own to the test. Aunt Honora, who was such a cold, suspicious fish. . .how could she have given Gustave a welcome like this? That remained to be seen. You'd have thought my mother felt a little resentful.

We were certainly glad to get the news, in any case. Lazy about writing, we had never, for all our good resolutions, renewed a correspondence (which in fact had never begun) with our western uncles. And it seemed that Gustave, by taking this duty over, took our bad conscience with it.

This was all very well, but my mother took the opportunity of giving a little lesson to my father, indirectly, as she well knew how to do.

Her head thrown back, shaking a mat, she remarked one day: "I must say, there's strangers that have more family feeling than. . .than. . ."

My father refused to take offence. He smiled the serene smile of one whose confidence is sheltered from all doubt.

And so time passed. We had another letter six months later, not from British Columbia but from the Yukon, where Gustave vaguely gave us to understand he had turned trapper. Years passed. We might even have forgotten him had he not, by coming to see us long ago, awakened that mysterious thing: interest in one's family, that bewildering affinity that makes a Marcelline, unknown though she may be, less of a stranger than any other old woman in the village. Or, above all, if he hadn't left in our house the memory of so many places and things and people that still carried us through the long evenings, when boredom was not far and we grasped at dreams to drive it off. At those times, rising behind our hazy imaginings, the slightly drawling voice of Gustave would come back from the depths of our recollections.

We no longer talked of him, but thought of him often, each of us, in the evening when a shadow grew long on the road outside.

VI

He came back on a foggy, rainy night like the first one. And Farouche was the only one that knew him, from the smell of wet leaves and mud that his clothing gave off. They recognized each other, the man and the dog, the one perhaps luckier than the other because he had obeyed the mysterious call of the roads and the moonlit nights. But the man seemed weary. Leaning over the anxious dog, patting his head, you would have said he was advising him to appreciate the comfort of his kennel and perhaps even the benevolent servitude of the chain.

He straightened up, examined with the same slow, sad smile the roof of our house and the smoking chimney.

My mother uttered a few excited words: "Good Lord! It looks like. . ."

The man hesitated, then, as he had the first time, detoured around to tap on the back door.

I went to open it. His eyes, deep in their sockets, shone for a second. There was no more gaiety in those eyes, not even in their depths. The lustreless blue of water sleeping on the road after heavy storms!

But he exclaimed: "Ghislaine! I'd have known you anywhere, but my land, you've grown!"

I showed him into the big room. He followed me. He was just raising his arms in a great gesture to the reunited family when suddenly we saw him totter, then stagger against the stove and fall, his thin face turned toward us, a little spittle at his lips, his eyes fixed on the shadows like trickles of stagnant water.

My mother touched his reddened forehead. She said: "He has a high fever."

My father took Gustave's feet, my mother his shoulders, and they carried him to their bed.

Then his delirium began.

"I'm Barthélémy," he said. "Son of your brother Alcide. I come from Saint-Jerome. Yep, from Saint-Jerome."

Then he sighed.

"You've got to be friends with your folks, even if they're not always up to the mark."

Then again, in a wheezing voice, between coughing fits: "Come on! You don't know me? I'm Honoré, old man Phidime's boy, the one they thought was dead. I'm his Honoré!"

And suddenly he was muttering about tapers, the monstrance on the altar, the great piety of the world. In the middle of a brisk little laugh he exclaimed: "Good day to you, cousin Anastasie! Well, hello there!"

My father and mother exchanged a long look, then one after the other pulled a blanket over the sick man's body.

It snowed that night, and the next day too, and then another whole day. Then it blew. You could hear the coyotes that had ventured right to the doors of the barns, hear them howling and fighting over the carcass of a white hare that had fallen into their ambush. At times, from the growls that shook

41

Farouche's kennel, we concluded that a great wolf was stalking around the house. Powerful gusts swept the prairie, piled the snow high near the stables, sheds and all the buildings of the farm, which next morning would be half-buried. Snow was already up to our windows. Suddenly a great gust hurled itself against them as if to have a try through glass at blowing out our lamp, last visible sign of life struggling against the unleashed passion of the blizzard.

"No use talking," said my father. "We'll have to try and get out before all the roads are blocked. He could die, that fellow. At least we need some medicine."

He spoke with no warmth. You could feel that his grave affection for the poor wretch had not outlasted the confessions murmured in his delirium; he was being torn by an inner tempest as powerful as the one outside.

Just then, as if mysteriously aware of our concern and his own great danger, Gustave murmured among other unintelligible phrases: "Ephrem Brabant!"

Inspired, my mother fumbled in the pockets of his old overcoat hanging on a nail in the wall. She discovered a small brown bottle. On its label, the face with the white beard, that of the charlatan of Saint-Alphonse, seemed to us familiar and reassuring.

"It can't do him any harm, anyhow," said my mother.

She gave the poor man a gulp of the elixir.

"After all, he believed in it," she added.

My father was getting ready to go out just the same. He wrapped himself in a heavy coat with a fur collar and, to calm my mother, assured her he was just going to the nearest neighbour who had a phone.

My mother calculated: "Six miles there and back. I'll be worried."

A few minutes later we heard a faint sound of sleigh bells

42

whipped by the wind, then the horse whinnying as it plunged past the fence into an immense, tumultuous tempest.

Gustave was quieter after he had swallowed Ephrem Brabant's remedy. Soon he was sleeping deeply, his hands open on the white sheet.

"Now who'd have thought it!" my mother sighed.

Several times she went to sniff at the few drops of brown syrup left in the bottle.

"Just because he believed in it."

Her remark, however, seemed to refer less to the remedy than to a possible thought that arose in her, illuminating her solitary wonderment. She resisted it still at times, as you could see from her restive look; then, with a little shrug of her shoulders, she seemed to give in to the undeniable evidence.

The hours passed. The sick man was still asleep. My mother had finally dozed off. But, waking suddenly, she looked at the clock with growing anguish. Then she struggled to keep awake, and watched over Gustave as she had watched over us, her children, through our illnesses.

Then came the crunching of the cutter's runners in the snow, as if it were still far off, though it was in fact close by the house. A little later my father came in. He was pale, despite the cold, and in a shaking rage.

"How is he?" he asked.

My mother pointed to Gustave, sleeping, and indicated that it was all right to talk.

Then my father turned on her violently as if he were going to accuse her: "The very idea! . . . Albertine. . . . Who'd have thought it? Do you know the police may be here tomorrow because of him?"

"What! He's not a criminal? Oh, no!" stammered my mother, her hands fluttering to her heart.

"No. Maybe worse."

"Is he crazy? Sick?" she asked, pressing her hands to her heaving breasts.

"No. But I'd just as soon it was that."

"What then? Tell me, Arthur."

My father strode across the room, darting wounded glances to one side and the other. His thick overcoat, which he had forgotten to take off, gave an impressive form to his shadow on the wall.

"Oh," he shouted, with lively rancour, "he'd be just as well off dead, that fellow. Imagine, Albertine, and you looked after him so well! Imagine, he passed himself off for a Lafrenière at the Lafrenières below the big hill. And for a Poirier at the Poiriers. And so on. He hasn't one name, that man, he has ten, twenty, as many families as he likes."

"What then?" asked my mother. She had grown strangely calm.

"An impostor!" my father exploded. "Don't you realize, Albertine? An impostor!"

He tried to control his voice: "Somebody reported him. The police have started an inquiry. When people find out he's here. . ."

"What then, Arthur?"

My mother had taken up her stand at the door of the bedroom as if to forbid all entry. Tiny as she was, when she stood this way, her head high, her eyes flashing with determination, not many would have dared defy her.

"Well?" she said. "Don't we know what to say? Don't we know it?" she repeated, questioning each of us in turn with her clear, open gaze.

Suddenly the violence that had seized my father was broken. He seemed infinitely tired. Almost feeling his way, he sought out his chair in the corner by the fire and sank down in it. And at last we understood the disenchantment, worse than anger, that he had to bear. A Marcelline who could laugh and dance at her second wedding; Eustache, attached to the memory of his parents; a tender, affectionate Philomène; these characters, like a mirage that had for some time fed my father's dreams, had already disappeared from before his eyes. They were replaced by a dried-up, hardened little woman, by the bad son who had deceived his parents, by Philomène, frightful and graceless. In my father's eyes we saw the return of that absence of love with which he had had to live for so long.

"Good gracious now!" my mother said in a curiously persuasive tone. "Who's to prove it isn't true? He has to be somebody's relative. What's to prove to us it isn't true?"

Next morning Gustave awoke practically cured. He accepted the warm clothing my mother had taken from the trunks for him. He thanked her without effusiveness. You'd have thought he'd left a few of his things with us, and was grateful to get them back clean and mended. Gradually our wrath, our shame at having liked him, quieted down.

That day the sky swept the snow away with great waves of sunlight. The buildings, the cutters with their shafts pointed skyward, the buckets and barrels, all our everyday things, projected only the flimsiest of shadows in the immense plain all trembling with light. In the distance, on the hardened crust of the prairie, tiny tracks made their way toward the woods. At dawn, when the storm grew still, the wolves and coyotes had again sought the refuge of the trees.

Gustave was getting ready to go. He went to the door, downcast, but paused, his hand on the latch. My mother was preparing a splendid stew of jack rabbit and beef.

"There's no rush," she said, paying no attention to my father's silence. "You were a sick man. There's no rush at all."

Gustave made a despairing gesture with his arms. Then a shiver passed through his whole body. He seemed to be struggling against the temptation of warmth and the odour of the stew. Had some echo of our words of yesterday floated up in his memory? Or was it his old mania taking over again? He began to lift the latch.

"I suppose you have to get along to see some relatives?"

My mother had spoken in a friendly and reassuring voice. The man pricked up his ears. His stooped shoulders straightened. He looked back at the room. Greedily, as if to make a memory of it, he contemplated a ray of sunlight slanting through it, delicately lighting up the steam from the pots simmering on the stove. Finally he glanced up at my mother. His old eyes with their worn gaze were shining again.

"Yes," he said.

"Well! And which way are you heading this time?"

"I have some folks on my mother's side. . .in Ontario. . ." he began uncertainly.

"Would that be down Hawkesbury way?" asked my mother, with every sign of lively interest. "They say there's a lot of our people there still speak French."

She had thrown a shawl over her shoulders. She went with the man past the threshold. She encouraged him with her eyes. He went off, walking backward a few steps, as if he couldn't decide whether to give up my mother's accepting gaze. Then he turned to face the naked, empty plain.

Farouche, straining at his leash, was whining, almost choking himself in the attempt to leave with that miserable silhouette.

"Quiet, Farouche, quiet!" said my mother.

Then she did something so simple, so splendid. Cupping her hands to her mouth, she shouted loudly into the wind, her apron flying around her: "Take care! Take good care. . .Cousin Gustave!"

Did he hear? Perhaps. In any case, he had cut a branch in our garden for a walking stick.

Where Will You Go, Sam Lee Wong?

Where Will You Go, Sam Lee Wong?

Had his life begun in a land of hills? At times he fancied he found their contours in himself, intimate as breathing. Then he would gaze downward to see them better, in self-communion with his memory. Vague, rounded shapes, half-blurred, gathered along an uncertain horizon, then dissolved. Did the vision come from a recollection of real hills, or from some picture that had struck his imagination? In a sense they were more real than his own existence had ever seemed, whether in Canton or Fuchow or elsewhere: a yellow face among an infinity of yellow faces; at times, a face borne only on a sea of crowds, noise and hunger; also, it was true, amid the stream of humans, a small, barely audible voice that dared to call itself Me.

A stevedore among clouds of stevedores, and at the docks one grain of humanity, a particle of the dust of life. What could he remember as being his except perhaps his name, and even that was common as air around the waterfront. Only in the dark recess where he slept—a hole in the wall—could he escape from the multitude that worried him along.

At last, one day he came to a kind of personal conclusion: there are too many of us in China. Couldn't one live more at ease in other parts of the world? He heard tell of a country as vast as all the provinces of China put together, but almost empty of all human presence. So much room, so few people, was it possible? Sam Lee Wong listened. . . . He could hardly believe such tales. . . .

Nonetheless, a few months later, with almost a thousand of his countrymen, he embarked on a ship leaving for that land of youth and hope. Gathered on deck, the Asians kept watch for its appearance with all their souls, but with their usual expression of humility, and eyes so weary you might have thought them devoid of interest even in their own destiny.

But it was then that Sam Lee Wong, leaning on the railing, found a firmer grasp on the tenuous thread that linked him to the ancient hills in the back of his memory. He remembered rice bowls filled to the brim. He recalled a little coat made of several layers of quilted cotton. He even thought he glimpsed a little boy with chubby cheeks, comfortable in the warm coat. Was there some connection between Sam Lee Wong and this apparently well-fed child? Sam Lee Wong wondered about it, staring perplexed at the heaving water. But the ocean, which by some mystery had brought back a forgotten scene, now bore it off again on its heavy swell.

At last they could see a shoreline trimmed with high mountains. The sight of them recalled again to Sam Lee Wong the relief of his ancient hills. This time he saw them leaning, all in the same direction, like a row of old trees in the wind. He could see, without understanding how it all belonged together, an offered bowl of rice, protective hilltops, a coat of quilted cotton; and he set foot in Vancouver, still

52

in a press of his own countrymen, and far from persuaded that there was space here that could leave you breathless, and yet so few mouths to feed.

In Vancouver, the Sons of the Orient Aid Society took them in charge. For each one it tried to discover, in the breadth and length of this almost unpeopled country, the spot that might be most suitable. They were made to take a course of several weeks in English to at least learn its rudiments. Each immigrant also received a loan to get him started. Paid back, little by little, the money would be lent again to some new son of the Orient arriving, so to speak, on the heels of his predecessor. Thus there would be no drying-up of the thin flow of money or the thin trickle, tightly controlled, of Chinese immigration.

In fact the Aid Society had very few jobs to offer the little yellow men arriving from Canton, Peking or Manchuria. They almost all, therefore, ended up in the same odd occupation. In the distances of the endless plains, flat and without contours, minuscule villages had sprung up ten or fifteen years before. If they were big enough to contain one China-man they put him in a restaurant. If a village were even more flourishing and could afford a second Chinaman, the latter of necessity opened a laundry. That's how it went in these poor villages, almost deprived of all tradition except that of always putting their newcomers from Asia into the same occupations. The astonishing thing was that the Chinese laundrymen soon acquired the reputation of being the best in the world. As for the restaurants, it is less certain that they were the first in their field. Yet who but a Chinese with nothing to lose would have opened a café in one of these scrawny little towns where catching a single customer was a major feat!

In the headquarters of the Sons of the Orient Aid Society, Sam Lee Wong patiently studied the map of this immense country with its unfamiliar names, among which he had a choice almost as disconcerting as the map itself. What would be the new countenance of solitude? Would it be still more intense than in the teeming crowd? Or just the same as ever? Sam Lee Wong's gaze wandered over the map's puzzling spaces and was truly at a loss where to stop.

"Take your pick!" they told him. "Here! There! Anywhere! It's your choice, Sam Lee Wong. There's nothing to stop you."

Perhaps, tired of his own hesitation, he was about to put his finger on one or the other of the signs scattered across the map, when one of his compatriots charitably pointed out that such and such an area was not really to be recommended. A little chain of hills, wild and barren, rose from the plain. Most likely the soil was poor there, and business would suffer.

Hills!

Sam Lee Wong's eyelids fluttered as if he had heard someone softly call his name.

He pretended to study intently this portion of the map which was not to be recommended. In fact he was trying to see the elusive hills of his most distant memories. They alone managed to endow him with a kind of identity and the feeling that even here in Canada he was still somehow Sam Lee Wong. A moment earlier he had begun to doubt it, as he searched hopelessly among the undecipherable names on the map. He had had the impression that he was no one, just a fragment of being, nothing but a wandering thought stranded here, without the support of soul or body.

Now he was able to place himself within his personality and life, because of a horizon and the recurring image of a steaming bowl of rice.

And so he put his finger on the map at the place said to be so unexpectedly traversed by a little chain of hills.

That was how he learned that he had chosen Saskatchewan, and that he had attached his life to a village therein which, curiously enough, was called Horizon.

II

And in fact that's about all there was to it: a horizon so distant, so lonely, so poignant, that your heart was gripped by it again and again.

Luckily, a chain of little hills far to the right put a stop on that one side to the flight of the landscape. As the village lay perfectly open, wherever you were you couldn't miss seeing those surprising hills, and, on finding them again each morning, feeling in them a kind of refuge against the dizziness produced after a time by the flat, unmoving plain.

It was when the sun went down among their folds that the hills, filled with a strange light, exercised the strongest fascination on the people down below in the stagnant village. That was how things were between hills and village when, one September day, Sam Lee Wong, his wicker suitcase in his hand, got off the train and set foot in Horizon.

The day was hot and windy. When the train had gone, Sam Lee Wong, alone on the wooden platform, looked like a human being set down there by sleight of hand.

The Society had dressed him in occidental clothes. Beneath

a broad, black felt hat, in a light gabardine, his frail neck choking in a flowered tie, Sam Lee Wong seemed less than ever to belong. He almost gave the impression of waiting until fate would see her way clear to taking him by the collar once again.

The wind raised powdered earth in eddies of dust. Not a soul was about in the village. Even the stationmaster behind his dusty window didn't trouble to raise his nose from the report he was skimming.

Sam Lee Wong, supremely conspicuous in the very centre of the small, wooden platform between the station and the dark-red water tank, might as well have been invisible, for no one appeared to see him. He stayed motionless for a moment, not even thinking to set down his suitcase. He looked at the space surrounding him. Finally, after leaving his case by the empty bench in front of the station, he crossed the rails, with their rustling border of tall weeds, and then the road, and came to the board sidewalk.

He hesitated a moment as to which way to go, then started toward the plain on the right. He walked slowly, noislessly, looking around but with furtive glances as if he didn't yet dare take a good long look.

Apart from the beginnings of a side street at right angles – only two houses were on it – the whole village was strung out along the highway, and the wind rushed through incessantly, finding no obstacle in its path.

At the sidewalk's end, Sam Lee Wong gazed out at the prairie which went on and on, without a wrinkle or an undulation. Two more houses, farther along, might belong to the village, but after that it was emptiness.

Sam Lee Wong retraced his steps. Now he was facing the little hills that rose up two or three miles away. The moment they entered the landscape it grew less desolate, less overpowering. A touch of fancy, a certain grace, you might have said, came at last to the frightful stretch of flatness.

This time Sam Lee Wong went a little more quickly and looked more boldly on either side. In any case, he now had a good notion of this village where his fate had brought him. The most important thing in Horizon was beyond a doubt those two strange towers that gave off a smell of grain, near the railway station, with enormous letters standing out in white. Sam Lee Wong had already understood that this was where the village stored its riches, enough to see it through any famine; and the descendant of hungry generations stared with infinite respect at the tall letters making up the words: Saskatchewan Wheat Pool.

A strange thing: apart from the station, the water tank and the other railway outbuildings, all in the same dark red, the whole village lay not only along the highway but on one side of it, facing the endless fields, as if prepared to wait till eternity for the curtain to go up.

Sam Lee Wong was now taking in details that he'd noted only from the corner of his eye the first time around. He recognized a tall house surmounted by a cross. Before the door a man in black walked to and fro reading a book, never interrupting his reading to glance at the passer-by. Unless he was peeking, like Sam Wong, who today seemed to look about freely only when people's attention was elsewhere.

Then the school set free a troop of excited children who started playing football. This time Sam Lee Wong stopped and stared. He stayed for a long moment on the edge of the walk following the children's play, while his silent laughter accompanied their rowdiness. It was the first time since he arrived on this continent that he had stopped to contemplate a spectacle from which he himself was not totally excluded. And yet the playing children seemed to pay no attention to

58

his presence, obvious though it was. Perhaps its very oddity made it inaccessible. After awhile a young girl appeared in the school doorway and rang a hand bell. The children went back inside. Sam Lee Wong continued on his way. He began seriously looking for what he needed.

Not much, in fact: an abandoned house, even a little decrepit if that made it cheaper, no more than a shelter, in short; but well located. And that wasn't as easy as you might think, for with the children gone and the sound of their voices silent, all seemed empty again.

With time Sam Lee Wong was to grow used to the idea of a village so swallowed in silence that it seemed deserted; with little grey houses, morose, from which a sound, if one escaped, was at once swept off by the wind and smothered in its perpetual wailing. He would get used to this kind of solitude, but for the moment he simply thought that everyone had left.

Just to be sure, he put his thin face to the window of a house that was particularly lifeless. His hands beside his eyes to intercept the light and see inside, he gave it a searching going-over until, to his profound stupefaction, he met the gaze of someone staring at him with a surprise as great as his own, perhaps even indignation. He drew back instinctively, then pressed his face to the glass again to offer in apology – whether to the dark pane or the astonished face – an immense and humble smile.

This smile, by the way, was now to become a part of Sam Lee Wong and appear for every purpose on his melancholy face. Making-do as a language? Because there was no other way he could be understood? Whatever the answer, this broad smile on a sad Chinese face was to astonish no one here. A Chinaman who didn't smile – that might have shocked them.

After going over the whole village twice, Sam Lee Wong

59

was able to count the shanties that were really empty: three in all. One of them tempted him more than the others, though it was in wretched condition. The façade had a curious bulge, as though it had long ago half given way to some internal pressure. It must have been used as a granary, for there was still a smell of wheat about. In fact, Sam Lee Wong could see through the window that grain still lay in a pile on the floor. But this house with its smell of wheat was right across from the station, at the point of heaviest traffic in the village, if traffic there ever should be. Moreover, it had an unusually large window that took up a good half of the front. Sam Lee Wong didn't mind the façade either. It gave the shack a Far West look such as he had seen on postcards.

Pensive, Sam Lee Wong saw himself partly reflected in the dirty window pane, and he also saw a kind of future taking shape there. Business couldn't turn out so badly, even in this sleepy village, with such a big window to attract the public. When Sam Lee Wong would finally hear the history of the shack he'd be even more drawn to it, for before being a granary, at a time when the village had achieved an almost sensational boom, it had housed the branch of a bank, and this was the reason for the big window. Then it had been turned into an office for the municipality, and that was when they'd installed a counter dividing its space laterally. When Sam Lee Wong, growing used to the dim light inside, saw the counter, he was almost as happy as he had been about the window. No need to search farther. Everything he could wish for was here.

The hard thing to find out would be: who was the owner of this former municipal office? And when he had found the present owner (a farmer who lived at the edge of the village), how to make him understand that he wanted to rent the ruin? At last the deal was made. For six dollars a month and repairs the office-granary was Sam Lee Wong's.

Before nightfall he had moved in. On his way back from the owner's house he had bought a pail, some soap and a broom. Late that night, a feeble lamp on the counter lit the comings and goings of Sam Lee Wong, his fine duds removed and replaced by a kind of apron-robe, sweeping and tidying as if he were already mysteriously at home. Whether it was the room that seemed to grow larger and emptier as he tidied it, or the enormous shadow moving on the walls, the fact is that the few passing villagers who cast a glance inside drew back in their turn, perhaps embarrassed at coming unexpectedly upon this too-naked image of solitude. Why, of a sudden, in their already solitary midst, should there be this Chinaman, unconnected, destitute? They went home trying to forget the picture they had seized in passing, of a man setting up house much as a bird makes its nest, at the world's whim.

On his clothes rolled into a pillow at the back of the great, empty room, Sam Lee Wong laid down his head and slept. Elsewhere in the village people were also retiring for the night, and all had a moment of afterthought, sharpened as it often is before the regrets and bad memories of the day drift off. For at the moment when she rang the bell the schoolteacher had indeed seen the Chinaman standing halfway along the sidewalk; and the priest between two phrases of his breviary had glimpsed him out of the corner of an eye; and of course the Saskatchewan Wheat Pool dealer, who from the top of the grain elevator had the best view of the stranger's comings and goings; and Pete Finlinson, section boss for the railway, from his residence, an old freight car set flat among the thistles close by the tracks; and many others whom the timidity of the Chinese had somehow frozen – or what was it then that kept them from making some gesture of kindness? Little by little, night stretched across the isolated village, in the distance of the naked plains. The wind rose and rattled at the flimsy frame houses and blew dust along the main street, where three lampposts, far apart, kept their reflective watch. What was the meaning of Sam Lee Wong's appearance in Horizon? Another unanswered enigma. No doubt, at last and luckily, they all slipped into slumber, Sam Lee Wong among them, his head on his roll of clothes.

A few days later, in the middle of the big window, now washed and shining, you could read, drawn in soap, the following advertisement:

RESTAURANT SAM LEE WONG
GOOD FOOD
MEALS AT ALL HOURS

III

Some time later, on a fine, dry morning, old man Smouillya happened along in the front of the café. For twenty years or more he'd been searching for a sympathetic ear in which to pour the too-incredible story of his life, of which you couldn't make head or tail. As a very young man he had left his village in the French Pyrenees and wakened one fine day in Horizon without ever really knowing how it had come about. A mountaineer transplanted into this naked plain! From then on, all his efforts had been directed toward getting out. But misfortunes had piled up and swamped him. Finally he had lost everything – his land and buildings, for debts; then his wife, from illness; and at last his children. All he had left was a shack at the end of the village. There he passed the winter, in such filth that you couldn't see your way around. When spring came he would move out pots and pans and camp beside his house, never setting foot in it for the three or four months of decent weather. Always half-drunk – on his home-made chokecherry wine, some said, or under the influence of a strange and tenacious aberration – you couldn't understand a word of old Smouillya's wanderings. Some people affirmed, however, that they'd come upon him by surprise, sitting on the ground, his back turned to the houses, weeping silently as he stared at the distant hills fired by the setting sun. But was he really weeping? Or was it his catarrh that left his face running with water?

Well, this old Smouillya happened by the restaurant. In the doorway was Sam Lee Wong, all smiles.

"Good molnin! Nice molnin!" he said to old Smouillya.

The latter, in astonishment, stopped cold. For years no one had given him more than a nod, for fear that if you even said good-day he'd take you by the sleeve and start into his endless monologue of which you wouldn't understand a word. Even in his youth he'd been barely comprehensible, what with his strong Basque accent and a speech defect. But now that he'd lost his teeth, and little jets of spit whistled from his mouth, and chronic asthma wheezed in his lungs...! It's very trying, one must admit, listening to someone tell you with great enthusiasm something important, perhaps his life story, perhaps his troubles, and not catch a single word or even know which expression to put on, pitying or happy! It was to spare themselves this embarrassment that people gradually, without really meaning to be unkind, started avoiding old Smouillya.

"Nice days todays," Sam Lee Wong said chattily.

Now old Smouillya could understand Sam Lee Wong. Understood by so few himself, there was practically no jargon or patois that he didn't succeed in deciphering.

In his impossible accent he replied: "Why, yes, a fine day, Son of the Celestial Empire."

That seemed to please Sam Lee Wong, whose smile grew even broader.

The aroma of sausages and fried onions drifted out from the back of the restaurant. Old Smouillya sniffed, strongly tempted. On this, his very first day in business, Sam Lee Wong discovered in himself an extreme facility for reading the faces and gestures of men. He quickly said, "Come. . .come. . .come" – moving back to let Smouillya in, and pointing with a courteous gesture to one of the two lonely little tables covered with oilcloth.

"Sit, sit, sit," he said, then ran to turn the sausages in the pan. They were already cooked and re-cooked.

Was it the glow of the fire that brought up from the depths of his slanted eyes an expression of tranquility? In any case, the Chinese seemed that morning to have found his place as a restaurant-keeper. Old Smouillya, for his part, was barely seated before he took on the airs of a customer, with just a touch of superiority over the one who serves, attenuated by polite camaraderie. At the same time the old fellow examined the place and nodded approvingly at the transformation effected in the old granary. It didn't feel in the least like a granary now, and still less like a bank. In fact, it had everything that constitutes a restaurant in a western village, from the two little tables with their four chairs each and a highly typical greasy smell, to the flies that buzzed around so gaily.

No sooner was Smouillya served than he attacked the sausages, spearing them three at a time on his knife. It made the trip to his mouth only twice and the lot had disappeared.

His meal ended, he took a toothpick from the table, poked it about inside his mouth, and ended up chewing it. Then, leaning back in his chair, he began to tell Sam Lee Wong, who stood deferentially before him in his white apron, the story that no one in the village had fully understood: first the drought years; then the wheat rust, which ruined two of his best harvests; finally the seizure of his machinery. All this he told with spittle flying in every direction and a rattling deep in the lungs, but also with a kind of leisureliness, of unexpected relaxation, because for the first time he was heard out with patient silence, and in his listener's eye he could read neither the desire to flee nor the impulse to plug his ears. This was so pleasantly surprising that Smouillya made his story longer and more picturesque than ever. For he didn't lack education, imagination, the power of invention or telling imagery; and perhaps the most painful thing in his life was that he had never been able to make these gifts apparent to anyone. With a new serenity and smiling almost as broadly as Sam Lee Wong, Smouillya finally managed to tell someone all his troubles.

But, he said, they were just about at an end. He was expecting some money, it was bound to arrive any day now. Then he'd pay his debts and go back to live in his country, in the mountains. There, beside the French Pyrenees, said Smouillya, he'd find his place; if not to live, at least to die in peace.

Suddenly the old man realized that he was in a public place, that the Chinese had obligations to other possible customers, and he hastily began fumbling in his pockets, which he knew were empty. With an energetic gesture, shaking his head, Sam Lee Wong put an end to the fumbling. Smouillya willingly got the message that Sam Lee Wong was refusing to be paid this one time and considered his first customer as his guest, for good luck.

"Oh, well, in that case I'll accept," said Smouillya magnanimously. "But from now on, oh! Son of the Celestial Empire, take note of the meals I undertake to eat in your café. Write them all down, for before I go back to my native

Pyrenees I'll pay all my debts, starting with you, you man of gentle heart!"

Sam Lee Wong accompanied the old man to the door. He too seemed to have something on his mind, something he wanted to relate. His gaze was an inward one. He tried and tried, and finally with infinite pains and trouble put a few words together: "China too many people, much people. Here big, not much people. Everywhere Chinaman all alone. World very funny. Little hills, over there, good!"

From being understood by no one, Smouillya had come to understand even stray cats, and that was enough for him to grasp the longing of the café-keeper. He put one arm around Sam Lee Wong's thin shoulder. He encouraged him. What was more, until other customers started to come he undertook to drop in almost every day – on his days off, of course – to occupy his place in the restaurant. That would bring the others along. Nothing like a good example! He would even spread the word about Sam Lee Wong's good cooking, and soon they'd be there in droves; and when the two of them had made their fortune they could go back to their own countries, he to his majestic Pyrenees and Sam Lee Wong to the little round hills of his childhood.

He kept his word. It was very seldom, as long as the weather was good, that he didn't turn up for his midday meal, for which he paid provisionally by telling of the world as he saw it: a tremendous merry-go-round where no one ever understood anyone else. There was nothing like mountains for saving mankind, mountains which by their nobility and unchanging nature obliged the species to arrest its endless chase.

He didn't stop coming until the severe cold forced him to move back into his shack, where he stayed for the winter. Lacking his chokecherry wine, he lost appetite and hope.

Then the profile of the Pyrenees grew distant, distant in his mind. Sometimes, taking his head in his hands, he would shake it as if trying to bring back some consoling image; for in his dark cabin, its windows boarded up to keep him from freezing alive, he could truly no longer see where to get the money to pay his debts and buy his ticket home.

IV

With the months and then the years, Sam Lee Wong's business prospered in a small way. Jim Farrell, the stationmaster, had a big argument with his young wife, Margot. She took the train for Moose Jaw one Thursday morning and was never seen again.

After a week of mortification Farrell had had enough of fried eggs three times a day, alone, at the corner of his table. He came over to try the food at the "Chink's place," as he called it, and must have liked it, for he came back. Perhaps best of all, he could say what he liked about women and not risk being quoted around town. Or perhaps he was too drunk those days to care much.

To hear him talk, they were crazy. All of them, crazy! Spenders, too, and extravagant, and man-crazy! Anybody said you couldn't get on without them was a fool. No sir, them silly articles, good riddance to them, a fellow could breathe easy at last!

At the times when Farrell was pouring out his most whole-hearted resentment, Sam Lee Wong made himself as invisible as possible and finally almost disappeared in his own restaurant. But one evening when Farrell was more dishevelled than usual, he addressed himself directly to the Chink.

"You, Chinaman, darn lucky not have woman!"

Though he still didn't have a big vocabulary, Sam Lee Wong would have learned to express himself quite well if people had only helped a little. He learned quickly. But they went on talking to him as if he were retarded. And he, out of politeness, so as not to shame those who spoke in this way, would answer in much the same style.

"Yes, Wong lucky no woman!" he acquiesced.

At that time there was a very cruel immigration law regulating the entry of Chinese immigrants into Canada. Men – a few thousand of them a year – were admitted, but no women, no children. Later the law was made more humane. In those western villages lost in boredom and tawdry dreams, in those same little restaurants with their smell of grease, you could henceforth see beside each Sam Lee Wong a little woman, probably on the plump side, doing her best to help him; and sometimes a swarm of yellow children pushing around in the back of the café; and if all of these were still outsiders in the village, at least they were outsiders together. But in Sam Lee Wong's time a Chinese woman beside him was as unthinkable as the King of England coming to Horizon.

"Yes, good no woman," Sam Lee Wong approved sadly.

Sometimes, rediscovering the vague memory of the quilted cotton coat and the bowl of rice, he also fancied he glimpsed a woman's loving face. His mother? An older sister? He didn't know.

Soon his two little tables with their four places each were filled at seven in the morning, at midday sharp, and six o'clock at night. From one meal to the next the smell of bacon grease had no time to escape into the distance. The overflow reached the sidewalk and built up there. It became a part of Horizon, like the dominant sour smell escaping from the tavern Saturday evenings, like the acrid perfume of wheat when they were filling the Saskatchewan Wheat Pool elevators.

After Farrell, Sam Lee Wong acquired Pete Finlinson as a regular. A heavy-set man with thick, straw-coloured hair, the Icelander had grown tired of coming back from the tour of his railway section and going straight to his freight-car home, feeling literally as if he were on the rails. He too began to like Sam Lee Wong's fried food, or perhaps more Sam Lee Wong himself, for though Pete was not a man who made friends, there he'd be, long after he'd eaten, watching the Chinaman's perpetual comings and goings. In fact no one, not Farrell, not even Finlinson who after all spent hours in his corner in the café, could say that he had ever seen the Chinaman sitting down.

Motionless at times, yes, but sitting in one of his own chairs? Never! What the devil kept this little man on the go all the time? (Between his four walls, of course. He almost never went beyond them.) Inside only, then. But there he went, trot, trot, trot, as if he had a thousand chores to do at once, though his place remained as greasy as ever.

"Where do you come from, Wong?" asked Finlinson one evening when he happened to feel talkative.

Sam Lee Wong opened his mouth in a vast smile. He pointed beyond the plain. "Far!"

"I well believe you. Indeed it must be from far. There's nobody here doesn't come from some end of the earth. Me, it's Iceland, and I came all this way to turn into a section hand in Horizon. Isn't that a hell of a funny story? Here we are, you from Far, like you say, and me from Iceland, Farrell from the Isle of Man, Smouillya from the Pyrenees and Jacob from old Quebec. . . ."

Then he forgot how strange it all was and began dreaming aloud about Iceland. It was the smells he missed most, smells of iodine and fish and the open sea, penetrating the whole life of the immense island.

Then the Saskatchewan Wheat Pool dealer got the habit of passing time in the café when he was tipsy, rather than face his wife, Lilly.

Yes, Sam Lee Wong had a lot of strange customers, more of them lonely and discontented than happy, and it seemed he took pains to fit their mood, though perhaps that was not so hard for him.

But when he at last acquired an ice-cream cooler, his café began to be invaded on Saturday nights by the young people from nearby farms and hamlets, sitting around for hours and making a splendid racket. The whole atmosphere changed. Instead of lamentations the air was filled with hearty laughter and endless jokes. It was then that Sam Lee Wong installed two tables with high-backed benches attached, on one side of the room. When the gangs of young couples came in Sam would invite them, with a gesture and a smile, to be seated in these booths. They would occupy them for hours on end, sucking away at the straws of their milkshakes or cream sodas, their feet and hands seeking each other out beneath the table.

Sam Lee Wong served these customers with perhaps a little more alacrity than he had demonstrated to those who complained about women or life in general. But this preference, if it really existed, was barely measurable. In fact, the only one to reproach him about it was Smouillya, who was unusually sensitive.

"What's the idea, spoiling these snot-nosed brats? You can't even come here and think in peace and quiet, the way we used to. What a racket they make!"

"Tut-tut," said Sam Lee Wong, allowing himself to make a mild reproach. "You young one time. You not remember?"

"Oh, that's so long ago," sighed the old man. "So long ago! And anyway, in our time we weren't bold like this lot."

"Always old men say that," Sam Lee Wong observed.

Just the same, there was soon no room for doubt that he put up with just about anything from the young folk, a real shivaree going on till all hours, glasses broken, Coke splattered on the tables. But with the same impassive face he had also put up with Farrell's grumbling, or the chronic belching of one Charrette, or the ponderous reminiscences of the Icelander. What hadn't he put up with? At times you might even surmise that he was the one in the village who cramped people's style the least, and that, consequently, he knew them better than anyone in the world.

V

Month by month Sam Lee Wong came closer to paying off his debt to the Sons of the Orient Aid Society. Smouillya, never very particular in money questions, openly tried to dissuade him from undue haste in acquitting his debt or even from worrying about it at all. The Aid Society had lots of money, he'd say. It could wait for Sam's. It could wait indefinitely. What was more, it would never sue a bad creditor, for that would reveal its racket to the public.

Sam Lee Wong was stubbornly deaf to these arguments. As he saw it, some poor Chinese in Vancouver, or maybe even in Canton, was waiting for that money to come and set up business in the Canadian prairies. Not for anything in the world would he be the one to block or slow down the trickle of immigration.

"You're crazy, you know," the Basque would go at him time and again, with a touch of resentment, as if the Chinaman had thrown away good money that somehow should have gone Smouillya's way. "Just be sure you keep a bit for yourself, if you want us to go back to our home countries some day, you and me. You in your coffin, all doctored up, and me on my two legs if things go my way. You'll make the trip in a special boat," he explained, "fitted up special to bring the deceased back to the Celestial Empire. Some kind of a refrigerator boat, I expect."

Then he'd come back to his theme for the hundredth time.

"But if they don't treat you right, according to the deal, you're in no shape to complain. And it's a poor deal, at that. If you can't go back alive, why in the sam hill do you want to go back dead?"

Sam Lee Wong had given him the answer time and again: it was to be reunited with his ancestors.

"But you never even saw them!"

"They'll know me," Sam Lee Wong would say.

"It's just this crazy idea of yours and all you ex-coolies," Smouillya would go on, "this idea of going back to China to be buried, it's making your crooked countrymen rich in Vancouver. When you're dead you've no comeback against their tricks. I hear they pile you up in the hold like cordwood. And they hold the shipment till they get a payload!"

Never mind! Sam Lee Wong contributed a little money every month toward his eternal retirement fund.

"You write. You send money for me, same as always."

Smouillya had a fine, clear and delicate hand, which Sam Lee Wong admired as much as the frost patterns on his windows. And no matter how the man went off on endless digressions or lost the thread of his own remarks in conversation, when he wrote, his sentences were concise and to the point. This was the old Basque's one priceless gift, and only Sam Lee Wong was aware of it, for only he had called upon it. The old man wrote his letters for him, and orders for sausages and supplies, and the tireless expressions of gratitude that accompanied each instalment of money to Vancouver.

When Smouillya brought these extraordinary letters and read them to Sam Lee Wong, the latter went into ecstasies. He even stopped smiling, lost in a kind of blissful gravity.

"It's me said that?" he would ask at the finest passages.

"That was you. Anyhow, that's what you wanted to say, oh Son of the Celestial Empire. Isn't it? For you and yours were always given a great gift of self-expression. That's what I read, anyway, in accounts of travels to ancient Cathay. Have you read them?"

"No," said Sam Lee Wong, regretfully. "I will know my people when I am dead."

Then he would admire his name, which when written occidental-style looked very impressive indeed, as Smouillya decorated his capitals with a kind of flying stroke, as if they were about to take wing.

"That's me?" Sam Lee Wong would ask, overwhelmed at last by emotion.

"Well, I should say! Look here: Sam Lee Wong, Esquire."

"I'm esquire?" the café owner asked.

"Just like me! Just like everybody!"

Sometimes on these occasions the memory of the hills before Horizon's hills came back to Sam Lee Wong. A woman's face emerged from the mist of years. He felt a kind of continuity with certain lost things, he wasn't sure exactly what. In a burst of gratitude he cried out one day: "You, Smouillya, not owe meals eight years. You owe four years, no more."

Always magnanimous, Smouillya, sputtering in all directions, protested vehemently: "Never on your life! I owe you eight years. All right, take off one year for secretarial services. Maybe another year for cogitation on your best interests. And take off the days my asthma kept me from looking after your

76

business. But don't you worry. It's all written down on the back of my calendar."

Then, forgetting it was only yesterday he'd been counting on Sam Lee Wong's savings to see them both back in their native lands, he added: "With what I owe you, you're sure of a ride back in a first-class coffin. It's as good as money in the bank."

And he would sigh: "At least you, you've got some money in the bank!"

Sam Lee Wong, not quite as innocent as all that, gave in to a significant little smile one day as the Basque was harping on the same old theme.

Smouillya, catching the smile in mid-flight, was offended. He struck the rickety table with a fist.

"Money in the bank, I tell you! Your money, whenever you want it!"

VI

And now a great drought, just like the ones that had driven Sam Lee Wong and so many like him from their homeland, swept down upon Horizon and the surrounding country. On the plains it traced an enormous circle haunted by the lament of scorching air in which you could almost hear the plant life crackle, where you could watch the burnt earth crumble and turn to powder. In the rich landscape it singled out this ring of misery that came to be called the Desert Bowl. Within it, indeed, nothing was left but arid desert!

Farmers left home, leaving all behind them except a few skin-and-bone animals half dead of thirst, led away behind wagons or cars driven at a snail's pace. Nothing could have been more strange than to glimpse through the flying dust these weird processions, dimly seen and lost at once in the opaque daylight.

Doors everywhere, of houses, barns and stables, flapped half unhinged in the wind. Their banging, and the occasional squeaking of a pulley or the cry of some bird flying past the dead land – these were the components, so to speak, of the frightful silence.

Nowhere was a sign of life to be discerned. The inhabited houses scarcely differed from the others, their doors and windows blocked against the dust, which succeeded anyway in sifting through.

Sometimes, in this floating dust as thick as fog, you could see beside a fence that managed to stay half upright a poor workhorse, its ribs protruding, its head down in the wind, rocking on its legs. Occasionally a small car crossed through this wasteland, so covered with dust you couldn't see its colour, its windows rolled up tight, its lights on in broad daylight, sputtering along toward Horizon.

Like everyone else, Sam Lee Wong hoped for rain. A hundred times a day he would stand in his doorway looking for a clearing in the dust-coloured sky.

The station had closed down, for there were no passengers. Jim Farrell, luckily for him, had managed to find a spot for himself somewhere in northern Saskatchewan where things were a little better. The Saskatchewan Wheat Pool dealer was fired. There was no wheat to buy. Two section supervisors on the railway, regulars in the Chinese café, were laid off as well. Pete Finlinson stayed, but he was possessed again by his savagery and went back to his lonely meals and his endless solitaire, his cat on the table sole witness to his game. The young had left for the cities in search of jobs. The high-backed booths were almost always empty now. Even the bacon smell that had so long pervaded the place began to fade. It gave way to the stronger smell of grasses burnt by the wind and the smell of the earth itself, rasping, catching you by the throat.

In Sam Lee Wong's place things were almost as dreary as in the first days after his arrival in Horizon. At long intervals someone covered with the dust of the land would come in and quickly shut the door behind him It would be an agronomist, one of the experts sent by the government to see if something couldn't be done for the population; or, very rarely, a frightened travelling salesman who had ventured too far into the dust storm to turn back, and had no choice but to go on to the next village.

With these exceptions Sam Lee Wong saw no one but Smouillya, with whom he spent hours chatting, the Basque straddling a chair – at least you didn't have to mind your manners anymore – and recounting once again from the very start the shaggy tale of his life and hardships. In those days it was drought that had brought him ill-fortune. Now this drought brought it back in force. Across the years misfortune was shaking hands with itself – the eternal repetition of things! Smouillya saw in this a fate that in a way absolved him of his personal failure, a fraternal fate that put everyone on the same footing. You might even get the impression at times that Smouillya was reassured by this monstrous calamity.

Meantime Sam Lee Wong would stare, dazed, at Jim Farrell's favourite chair and imagine him still missing his Margot, whatever he might say; or at Pete Finlinson's, and he would see again the big head with its blond hair; or, longer still, he would stare across at the high-backed booths. Then, with a sigh, he would look down between his feet at the linoleum, paid for by instalments after a public health inspector had lectured him on the virtues of cleanliness. Alas! The linoleum was not quite his yet, but already showed signs of wear, especially in front of the counter, and still more at Finlinson's place, for as he told his tales of Iceland he had a habit of scraping the floor with his hobnailed boots.

At times it happened then that Sam Lee Wong, who had after all seen a few things in his day, allowed a shade of astonishment to appear in his expression.

Had he grown much older? It was hard to say. He had

looked ageless even on his arrival. Since then he had grown very thin, quite dried-out, even skinny, but this had happened so slowly that no one remembered how he had looked before: slightly plump. With the years he had acquired a trembling chin, soft and receding, especially when he sank into one of his reveries, his eyes gazing out toward the hills, now barely visible behind the storm and its dark snow.

Once so polite, he was now so altered that he no longer listened to the tireless drone of Smouillya's voice. Smouillya's sight had grown bad, so he didn't notice. To him the absent-minded silence of the Son of the Celestial Empire passed for the profound and smiling attentiveness of other days.

The old man took to leaving late, announcing like a regular whether or not he'd be there for his meals next day.

Sam Lee Wong, behind him, would stand in the doorway for a moment, searching as usual for the profile of the hills.

He had seen many droughts in his time. The memories of them went back as far as his vaguest recollections. His whole life seemed to have been one long drought, apart from a few moments of communication with others. And yet one got over it. People managed to get over it. Standing there in his doorway before going to bed, he waited a long time. In the moonlight, when the wind dropped a little, the hills would reappear, just long enough to give you a glimpse and then another.

The winter was a rough one. The horizon, freed of its dust clouds, grew precise and hard, a cutting edge, and the cold was pitiless as the dry season had been.

Smouillya, with a relapse of his old bronchitis, was unable to leave his cabin for weeks on end. When he emerged he was no more than a string of bones wrapped in sweater after sweater, the whole parcel racked by an incessant wheeze. As soon as it let up for an instant he would go back to his refrain:

money was bound to arrive any day now; he'd come into a heritage over there. With that in his pocket, after his debts, he'd get the heck out of this wretched country.

On these winter nights the contour of the hills beneath the snow was sweet to see. It seemed they were ancient hills, linked to the earth's most distant past. Under the stars, their round heads capped in white, they evoked for Sam Lee Wong a notion of infinite old age, a past profound and unmarked, an anchor post at last for this errant life.

He asked Smouillya, then, if he had remembered to send off the monthly payment for his return fare in the coffin. Smouillya grunted that it had been done, for what it was worth, and to the Son of the Celestial Empire that wasn't much.

He went off puffing like a forge, his woollens clutched with both hands across his chest.

Sam Lee Wong returned to his contemplation of the distant hills. Shrivelled, hunched, half frozen, watching motionless from his doorway, he himself took on the form of all things conquered and worn by time.

VII

But the final blow was not dealt by four years of drought. He was built to resist that, shrunken to the very limit, needing little food – and as for other wants, had he ever had any? No, what dealt the final blow was sudden prosperity.

It fell almost like a catastrophe on the impoverished land, which from one day to the next was found to be rich in oil, now in one spot, an hour later in another, and finally almost everywhere for thirty, forty miles around.

As soon as the track was reopened geologists and prospectors came in by the trainload. Then a drilling team, that found lodging anywhere it could in the little village houses. The smallest room rented for exorbitant prices, even a bed in a corner. Soon there were secretaries arriving. The station hummed with constant activity. The bank set up temporary business in a cabin long deserted, while its future home grew up alongside with great glass panels. The village began to look a little as it had in its first days of growth, in the pioneer times, but more agitated, more feverish.

For example, take the old spinster on the switchboard, Amanda Lecouvreur! Up to now nobody had had an easier time of it: a call here, a call there…and in the meantime she'd get on with her knitting, warm up her soup, doze a little and, on the really dead days, ring up one of the distant farms to ask, "Anything new out your way?" But now her board was lit up like a Christmas tree. People wanting Regina, Moose Jaw, Swift Current. In ten minutes they wanted more lines than she used to hook up in a whole year. The telephone company, pushed by the oil company, pushed in its turn by Regina, threatened to replace Amanda with someone more efficient.

From a placid old maid she turned brusque, irritable, nervous, and perhaps a little more efficient, with no time for news of people's health or personal affairs, tending only and strictly to business. She could no longer see the human beings behind the flashing lights, behind all these voices, familiar or new, that jostled each other in her earphone. But as she was paid a commission on long-distance calls, she made a fortune.

For a few months Sam Lee Wong also picked up a share of the profits raining on the village. The café was never empty. He had built up a reasonable clientele that accepted without too much grumbling what he had to offer: fresh eggs when he'd just bought them, less fresh a little later. But now at the same table they'd order one steak medium, one rare and another medium rare. Sam Lee Wong would go off running, his eyes staring inward so as to engrave the order on his memory; and he might even have managed, but as he passed another table someone would snap his fingers, shouting: "Hey, Charlie! Coffee over here!"

Why did they go calling him Charlie? That put him off his stride for good and all.

And somebody else wanted ice water. Charlie had good cold water, with no bad taste to it, out behind in his well. But it took five minutes to let the bucket down and bring it up full. Meanwhile the steaks were all done the same.

"Hey! I wanted this rare!"

"We're in a rush," they'd say, almost all of them.

"What about that ice cream? Is it gonna be here today?"

Some of them dared to call him back to give a lick of the rag to a table with a little grease on it. Others wanted a "clean" fork.

One day Sam Lee Wong was seen to give up, to do a thing that was completely out of character. He stopped running, remained stock still, took his head in his hands and stared ahead vacantly as if trying to summon up something of his own, an idea, an image, that would reestablish contact between himself and his own reality. He remained thus, frozen in his tracks, quite absent, most disconcerting in the midst of people with not a minute to spare. Then he again became the man they had known since business had picked up: a conscientious Chinaman, a little absent-minded, no longer smiling, even at times daring to raise his voice: "You not satisfied? There a door!" But it should be added that he had heard this phrase a thousand times from Smouillya and had ended by making it his own, not really noticing.

That's how things stood when the mobile kitchen arrived in Horizon, all finished in chrome and aluminum, with hot and cold water and even a refrigerator. The company also moved in trailer sleepers.

Then one day at noon a young woman, a stranger, came and ordered a meal which she never touched. Instead of eating she wrote in a little notebook. Sam Lee Wong hovered some distance away from her, wanting to ask why she didn't eat but not daring. Never had he been subjected to such an indignity. Finally the young person got up. She paid for the meal she had not touched and left without a word. Was she from the Health Department? Was she making a report?

In any case, the inspector came back for a visit shortly after. He had never been very severe in his objections in the past.

Sam Lee Wong received him humbly but without too much apprehension. Instinctively he put on his worst English: "You make trip. . .good?"

The inspector pushed past Sam Lee Wong. He went about running his finger along the underside of tables, where people had stuck their used gum, and then along the counter, where it came up greasy.

"Not much time clean lately," Sam Lee Wong apologized. "All the time rush, rush, rush!"

Frowning, the inspector turned to the enclosure at the back. He eyed the contents of a saucepan, tasted a blackish soup, made a face. . . .

A greasy curtain separated this nook, which was the kitchen, from another smaller one. Not standing on ceremony, the inspector lifted it up and peered inside the smaller nook. A few clothes were hanging on nails in the wall. A tiny window, its panes patched with bits of paper, let in a faint gleam of light through its thick coat of grease. The inspector bent down to look under the poor cot, picked up a few rolls of dusty lint and examined the grubby bed with its one grey blanket, turning his nose away as if to inhale as little as possible.

Anxious at the turn the visit was taking, Sam Lee Wong promised a major housecleaning no later than tomorrow.

"Me buy soap very strong and all scrub."

The inspector was still not speaking, except with his eyes and lips which expressed strong disapproval. Finally, asking Sam Lee Wong to sit down for the bad news, he told him the following: unless he refinished the whole place, the mouldy floor, the rotting kitchen, the greasy partitions – in fact the whole works – he would have his restaurant permit cancelled.

Sam Lee Wong was still not upset. After all, he'd been lectured more than once about cleanliness and then they'd let him alone. Yet it was true that today for the first time the inspector had bothered to look in his cooking pots and under the bed. And it just happened, as if on purpose, that on that morning, feeling a little discouraged, Sam Lee Wong had neglected to draw the blanket up over his cot. When it was pulled tight it hung to the floor and hid the dust and lint beneath the bed. He imagined that his misfortune had something to do with this tiny oversight and hastened to make his bed up properly. Then he closed his restaurant, hanging a sign on the door written in Smouillya's fine hand: "Gone on serious business. Back in a few hours."

He went off with short, mincing steps, unused to walking and a little dazzled at finding himself outside in broad daylight – he who for years had barely stuck his nose past his own doorway. And so he was astounded by the changes that had taken place in the village without his noticing. Derricks rose up everywhere on the surrounding plain. Men, black with oil from head to foot, were busy around the drilling rigs. It seemed to him that before, in the sun and wind, with the ripe grain waving in harvest time, the landscape had been a happier one. He remembered the endless fields of wheat and seemed to discover that they had been woven into his life, like the gentle hills of his other memory which still returned at times. Then he became conscious, with a feeling of distress, that in a certain way he had been happy surrounded by the wide, pure spaces of his adopted land but that, like most men, he had allowed his happiness to pass without recognition. Perhaps you had to lose it to know that it had been happiness.

At first he met no one he knew, no one that knew him. Still, a few might have recognized him if they had been able to

87

imagine him out walking in broad daylight like anyone else.

Gradually Sam Lee Wong was filled with a great melancholy and gentle affection for things as they had been, the silent little village to which he had been carried by a memory of hills he might have seen at his life's beginnings; and the people of his first days here and their cordiality!

At least the warm dust blowing around him was the same as then. He made his way to his landlord's house. Each month he had faithfully mailed the amount of his rent, first ten, then fifteen, then suddenly, of late, twenty-five dollars.

He spoke at first, and with a certain self-assurance, of the improvements the Health Department wanted, saying he was willing to assume a part of the cost if the owner – who would have a better property afterwards – would pay his share.

The owner listened in silence, without looking at him, embarrassed. Well, he explained at last, the company had just offered him three thousand dollars for the land where the café stood. The shack was to be torn down. It was a good thing Sam Lee Wong had come along. It saved him the trouble of going into town to tell him about the deal, which was almost closed. He was sorry, but maybe Sam Lee Wong could find another spot, though the little land remaining along the main street had gone sky-high. He was sorry, really sorry! And yet, who could tell? Perhaps it was for the best! Sometimes in life you'd get in a rut and never see it was for your own good to get out of it. Anyway, he wished Sam Lee Wong the best of luck. . .and, oh, by the way, did Sam think he could get out of the place a bit before the three months' notice was up? He'd be paid the difference. . . .

Sam Lee Wong went home so stunned that he didn't even notice several people who this time seemed to recognize him, astonished as they were. "What! Is he still around? It's been years since anybody laid eyes on him!" That's what they

88

seemed to think. It had taken this little daytime excursion of his to remind people of the Chinaman's presence in Horizon.

It was recess and children were playing, just as they had the day he arrived. And what was getting into them now, all of a sudden? They ran up and trapped Sam Lee Wong inside their ring, chanting: "Chinky, chinky Chinaman!" Sam Lee Wong did his best to get in the spirit of the joke. Could he be just arriving in Horizon today? For a moment everything swam inside his head. He'd have to go back where he'd been a moment ago and announce his intention of renting the abandoned granary. He remembered that he had to buy some strong soap. Then he searched his pockets for candies to appease the children. He found only bits of paper he had used as reminders when he was learning by heart the phrases he'd need that day, the kind that would please his customers. "It's a fine day today." Or "spring's coming!" Little by little he recaptured the memory of years gone by, of time irrevocable, and his gaze, like a cry for help, went searching at the plain's end for the gentle, undulating line of the ancient hills.

For a time he was stirred by a desire to fight back. But how to go about it? Write to the Sons of the Orient Aid Society? His dealings with the society had been wound up long ago – ever since he had paid back his debt. If he started writing now the society wouldn't even remember him, and they'd be quite right to ask, "Who's this Sam Lee Wong, asking for money?" Or, if they did remember, they could rightly say, "What! He wants more money now? What a nerve!"

How much would he need? Sam Lee Wong tried to calculate. He thought of the price the owner was getting for the land alone, and reckoned that a modern restaurant would cost as much again, and then he lost his way. He wasn't used to juggling such amounts.

Maybe, he thought, if Sam Lee Wong could arrive nowadays, with Horizon prosperous, but young and enterprising as he had been then, maybe he'd do a big business. That other Sam Lee Wong would know how to go about it. The restaurant would have neon lights, a ventilation hood, even an inside toilet, and perhaps two or three rooms on the first floor up, for company presidents. Fine rooms, with a washbowl in every one. Real style! He dreamed awhile about that younger Sam Lee Wong, saw him grappling with the complications of life today, while he stayed on the sidelines, a spectator, overwhelmed.

For he couldn't make up his mind whether to write to the society. To write, "It's me again, Sam Lee Wong. I need a loan."

"What!" the society would answer. "You had your chance, Sam Lee Wong!"

"That's right," said Sam Lee Wong, bowing his head. "I had my chance."

He simply couldn't see himself rejoining the lineup – which he imagined as having been continuous all these years – from the ship's deck to the most forsaken outposts of this space-rich land. He couldn't see himself stealing the place that belonged to someone else, someone such as he had been – in fact, another Sam Lee Wong.

VIII

There was no one but Smouillya to notice how this skinny Sam Lee Wong was wasting away, sickly from thinking and insomnia, eating less and less, yet never losing his smile. But it was a smile left behind by his gentle humour in retreat, as the sea leaves its mark upon the sand.

During the drought Smouillya had not felt too unhappy, for everyone in those days was more or less in the same boat. But now that people went riding around in Buicks, going to the bank once a day, planning trips to Texas, how could he help feeling like the only one of his kind! Himself abandoned, Smouillya began to realize what might be in store for Sam Lee Wong. He succeeded in getting him to talk. He discovered the impossible tangle of difficulties in which the Chinaman was struggling. Filled with indignation and the energy it gave his feeble body, he went off at once down the main street to alert people to the news, stopping this one and that one, shouting at each of them. "Listen, we've got to do something for Sam Lee Wong, damn it! He's been living in this

91

town twenty-five years. He's one of us, we can't just let him go to pot without doing something for him. Come on, have a heart, let's do something together for Sam Lee Wong!"

At first when they saw old Smouillya veering toward them, people tried to dodge him, thinking, Oh oh! Here he comes! He's good for half an hour, let's get going! But Smouillya would grab them by the sleeve or simply bar the way. And talk and talk and talk! In the whine of the hot wind he put his whole talent into the wretched story, sputtering in the faces of his listeners who would back off as he advanced, keeping the distance about the same. All the while Smouillya's eyes, filled with a surprising eloquence, begged for attention as they had never done. But it was a waste of time. Nobody understood him. He tried English. If anything, that was worse. Out of politeness or laziness a few people pretended to understand, but Smouillya knew from their eyes that they did nothing of the sort, and he was taken by a kind of despair.

Where could he go? Who would listen to him? Suddenly he saw the light and dashed to the telephone company's switchboard. In the days when he'd been a good-looking fellow and people put up with his speech defect, he had paid court to Miss Lecouvreur, who had, it was not impossible to believe, been in love with him. He turned up in front of her and shouted over the buzzing of her board: "Amanda! Amanda! Listen with the heart you used to have. For God's sake, listen to me. Hear what's happened to Lee Wong!"

Amanda, her head gripped by her earphones, looking like a traveller about to leave, an aviator or a deep-sea diver, frowned, saying to herself, If I listen to him, Lord knows what I'm getting into. He'll still be here this time tomorrow. But hooked by who knows what sudden curiosity she switched everything off and removed her earphones.

92

"All right, make it fast. It could cost me my job, you know, listening to you."

Then, perhaps feeling a little remorse, Amanda realized that when she paid complete attention she could grasp a word of his gibberish here and there. Perhaps the old man was making a special effort to be understood today. Amanda, reading his lips, watching his eyes – their expression filled in the meaning – began to get the thread of this irregular torrent of language. She finally understood that it was about Sam Lee Wong and that he had to leave, but she got the rest all wrong. She understood that Sam was retiring from business to go back to China. And she said, "Fine, just leave it to me. I'll look after the whole thing, don't worry." And she went back inside her earphone.

She had already decided that if Sam Lee Wong was leaving they certainly couldn't let him go without giving him a party. In the old days, when Amanda's life had been monotonous, there'd been no one like her for organizing parties. Arrival parties, going-away parties; paper weddings, tin weddings, gold and silver weddings and jubilees of every kind.

Now a little of the old fever overtook her again. For a few minutes she let the executives in Calgary and Moose Jaw and Swift Current languish at their phones while she busied herself calling as many people as possible in the village and on the farms.

As she went on explaining her plan for a party in Sam Lee Wong's honour, the plan grew bigger and bigger and she herself was caught up in the game.

"It's almost twenty-five years," she'd say, "that Sam Lee Wong's been living here among us. You could say he's an early bird, an old-timer. Now, are we going to let an old-timer leave without getting back a taste of the good old days? For he was part of those days!"

The good old days! Now that they were rich, people thought nostalgically of the past. Amanda had them all on the string when she talked that way. Neighbourliness, loyalty, fidelity to the good old days! This emotion, revived, turned to Sam Lee Wong's benefit. He was leaving! You couldn't let him go without marking your regret.

At once a flock of good-wills were on the wing. Mrs. Connoly would take care of the cakes and cookies, Madame Toutant would do the turkey. A committee of honour was formed. They reserved the town hall for the evening of the second Saturday in November. And in the meantime, shhhhh! not a word that could spoil Sam Lee Wong's surprise. One of the committee ladies, thinking of Sam Lee Wong's origins, had the idea of decorating the hall with Chinese lanterns. Adopted unanimously! Making the lanterns was left to the schoolteacher, who found a pattern in the *Encyclopedia Britannica*. She had her pupils cut them out in quantity from brightly coloured paper. The class was overjoyed. The children clipped and assembled and glued the paper after the model. The teacher took the opportunity of saying a few things about China, a great country that produced much rice and many floods, and told them all about mandarins and coolies, and how the latter pulled the former in rickshaws.

The hardest thing was to keep the project from getting out of hand, as the village hadn't had a going-away party for a long time. Why not hire a little square-dance group like in the old days? Done. They found a fiddler and a caller unequalled for getting the sets on their feet. They asked the priest to say a few words. Baptists, Catholics, Lutherans, Swedes, Finns, Russians, French – they all found it exciting to catch the spirit of the party. In the first place, it had one most original aspect: giving a party for an Oriental was somehow a sign of rare cosmopolitanism, and it pushed back

Horizon's frontiers considerably. And then, it was for Sam Lee Wong, who had gone through the good and bad years with them – a whole quarter-century. That was really something in a province like Saskatchewan which itself had barely more years than that to its credit.

But what should they give the café owner as a going-away present? The argument was heated. If only they had listened to the sensible voices who favoured a sum of money! Alas, it was the eternal gold watch that prevailed. With a gold chain as well, the whole works! They ordered it from a jeweller in Moose Jaw. Sam Lee Wong's name was to be engraved on it.

Then they started hanging the lanterns in the hall. They looked simply splendid. Old Smouillya held his tongue the whole time, though with difficulty, for he watched Sam Lee Wong sink ever deeper in his distress and could hardly resist the temptation to reveal the joys that awaited him.

IX

The autumn passed quickly. That Saturday it already felt like winter. In Sam Lee Wong's rickety cabin the nails in the walls creaked with the dry cold. He was all alone at one of his little tables; from time to time he looked up and smiled vaguely as if following with his gaze someone who had just come in and gone to sit at the other side of the room. In his boredom he nearly began to talk aloud to these imaginary customers, all phantoms from the past. In fact, Sam Lee Wong had an excellent memory. In a sense he had not forgotten a single person who had come to his restaurant, even if it were only to buy a package of cigarettes; but of course it was with his regulars that he was having his imaginary conversation. He invoked those who had been meticulous and polite, those who said thank you when their soup came – nothing much, but Sam Lee Wong remembered it – and those who carved at his tables with their penknives. He thought of them all with almost equal regret. Suddenly the door opened on the bitter cold and Smouillya appeared, unrecognizable, washed, shaven and combed. He headed for the nook at the back and

Sam Lee Wong's good suit, which he brought out to him, saying: "Come on, get into your Sunday suit. It's a special night!"

Sam Lee Wong thought Smouillya was playing a joke, and he was so pleased to see him happy that he did as he was asked. He put on the suit, and it hung so loose that the two of them burst out laughing, partly in nervousness and partly because it was funny, for Sam Lee Wong had to take very short steps in order not to lose his pants. Smouillya took care of that with a piece of binder-twine, and away they went, walking slowly because of the flapping pants, on snow that squeaked with little, soft cries under their feet. It was a night for a feast. The stars shone brightly, and so did the windows of the distant town hall. Sam Lee Wong saw nothing surprising in that, nor in being dragged thither by Smouillya, who couldn't stop laughing. There was a touch of festivity in the air, and in Sam Lee Wong's heart a contentment that corresponded a little to it. For yesterday he had glimpsed a kind of solution. Why not, in fact, make way for a young and enterprising Chinese like the Sam Lee Wong of former times, while he himself would become a laundryman? With all these newly rich in Horizon there'd be no lack of fine shirts to wash and iron by hand. And if he'd learned before to be a restaurant-keeper, why couldn't he learn the laundry business now? All in all, it was less complicated than the other.

His relief was so great that he felt like telling Smouillya. But it was Smouillya's turn, in his joy at having a surprise for Sam Lee Wong, to listen to no one, still less to poor Sam Lee Wong trotting along at his side.

In single file they entered the hall with its splendour of lanterns and its crowd of happy faces. There was a burst of applause. Sam Lee Wong smiled to the right, then to the left, at all these people who (wasn't it odd?) seemed to be looking at him with the same warm expression; but it must be for Smouillya. Then a catchy tune was struck up, and at the same time everyone gathered around him to sing, "For he's a jolly good fellow, for he's a jolly good fellow. . . ." And then more applause! People laughed when they saw Sam Lee Wong's expression and gave him friendly slaps on the shoulder, and he too began to laugh a little, though a touch of anxiety showed in his eyes.

Then Amanda came to take his hand and lead him up on the platform where the dignitaries were already seated. And there was Sam Lee Wong sitting between the priest and the mayor, exposed to the gaze of all, trying at least to hide his feet under the chair, for he had changed everything but his shoes.

The mayor stood up. He spoke for rather a long time about someone who had arrived in Horizon twenty-five years ago when the village, as they must remember, was just a few houses; and how he had worked hard with the others to make it the fine and prosperous little town it was today. A man who had laid his stone in the building and put his shoulder to the wheel! When he returned to the land of his birth, in honourable retirement from business, he could be sure that he had left behind a lasting memory.

Applause! Sam Lee Wong was just about to start clapping with the others but held back, pierced by a mysterious apprehension. The priest in his turn made a speech, and again the subject was honourable retirement and a memory that would never fade away.

Then a little girl in a white dress, her hair in a bow, curtsied in front of Sam Lee Wong and laid in his hands a slim box wrapped in tissue paper. From the dignitaries' looks he saw that he was supposed to open the little package. Sam Lee Wong stared long at the gold watch. He passed it to the mayor, who passed it to the priest, who gave it back to Sam Lee Wong. Then each of them turned to shake his hand, and everybody was clapping him on the back and saying, "Have a good trip, Sam Lee Wong! Happy retirement!"

Going home alone through the frozen night, abandoned even by Smouillya who had taken a drop and felt unwell, alone under the sky-vault so busy with stars that it made one think of the immeasurable exile of man on earth, Sam Lee Wong began to understand more or less clearly what was happening to him. He would have to leave. For he was the one they'd been saying goodbye to. It was he who had been congratulated by the mayor, who had been praised to the skies by the priest. What could he do here after all that? His eyes looked down at the earth and seemed to have dulled for all time.

For though he had lived apart from the village he had occasionally seen just this series of circumstances: someone would be treated like a king and almost immediately he'd be taking a train; he'd go away so far that no one would ever hear of him again. It must be the unwritten law of these parts. As soon as a whole village started to like someone publicly, that person had no choice but to be on his way.

On his way! Of course Sam Lee Wong had welcomed the notion, but only as a terminal adventure. When his short life here below was ended. When the time had come to go, in his coffin, to join his ancestors. Apart from them, who would care two cents whether he ever returned to great, swarming China? Perhaps even they, the ancestors, in their leaden slumber had ended by forgetting their lost child!

X

Through these slight hills, not really far from the village, that had attracted Sam Lee Wong from a much greater distance and then drawn him to his doorstep in contemplation almost every day, he had never once managed to travel as a simple sightseer. And here he was in the midst of them, sitting snugly in the train, his old suitcase beside him on the seat and, on the floor, a big parcel tied with cord.

A few of his old customers who had come to say goodbye at the station were surprised to see him take the eastbound train to go to China. Wouldn't it have been shorter to go back the way he had come, by Vancouver and the Pacific Ocean? But, they speculated, maybe Sam Lee Wong had finally decided to have a look around before leaving the country.

As long as he remained visible to his friends (who were stamping in the snow to keep warm, shouting through thick clouds of frosty breath, "Happy landings, Charlie! . . .") Sam Lee Wong had almost succeeded in getting into the high spirits of his send-off. Then he caught himself nodding and smiling at the fences and fields that had begun to slide past his window, but soon the old, familiar weariness took the place of nods and smiles and settled in again on his face. Now the train was labouring up the slope that led to the isolated little chain of hills. Sam Lee Wong moved closer to the window to at last have a good look at these cherished hills that had cast their spell over his whole life. But they no longer evoked or connected up with his childhood hills, which had somehow dissolved into these.

Inscribed on the horizon, he saw a slow-moving undulation, arrested and held for all time, as if (you might imagine) it were meant to rock asleep forever the immemorial distress of man. The hills were covered with snow. It rounded off their already rounded heads with their attitude of patience, of listening to some long story whispered up from the valleys' hollow. On the protected side, small trees bore brown and shrivelled leaves upon their branches, still trembling as if with a vestige of life in the breathing air. Sam Lee Wong saw no houses or outbuildings of any kind. Strange that a railway was there to carry you through such a wild and desolate scene.

In fact, it cut through the hills at the narrowest point, with a branch line that ran down as fast as it could to join the main track. The branch, and a whistle stop, had been built in former years to serve a few fine ranches located in the hills. Of these practically no trace remained. The train rushed through the whistle stop. A little later it emerged from the hills onto a plain so amazingly like the one he had left that Sam Lee Wong sat blinking, as if he couldn't believe his eyes. The same flat immensity. The same faint, dotted line of fence posts barely poking out of the snow, like the tracks of an animal in a straight line across the stretch of white. Human life reappeared in frail clusters of houses, then in bare villages. Sam Lee Wong scrutinized from afar the profile of each. He was on the lookout for one that would impress him.

He hoped for a village that would be big enough but not too big. Just enough to keep a café going. He had learned from the conductor that the first five or six villages on this side of the hills had no restaurant, and that two of them might just fill the bill for a café-keeper, if he wasn't fussy, of course.

Well, the train was slowing down just as it entered one of the villages that combined the qualities required. Sam Lee Wong could make out a snow-covered main street, little wooden houses on just one side of it, grain elevators – in short, a landscape as familiar as his memory of Horizon the day that he arrived. . . . But that had been on a sunny September day, and now the wind was whipping by in icy gusts. Never mind! Sam Lee Wong hastened to lug his suitcase and his big parcel to the steps of the carriage. He'd have to hurry. The train tarried no more than a minute or two at these almost lifeless whistle stops. Sam Lee Wong barely managed to drag his belongings down to the platform when the conductor ran out from the next car, waving his arms in protest, shouting: "You not get off here. Ticket good yet!"

From the platform, to reassure this kind man who seemed concerned about him, Sam Lee Wong shouted back: "Me not wish go further. Here all right! Very all right!"

The conductor threw up his arms as if to say, What can you do. . . for human beings! Already the train was picking up speed. It left behind the frail silhouette encumbered by its packages. A gust of wind caught Sam Lee Wong's grey scarf and wrapped it around his face, forcing him to grope for a few steps. At last he reached the station, set down his things and pulled away the scarf, which had half-blocked his vision. He found that his gaze was probing implacable and howling distances. He clambered over a high bank of snow ploughed up at the edge of the main street. He reached the trodden path that served as a sidewalk. There he stopped to empty snow from one felt boot. Then he went off in search of space to rent. That, it seemed, would not be hard to find, for a good part of the village was abandoned. Its only luxury, lying beyond its twenty-odd houses and set back a little in the fields, was a long hut with a corrugated tin roof: the curling rink. A good sign, that. It meant customers at night, after the game! And in fact that same evening some villagers going home from curling saw a light in the former barn that had been moved into the village to provide an office for the itinerant agronomist. One said, "Hey, that won't be bad, sandwich and coffee after the games!"

In the light of a naked bulb hanging by its cord from the ceiling they could see an old man with slanted eyes, his apron on, cleaning, tidying, like a bird that builds his nest where the world calls him. Some of them had the notion of going in to give him a hand or at least say a word of welcome. The others dragged them off, saying, "Aw, come on, you never know with these Chinks when they get old. Sometimes they get cranky. Let's wait and see, anyhow."

On a fine winter morning a few days later, you could read the following sign drawn in soap on the freshly washed window (less impressive, though, than the one in Horizon):

RESTAURANT SAM LEE WONG
FULL COURSE MEALS
SNACKS
SOFT DRINKS

And in a corner, in smaller letters:

Ice Cream, Soda, Cigars

Sam Lee Wong himself, in his apron, his grey scarf around his neck, stood in the half-open doorway, despite the biting

103

cold, waiting for his first customer. He knew from long experience that an open door was half the battle. Since no one showed up, he had all the time in the world to daydream as he gazed far across the snow-covered plain, blowing on his fingers to keep them warm.

And the miracle was there! From his new threshold he found that he could see as well as previously, but from the other side, the frail outline of the gentle hills imprinted on the winter blue of the horizon.

Before to his left, now on his right, they were still a part of his life. So there was no need to despair. Perhaps his ancestors hadn't quite lost track of their child who had landed. . .where? What was it now, the name of this village? Oh yes! Sweet Clover, Saskatchewan. . . .

He concentrated. He engraved the name in his mind with care, with diligence, as if it were a piece of information he must make known somewhere, if he were to be found at last.

He lifted his eyes up to the hills. The place he had been walking toward all his life could not be much farther now.

Hoodoo Valley

Hoodoo Valley

The group of Doukhobors newly arrived in Verigin, a prairie hamlet, were living for the time being in the round tents and converted railway cars that had been provided for them: a melancholy encampment on a hostile terrain invested by marshes, mosquitoes and, worse still, every evening, by boredom. Then, gathered like an immense family around a fire of branches, you could hear them intoning, all with the same low-pitched, afflicted voice, some song of their people.

No Doukhobor was ready to say it right out loud, but they were desolate.

"It's nothing like our Humid Mountains."

"Oh, no! Far it is from our green Caucasus!"

From the very start the plain had set about rebuffing them with its flat immensity, naked under the sky, this endless space, this too-vast exaggeration of a land where in winter, they said, it was cold enough to freeze your breath in your throat, and in summer hot enough to put an end to your days. And the people here, the ones who'd been living in this solitude awhile, what strange ones they were! Eaters of meat and other forbidden foods, they squabbled among themselves as if life wasn't hard enough already; or, carried away by a different madness, they'd dance till the tavern tables jumped. They couldn't be Christians, these folk who used alcohol and tobacco and never seemed to tire of spatting viciously among themselves.

The Doukhobor women, their blond hair carefully hidden under kerchiefs doubled to a point, had perhaps less time for boredom than their men. They cooked over little piles of embers, did the washing, laid it to dry on the grass, and went off across the naked plain, sometimes quite a distance, searching for bits of wood to burn. But their husbands, these great stalwarts, upright as oaks, with heavy moustaches, their blue eyes childlike and astonished, had all the leisure they needed for sighing and lamenting.

Their leaders, Streliov, Zibinov and Strekov, went out every day with their guide McPherson, the settlement agent, sometimes to the north, sometimes to the south, in search of land for their community. Up to now they had nowhere found a concession that in their eyes combined the qualities they obscurely felt would suit them.

The man McPherson, an ambitious and enterprising little Scot, had wagered that he'd settle his Doukhobors in no time, intending to use their success on Canadian soil as a stepping stone to promotion in his career.

The women, the children, the old men, would surround the three leaders on their return to the encampment and ask: "What did you see today, Zibinov, Streliov, Strekov?"

And these three, the men in whom they had placed their confidence, would reply: "Just the flat land. The same as here."

"And that was all?"

"Just prairie, I tell you. Nothing but prairie."

McPherson was fuming. What else did they expect to find here in the flattest stretch of all Canada?

A strange folk, gentle, dreaming, with only one foot in this world; but in their refusal, their disillusion, they had a tenacity that could outlast the most energetic. The people of the village, a handful of neighbours, immigrants themselves but resigned with good grace to their new land, began to grow impatient with these long-faced Doukhobors whose incessant plaintive songs reached them night after night in their scattered shacks. As if singing could change the prairie! It had heard other sighs, seen other regrets, this plain of exile and homesickness. In the end it always brought people around. Others, many others, had been through the same thing. The Doukhobors too would have to give in.

They didn't want to break up or settle in small groups as others did. That would have solved many problems, for the good land was by no means all in one place. Most often it was a patchwork created by ancient alluvia or waterways. But they absolutely refused to separate. They insisted on settling in a single region, old and young, grandchildren and grandparents together, along with nephews, cousins and friends – in short, the whole lost folk in one place.

So they sought a big stretch of arable land. At some distance from the camp such tracts of land were still to be found. McPherson took Strekov, Streliov and Zibinov to see them, across miles and miles of silent plain, often serene and inviting under the high, clear sky. Where the road stopped the wagon made its own trail through the grasses. In this way they'd seen a good part of the countryside: sandy, desert-like spaces overrun by the wind; others with a stubby growth like wire twisted and rolled together; others made almost livable by pretty groups of trees that showed from afar the presence of water. Nowhere did the Doukhobor leaders consent to stop.

"Nyet, nyet."

Here the country seemed too wild, too isolated; there they would spy tents or trappers' huts and suddenly were unwilling to have neighbours.

"Nyet, nyet!"

They shook their heads. Their eyes, blue and candid, wide with astonishment, always expressed the same tenacious estrangement.

And this had been going on for weeks.

The women were constantly on the lookout for the party's return.

"Come now, you must have seen something today that would suit us!"

"Nyet. We saw nothing but the flat land. Always the same."

They could find no other way to express their disappointment. Before they left the Caucasus, someone must have told them a very fancy story to attract them to the Canadian West, and they'd swallowed it whole. They always ended up singing their songs of lamentation. At such times the gentle landscape they had left behind, the land of acacias, of lemon trees and tender grass, came to life again behind their closed eyelids. For each new evil chases out the last; having forgotten the persecutions that had forced them to leave their native soil, their hearts retained nothing of it but the most tender recollections.

Oh, what nostalgia!

By now even the women were almost all infected by it.

This wretched plain all around! (At times you could see one of them stoop to pick up a pebble and hurl it violently as if to strike the immense countryside and take vengeance on its numb expanse.)

110

"What did you see today, Streliov?" asked Makaroff, the oldest and wisest, who thought the time had come to make the best of a bad job. Life wasn't so long, he often said. If we have to use up so much of it regretting the past, what's left for doing what's still to be done?

And Streliov, the oldest of the three leaders, a solid man with all the strength of his thirty years, began to sigh like a stripling.

"The same thing as here, Grandfather. The naked plain, always. And always, it seems, the same cruel indifference."

The old man drew nearer to poke the fire.

"I remember when I was young and we'd just been exiled to the Caucasus, life didn't seem so easy there either at the start. Did you say 'indifference,' Streliov? Do you have any idea how many trees – lemon trees and cherry trees and acacias – we had to plant there for every one that lived? Do you know that, Streliov?"

The immigrants, seated in a circle in the growing dark, were suddenly as struck by his words as they had been by their recurrent longing for their lost homeland. At once their eyes turned outward toward the plain which their imagination saw as endless: the mute, the enigmatic land. They did their best to see it covered with little whitewashed houses, with pens for the chickens, vegetable gardens, fences, milk pails upside down on the fence posts, busy comings and goings, and even their seesaw wells like the ones at home in the Caucasus, punctuating the prairie with the long strokes of their lever poles drawn dark against the sky. For awhile they were all comforted by the vision of the tremendous work to be redone and they burned with impatience to get started.

"True enough, you know," some of the more realistic women grumbled, "it's more than time we started in somewhere. You leaders, go off on your search again. And try to come back with some good news. It's high time to get on with our work."

But others, lulling their babies, held them tight to their breast as if defying the dark plain to steal them away. And suddenly they would begin to weep, doubtless because of some vague perception that the plain would finally take their children, would take thousands of others, would absorb as many lives as there were grains of sand, before this would even show. Still others, a few about to bear children, had an even stronger hatred of the stark land and the giant sky which their eyes probed in terror.

The ones with the most common sense were the very old women, tottering babushkas, come to this country with just enough time left to die and sleep in its foreign soil.

They scolded the younger ones: "What would our holy little father Verigin think, and him in exile in the wilds of Siberia, if he saw you now, downcast and fearful and always snivelling?"

And the others would reply: "Our little father Verigin promised we'd find peace at the end of the world, and harmony, and that in the place we went to we'd be of one heart and mind. Perhaps we didn't understand his orders. Did he really mean us to come to Canada?"

A very angry babushka scolded back: "There's no such thing as a country where we can be of one mind unless we try, each one of us, to make it so. Our little father Verigin promised us a land where they'd let us live in peace according to our ideal of non-violence and free conscience. He didn't promise the grass would be trimmed and the house all built and the bread on the table. Have you all gone mad? Tell me! The old Doukhobors of my time put more heart in their work and whined less. And they'd seen something of cruelty and injustice, before our good Loukeria, in those dark years when they wandered over Russia. What about those who fell under the knout of the Czarist soldiers rather than take arms against their brothers? Did you ever hear that they grumbled? Shame to these Doukhobors around me!"

In the end they prayed together under the great starlit sky. At least the stars were still familiar. Their eyes raised on high, they asked for a light to guide them on their earthly path.

"Little mother, it's not the work we're afraid of. It's the silence here. It's as if God no longer wanted to give us a sign. As if from now on he would be silent forever."

The wrinkled face, furrowed by life, was absorbed in contemplation of the flames.

"It is true. Since we came to Canada he has seldom spoken to us. But he is there, behind all that silence. Just wait, my lambs. Tomorrow, the next day, one day soon, he will surely give us a sign."

II

Forty miles north of the railway a great stretch of grassy plain, formerly pastureland to a herd of buffalo, was still there for the taking. That was the destination of the expedition that set out on a certain July morning.

The heavy wagon lumbered along at the trot – often a slow one – of the four prairie horses, all small but solidly built. Six men were in the party: the three Doukhobor leaders, then McPherson, flanked by his interpreter, James Craig, and the half-breed driver. They had left at dawn accompanied by particularly fervent women's voices raised in song, for after the long evening of prayer everyone had risen with the conviction that this day, at last, would be marked by divine favour.

At first they drove across a plain where a reddish grass waved as far as you could see; then others where a thick growth of weeds rose to the wagon's axles; saline patches harboured the noxious smells of many carcasses of young deer and dead birds; brushwood country, and muskegs where everyone had to get off and help the horses; morose land-

114

scapes where there was nothing living but the wind; and, from time to time, fresh little stands of elder trees or poplar. Almost everywhere the plain seemed uninhabited and silent.

Each patch of green in this limitless landscape could be seen for miles around, and this was all that kept the tired beasts going or altered the men's unblinking stare.

Evening was not far off. Still nothing hinted that they might be nearing the former buffalo pasture. McPherson was growing worried. Had they taken the wrong fork at the last faint crossing of the ways?

No path was visible now. They were navigating by guess-work across rocky soil or through virgin grass. The half-breed driver seemed as uncertain as the little horses themselves. Their ears pricked up anxiously from time to time. The leaders, impassive in the back, pretended to ignore these disturbing developments.

Suddenly McPherson exclaimed loudly in vexation. The land was changing without warning. For in fact, on emerging from a gulley of shadows that had hemmed them in for several minutes, they were met by an intense and gleaming light. There a new landscape stood revealed, one of surprising beauty, unsuspected even a moment ago.

It was Hoodoo Valley, so named by the Indians who were frightened of its strangeness and the curious power it had – precisely at this hour of day – over the unstable souls of men.

With an exotic splendour, more reminiscent of the Orient than of the plain with its assortment of quiet shades, it flamed up before them in the floods of copper light the sun spilled over it at this day's end. Countless flowers, pushing up through brambles and tall, sharp-bladed grass, gave off a glow in that light almost not to be borne. Flowers among which not one, so people said, was without its sting, its poison sap, its capacity to wound; but all strangely sumptuous, in umbels of garnet velvet, bunched heads of sombre gold, purple or milky corollas with stiff, smooth leaves shining with their lacquer.

In the distance clouds tinted blazing red enclosed this odd valley, surrounding it as with a chain of hills whose folds held an indefinable attraction. Each one appeared to open into the reddened sky a secret and mysterious passage toward a place where certainty and happiness must reign at last. From one minute to the next, moreover, beneath the constant flaming of the sky, the more distant clouds took on further depth and issued their silent call.

McPherson, almost caught in the spell for a moment, though he'd have been the last to admit it, got hold of himself. He hated this place above all others. He was about to give the order to leave at once when the three leaders, on their feet in the back of the wagon, began encouraging each other excitedly: "Da, da!"

This was the first time McPherson had heard them say yes.

Further words seemed torn from them by their excess of emotion and the infinite joy of being there together, all three unanimous.

"What's that they're saying?" asked McPherson.

The interpreter smiled with some commiseration.

"They want to get off here. They're talking about the Humid Mountains, something about receiving a sign at last. . .and I don't know what-all, it doesn't make much sense. . . ."

As if under a spell, they were barely recognizable, their faces lit up and transformed, their eyes gleaming. With one accord they leapt from the wagon and advanced toward the valley. Stones rolled beneath their feet, a fine dust rose from the earth where they walked, and this alone should have told

116

them of the poverty of the soil; but the Doukhobors paid no attention, their eyes dazzled, advancing in line toward the brilliance the setting sun had managed to extract from an inextricable tangle of thorn and thistle.

They stopped. One raised his arm and pointed to the mass of clouds resting on the sky's edge, forming enchanting hills that rolled back to beyond this world. Another pointed at the long streak of light that wound across the valley like a river of pale waters. The third fervently stared out at the fiery horizon.

"What do they say?"

"That there's all you need here to rejoice the heart of man," the interpreter said. "Mountains in the distance, a river in the grass, a rare kind of peace and birds everywhere."

True enough, for look! The burning air was filled with the presence of birds! Nesting in the serried thickets, calling from bush to bush, then, all at once, with great cries and whirring of wings, bursting into flight; creatures with flaming throats, crested with red or light yellow, thronged into the air. But these were unsociable birds and fled from men: their presence here, like that of the strange flowers, spoke further of the wildness of the place.

"But those aren't mountains yonder," McPherson tried to explain, "and that's no river in the valley. Tell them, Craig, that it's all mirage and trumpery. It's the sun and the time of day that make the cursed valley turn this way at sunset!"

But it was no use. The three Doukhobors had removed their hats as if to salute one of the most moving encounters of their lives. They stayed motionless a long time, their eyes moist, contemplating the landscape and listening to their conquered hearts.

"They know, at least I think they do," the interpreter reported, "that the mountains and rivers aren't real, but they

117

say, 'What's the difference, as long as we can see them? And if the three of us, by God's grace, can see again in this place the mountains and river of our sweet homeland, why should it be any different for our wives and children and old men? Won't they see these things too? And when they've seen them, won't they be reassured, as we are?'"

Then McPherson, forgetting that they couldn't understand him, shouted: "Just scratch that soil! See how poor it is! Look at that confounded brush, it's all that'll grow here. I can give you a hundred times better, a thousand times better! I can give you lovely flat fields where the grass is so tasty your horses'll whinny a mile away. Or if you want I'll find you land that's half woods and a real river running through it. Just a few hours from here, all that's waiting for you!"

But the Doukhobors would hear none of it. Beyond the call of reason now, exiled in elation, assured that they alone understood the world's mystery, they stood there, hat in hand, imagining that they had perhaps been shown an infallible sign of destiny. They took one pace forward and struck up a song of thanksgiving. The song found its way down the valley and echoed back twice, three times. The great, wild birds, and the dry leaves rustling at their passage, seemed shaken with surprise at hearing an old, exalted hymn rolling all the way from ancient Russia.

At last the three men ended their song. McPherson saw that they were weeping. Tears rushed impetuously from their eyes, washing the dust from their cheeks and disappearing in their blond moustaches. They wept without raising a hand to wipe their cheeks, in abandon and confidence, relieved once and for all of the cruelty of expectation.

McPherson waited yet awhile. Soon there would be an end to the fugitive beauty of the place. In a moment now it would be left bare: when the great footlight on the horizon dimmed, perhaps they would see that this was nothing but a wasteland under false, flamboyant colours.

But now the Doukhobors were showing their impatience to be gone. They were in a hurry to bring the good news to the others.

They sat on one side of the wagon, facing the same way. They were looking back when suddenly the valley dimmed into twilight and what was perhaps its true and poignant gloom. But in the shadow there still glowed on their inscrutable faces the flaming sky that their eyes had seen and their souls now bore away.

Garden
in the Wind

Garden in the Wind

*F*arther on, farther still than Codessa – that little Ukrainian capital of sorts in the Canadian North – after you've travelled for hours on an endless dirt road and beyond a wild stretch of plain, you suddenly see signs of what once upon a time tried to be a village. This is the place called Volhyn, in Alberta, and to tell the truth there's almost nothing to it, apart from the immensity and the solitary stroke of the road through it; above, the phone lines hum inexplicably in the air.

To one side of this poor track is an old-fashioned schoolhouse, with its *teacherage*, and beside it, a woodpile; all three abandoned. It's been a long time since the voices of children were heard here, or the bell that called them.

Even more enigmatic in its remoteness, all alone beyond the fields, there is a tiny prayer house, an odd kind of chapel. Barely seven or eight people could find room inside. Yet it was built just like a church and has all the parts: a bit of a porch preceded by three steps, a touch of stained-glass in the narrow slits that serve as windows, and even a little onion-shaped steeple. Nothing could be so strange in this flat expanse of uninhabited land as this reminder of the Orthodox faith.

Inside the prayer house spider webs cover the faces of aged icons. The dust of old bouquets of wild flowers lies where it has lain for years, at the feet of Saint Basil and Saint Vladimir. A madonna with faded features seems worn out by age and thankless labours. Outside, a never-ending moan: the prairie wind blows here like a sea wind, bringing the same unease, ceaselessly curling and whipping at the grasses as it does in water.

It was around the years 1919 and 1920 that this land was, as they say, opened for settlement. At that time a little group of peasants, most of them illiterates, came to these parts with their bundles and their babies, having left their native Volhynia months before. It was the first voyage of their lives, and they had crossed a continent, then the ocean, then most of another continent. Bewildered, they had pushed on with horses still farther across a solitude that grew from day to day, to reach at last, on a day in spring, this long, grassy plain that opened before their eyes like some endless reverie on man and his destiny.

Did they then have the feeling that all roads were wiped out behind them, that they would never come alive out of this extremity? And are they now all dead or disbanded?

Not quite. The road, straight for so long, at last bends slightly. A little aspen grove appears, all trembling with light, its leaves reversed, its branches trimmed to a man's height – the kind that in the West is a sign of an immigrant farm. Then a living house. And in the same moment, flowers. A mass of flaming colours that strike your eye, seize your heart.

So it was that one day, when a strange curiosity – or rather that melancholy, that taste for seeking out and sharing the most utter solitude which often possesses me – guided me along that road, I saw before me, under the enormous sky, against the hostile wind and among the tall grasses, this little garden, fairly bursting with flowers.

In those days I often said to myself: what's the point of this, what's the good of that? Writing was a chore for me. Why bother inventing yet another story – would it be closer to reality than the facts themselves? Who still believes in stories? And in any case, haven't they all been told? That's what I was thinking that day when, toward evening on that road which seemed to lead me nowhere, I saw in the very emptiness of drought and desolation that surge of splendid flowers.

Scarlet poppies with their dark core, others, their warm pink rimmed with a stronger hue, some like fine, white silk rumpled in your hand, offered their delicately pleated faces to the dry wind. How long could they cling to life in this rough wind? Perhaps not a single day. In double ranks lupines on their slender spikes wavered like candle flames in a wind-blown procession. But the delphiniums, now, turned back to the sky its own gaze of indifferent blue. Geraniums in brighter tones, fragile snapdragons, their small throats swollen as if from milk or honey, some flowers tall and haughty, others timid, all pressed close together as if in boundless surprise at being there. Had I ever, until that moment, seen flowers at all? Have I ever truly seen them since? Perhaps only on that deserted road from Volhyn have I been quite penetrated by the mystery of this world called flowers.

Sometimes even now when the vision of that little garden on the edge of the inhabited earth comes back to mind, I think: it was a dream and nothing more!

But then other things come back to mind as well: the face, the smile, the memory of Marta.

Her full name: Maria Marta Yaramko.

At least on her grave, hidden among the tall wild barley and meadow grass, on the wooden cross that barely rises clear, that's what is written, letter after shaky letter, as if by a hand that scarcely knew how to write.

Here then is her story as I discovered it, piece by piece.

II

Early that morning, despite the pain that woke in her body with her own awakening, Marta went out of the low, white-washed house, a white kerchief tied beneath her chin, her apron billowing, to reconnoitre the sprouts in her garden which were barely showing out of their seeds, just pushing into life. For springtime had managed to come once more, that spring which out Volhyn way surely had a longer and harder road to go than in any other corner of the world. The wind on high spoke of it in the heavens, and the lively plants, sowed in other days when Marta had faith and hope, showed themselves still full of health and youth. At her feet she recognized a leaf, so newly emerged from its sheath that it still had the shape of its former casing. With her hand she helped this birth along, brushing away a twig that could hinder it, crushing to dust around it a crumb of earth that could seem mountainous to such a tiny creature. She stood up, within sight of this small, unfolding life, and contemplated the disconcerting size of sky and earth. Why did her garden, started when she was young, still force her to take care of it? Why, in her old age, so much weariness in the service of life? She didn't know, sought no further. She bent down again, found another tip of green and tenderly uncovered it to the light of day.

Some weeks later the weeds in Marta's garden also sprang to life. She should have known by now that once you become the ally of anything in this world you have a thousand enemies and no more peace. Marta, a friend to flowers, had discovered an enormous hostility toward them in the created universe.

On this May morning she directed her attack against the grass shoots within an enclosure of chicken wire where for nearly thirty years now she had been growing vegetables, yes, but flowers as well, scattered everywhere amidst these nourishing plants. Thus her dull life had had this richer side, a little mad and fanatical. In no time she had weeded out one row. By now she believed she could tell the difference between good and bad. Yet once, having allowed a certain weed to grow to maturity (at first mistaken for a domestic plant), she had watched how, under her care and watering, it flourished and grew beautiful and finally bore flowers shaped like tiny bells, as gracious and well made as those of her favourite plants. Perhaps, then, all beings in this world bore fruit according to the love spent on them.

That's how it went with her thoughts these days. She no longer had the strength for heavy tasks. Now she gave herself solely to her little garden, and as she did so her thoughts, like plants well cared for, also sprang free from silence and routine. They became company for Marta. It seemed to her that they were beautiful, each with its loneliness. Sometimes she was astonished to find they were her own. On that day a feeling crept into her heart that they were too lofty to have come from her alone. But from whom else could she have had them? Perhaps she had always had them, but locked deep inside her, as indistinct as the flower-to-come in the heart of a dull seed. And if she had not lost her robust health, if she had not felt the idea of her death flapping at her soul like a frightened moth, would she have paid the least attention to her thoughts, would she have known that hers was a human life?

Moving awkwardly on her knees, she cleared the earth around the cosmos. She spoke to the flowers the whole time, congratulating them on their good nature – flowers of the poor, making no demands, living in almost any soil, born again of seeds they had dropped in autumn. But no less than these she had loved certain of her plants that she had taken great pains to save. Something like an angry thought crossed her mind. Why, she wondered, should a small life as tranquil as a flower's have so many enemies?

Now look: there she was scratching at the earth around a peony, and a stalk detached from its root came away in her hand, cut through at its most sensitive point, just where it left the earth. Och, she thought in vexation, because of a greedy grub it's turned to worm now, and it could have been two or three great flowers, moist and proud. And what good did it do, for the worm itself will surely be eaten today! But it was she who found him in the dark earth and crushed him, almost with pleasure, beneath her heel. There was nothing left but to protect the other young plants and there was only one way, long and tiring, which she had been obliged to follow. Each year the flowers appeared to her as a wonder she would never see clearly enough; but the care they demanded was equally inexhaustible.

She went back inside the house to cut from cardboard what looked like little collars, and then out again to force them into the earth around the roots. This done, she stood up, her face somehow shrunken, sagging and a little empty from fatigue.

129

She still had to support the plants in their struggle against the wind, with sticks planted beside them and attached with a bit of string. She went about her task with deliberate slowness, carefully avoiding any sudden move that might revive the pain momentarily asleep in her right side. It was the pain that caused her to give the impression of bearing within her something fragile, of great value.

Far away Stepan passed, gave her an irritated glance, then went on his way, scattering to the ends of their land the raging sound of hostile words. The whole day long you could hear this indistinct grumbling sound that traced his path from one place to the next, now nearby, now almost indecipherable in the strong western wind, itself a great complainer.

Marta stood up for a moment to watch this man go past, her husband, her life's companion: was it really possible? And what kind of thing was young love that could sometimes join natures so completely opposite?

His intermittent growling was lost in the hot wind, which today for a change whispered of tenderness but as if that were a far country infinitely hard to reach.

She went inside and began the chore of preparing something for the man to eat. When the soup was ready she brought it to the table and neatly set the places. She wasn't going to give up good manners just because Stepan had turned into a savage. For a centrepiece she placed among the dishes some blue cornflowers in a little bowl that she had once painted with flowers, blue as well, for that was her favourite colour. Blue seemed to her to have a gentle, dreamlike quality, the colour of day – but of night as well under certain kinds of clouds or moonlight. She went to the doorway to call Stepan. He was nowhere to be seen, and as her gaze settled on the distance she forgot why she was there and realized that she was looking with a completely new thrill of attention at things that had surrounded her for years.

She would likely have been most surprised if a passer-by familiar with the ways of the Canadian West, wandering by some miracle this far along the dusty road, had been able to say at once that this was a Polish or Slavic farm. Differ though they might in some respects, all these farms had in common their small grove of aspen, the lower branches pruned to give free passage to the air and sun, and under them a hundred little coops, some for broody hens, others still for geese or young ducks held captive. In these thin copses, already sparse, there would often be horned animals that grazed and cleared the space still more. This was the kind of little wood that Marta saw to the east of the house, like a protection against the infinity of the plain. Alas, it had turned into a junk yard: carcasses of buggies without wheels forming little settees in which no one ever sat, and stranded sleds or cutters. Yet something light and singing went through the place, as if the wind, wherever in the world it might have been, whatever despair it might have known, grew tranquil and regained its calm on coming back to this little wood.

Not until today, after thirty years of living in Volhyn, did Marta realize that she and old Stepan, perhaps unwittingly, had reproduced almost exactly the atmosphere of the poor farm in their native Volhynia from which they had come. Almost the same farm this was but surrounded by a savage silence. How strange it seemed to her, all of a sudden! But what had captured her attention was today's very peculiar sound of air in motion. She listened, poised like someone listening to a voice, a distant call, and suddenly she was filled with living joy. In this warm noontime, barely tempered by a breeze just strong enough to make the aspens tremble, this was what she heard: the faint clicking of their leaves, like festive castanets. The same sound Marta remembered hearing

131

in just such an aspen wood in Poland, when she was young and thinking only of the future. Oh, this dear aspen wood filled with music, she could count on it then to link her always with the wellspring of her life!

Then she remembered why she had come to the door and searched across the plain which seemed to be lying in a dream of expectation – she had never got over the notion, however often she looked out at it, that behind the emptiness someone was there. Not knowing where to direct her voice to reach Stepan, she simply shouted into the immensity: "Hey! Yaramko!"

That was what she called him these days. If she called him "Man!" as he nowadays said "Woman!" to her, it would have seemed an offence against their love of former years. On the other hand, a feeling of friendship still clung to the Christian name Stepan, and she could not bring herself to use it: it would have been like trying to call back a person who had long ceased to exist.

"Yaramko!" she shouted again. "Your soup!"

To make him come running there was really nothing left but this call to eat, as if he were a farm animal.

From the far fields, he straightened up and came toward her, a puny silhouette with short legs and large, bushy head. As a fly surrounds itself with buzzing, he walked surrounded by his own complaints, a constant, wearisome reiteration of wrongs, of defiance and threats directed at nothingness, grown to such a litany that he himself was perhaps no longer aware of it.

As he came alongside the little garden he stopped, saw where Marta had been working and seemed to take violent exception to it. He shook his head in a rage and broke out with a new attack of lamentations. Then, his cap pulled down to his ears, he sat down to eat, grabbed some bread and, as if this too was the object of his wrath, tore at it with his teeth.

Could this face that Marta saw before her still be called human? His forehead, his eyes, his mouth – features that even in the grimmest face would constitute a door of access – were concealed by hair. His great rake-like moustache covered the whole lower part of his face; the frightful briar patch of his hair spread daily on all sides, with enormous tangled eyebrows rising darkly to meet it; beneath them, deep-sunken wolf's eyes watched, black and defiant.

Tonight, thought Marta, she would dig out of her trunk their old wedding photograph so as to see Stepan's face and remind herself that this was indeed the man with whom, before the priest and for her lifetime, she had sworn an alliance of affection.

III

What kind of evenings did they spend together in Volhyn, in this season when evenings were long and astonishing pink skies hung in suspense over the darkened earth? From a pile of Ukrainian newspapers printed in Codessa Stepan would pull an old number – any one, he had read them all before. As he laboriously fitted words and phrases together he could still work himself into a rage at the absurd attempt of mankind everywhere to improve its lot.

Marta, for her part, would get out the Eaton's catalogue. For her it was a friend. It was from the catalogue that she had learned a few English words, though they were the farthest from the necessities of her life: dress, coat, hat, rug, curtains, garden swing. It was a good schoolmaster: it illustrated its words with pictures Marta could understand.

In the beginning, before it became a book of knowledge, it had perhaps, above all, been a book of covetousness. All she lacked at that time became clear to her as she leafed through this catalogue filled with pictures that made you want. This beautiful modern kitchen, for example, with a proper sink and gay plastic curtains; or that maroon coat with the fur collar. Marta had imagined that with such a coat she could run away from Volhyn, take her place in the civilized world and join her children who would no longer be ashamed of her. Now it was only the pages of garden seeds that made her heart beat with desire.

The catalogue opened of its own accord at these pages she had studied a hundred times. Once more she was touched at the infinite variety of flowers. She dreamed of seeing them this summer, perhaps her last, all represented in her garden.

Stepan rustled his paper, threw it aside, took the lamp and began to climb the stairs. She followed. The lamp blown out, they lay beside each other under the eiderdown of fine goose feathers sorted by hand. What had she not made with her hands? Pillows, also stuffed with goose down, coloured quilts, not to mention the thousands of meals she had prepared, and all the other thankless drudgery such as killing chickens or catching the warm blood of the still-screaming pig. If it had not been for her garden and her flowers, which testified in her favour, how much more terrified she might have been at the thought of leaving this world!

The night before her promised to be long, like a long journey of the soul turning, turning around itself. . . . The Eaton's book had taught her none of the words we call abstract. To recapture her thoughts of nostalgia and regret she had recourse to the old language of the Ukraine which she and Stepan would have used if they still used any with each other. Those feelings that we never express, that live crouched in the deepest crannies of the soul, that we never name – how do they manage not to die completely? Suddenly Marta was aware of the wind whining about the roof. She wondered if she was not already touched by the illness that would carry her off. Under her fingers, on her right side, was a tiny lump no bigger than a walnut. When she pressed it, the pain awoke.

And what would happen, she wondered, if she tried once more to make contact with Stepan, to confess her anxiety? What would happen then? Would he tell her to go and be looked after? But what for? She felt weary and discouraged at the thought of the long trip to Codessa, and then the train to McLennan where there was a little hospital. The worst cases were sent farther still, to Edmonton.

Edmonton, capital of Alberta, she rehearsed like a good schoolgirl who loses no opportunity of reinforcing a lesson learned.

Edmonton was, nonetheless, unreal to her. At times she had to make an effort to believe that beyond Volhyn there were cities and vast populations, and that all those things, the world and its countries and human societies, actually did exist.

Most of all she hated drawing attention to herself, having people fuss over her, perhaps being a nuisance. Her life didn't seem to be worth that trouble, and fear overcame her at the very notion of the slightest inconvenience she might cause. In fact, she could not follow too precisely what went on in her mind, and by dint of thinking silently to herself she came to be unsure of everything, even her melancholy.

Thus one night she reached the point of wanting to detach herself from all things so that nothing else would be taken from her. Her heart was like ice. No trace of a desire aroused her now. She even thought she might not plant flowers anymore. Good Lord, who would care? What passer-by, what other soul, would ever worry about the flowers at Volhyn!

But when summer came, under its excessive sun, there were perhaps more flowers than ever in this little garden at the end of the long dirt road from Codessa to Volhyn.

Lacking the strength to make rows or compose her intricate designs with groups of plants – diamonds, points or squares – that she had taken such pleasure improvising every spring, she had let them grow this time according to chance and providence, and the effect was perhaps the more striking because of it. Under giant clouds or a clear sky, the mass of packed and varied flowers mixing their brilliant colours formed a kind of serried round-dance, crying summer to the whole horizon.

Unable to go on caring for them, Marta now went near them only to rest and enjoy the show they made.

She would sit on a little stool right in their midst, closest to summer, in the very heart of this marvellous and incomprehensible summer. Yet she remembered how winter had piled the snow until the windows were covered; she remembered the fierce winds, she had not forgotten their fury. And she would sit there for hours, almost without moving, hands crossed on her knees, to all appearances just an old woman without much to expect of her life or of this world; but her soul, resolute and full of good will, was searching as it had never done before. She asked herself, gently astonished, "Summer, what is summer really?"

Pensively she considered this gilded light, this well-being of leaves and air, this health in all things, this fervent living, this joy, mute and secret, and said to herself, "Summer, summer, what is it anyway?"

Her white kerchief framed a face whose deep tan no longer disguised the clay-like tint that lay beneath, against which her eyes appeared each day to be a more striking blue. She looked again at her delicate poppies, her fragile snapdragons; she saw her flowers healthy and alive. A breeze stirred among them, and as they all together started tossing their heads they seemed to maintain that they were the true thing in this life:

its gentleness, its beauty, all its tenderness. Oh, the silly creatures! They seemed to claim they were the only ones who knew what it was about.

Marta caressed them with her hand as she would have caressed someone too innocent, too young to understand, such as a child. And were not flowers, in their innocence, a kind of eternal childhood of creation?

But when she caught herself thinking this way, in regions which she felt were so much beyond her, she would take herself to task: Stop that now. You'll never be any good at thinking. Stop it, it's not for you.

IV

A few days later she had the notion of bringing some of her scarlet lilies to the long-forgotten icons in the chapel. And away she went. Today the wind touched her lightly. Around her, as she walked with deliberate steps, one might have thought the wind indulged in mischievous games, now tugging upward at her long skirt, now raising little whorls of dust around her. Her lilies over her arm, her hair well hidden under the white kerchief, she made her way along this endless dirt road, straight and lonely as if it came from time's beginning. Marta contemplated the sky, so wide, and the horizon, so patient, and her own life, buried in so much silence that it seemed to have dissolved in it.

"What kind of life did you have anyway, Marta Yaramko?" she asked herself as candidly as if she had been talking to a mere acquaintance. But she didn't know what kind of life she'd had. The question is hard enough for anyone to answer. For her, with almost no points of comparison with other lives, the problem was insoluble.

But seeing herself underway on this long, long road which

after Codessa went on to other villages, bigger and bigger, and came at last to cities, she felt drawn onward, carried toward a human family, a murmur of voices. Notions of busy crowds awoke in her mind. She daydreamed of them as of something fantastic; she felt in her heart a little shock of adventure, of excitement. It seemed to her that she was travelling toward Canada.

She was a part of Canada, of course; somewhere, carefully tucked away, she even kept her naturalization certificate. To get it she had merely to declare before a witness that she loved the country and would be loyal to it. But Canada seemed to her less a country than an immense map with strange cutouts, especially in the North; or was it no more than a sky, a deep and dream-filled waiting, a future in suspense? Sometimes it seemed her life had been spent on the edge of the country, in some vague zone of wind and loneliness that Canada might yet embrace. For how could those in Volhyn, now reduced to a handful, old and complaining, have reached out and touched it? They were no longer quite Ukrainian but not quite Canadian either, poor lost folk, so discouraged it seemed there was no way they could help themselves except perhaps by disappearing.

She raised a baffled gaze to the sky, wide and immense.

"It's your fault as well," she reproached it, "you let us stray. You held back. It's true, it is!" she tried to explain, as if to someone or something. "We came into the world in our little villages in Poland, living on top of each other, where you could hear the neighbours crying or laughing in their house. And next thing you know we're lost away here in so much silence and sky, our lives small and forgotten as those of insects.

"You ask all the questions," she protested to the sky, "but do you ever give an answer? Will you ever tell us why we came so far, what wind blew us here, what we're doing here, the poor of the Ukraine, in these farthest prairies of Canada?"

Then, tired and upset at having dared to think such high-flown thoughts, she brought her attention back to her surroundings. On both sides of the road the grasses waved in the wind. Used to rougher treatment, today they bent gently over, and their furry heads in ripe, half-moulting panicles formed a golden florescence as far as you could see, a blond froth floating on the surface of their endless movement.

And Marta's heart melted in a mysterious way, as if in this eternal play of wind and grass and sunlight there was for her an inexhaustible consolation.

V

The state of disrepair in the little chapel shocked her
deeply – though she should have expected it, for she was the
only one in recent times to have cleaned it up at all. Dust,
ruins, silence! You could no longer make out the faces of the
saints in the pictures they had brought along from Volhynia
to have these uncertain friends at their sides in the great
uprooting. Who had withdrawn? God, forgetting his creatures
lost in the depths of the Canadian waste? Or they themselves,
the humans, through a failure of the imagination? Who could
understand these things, she wondered; but at once renounced
the dizzying thought. Then memories awoke in her heart, just
as, encouraged by the silence on the edge of humid marsh-
lands, innumerable birds arise out of the grasses, out of their
sleep.

Her youth appeared to her: confident, daring to the point
of foolhardiness. She was the one who had wanted to leave
and prodded at Stepan's will, for he was frightened by the
long journey toward the unknown. She was the one who had
swept him along in the ardour of her faith in this still undis-

covered country, about which they had known nothing but its name and immensity.

She remembered the amazement that had overcome them as day after day they rolled in their immigrants' train across an unchanging landscape.

She tried to remember how all those things had come about – the journey, their arrival, the frenzied pace of their labours. But that whole human adventure was so impregnated with silence that even those who had lived through it wondered about its reality. It was as if they had entered alive into a kind of limbo, between this life and the Eternal. How could you deal with such solitude? Yet they had tried. Oh yes! No one could reproach them for not trying, with their bare hands if need be, to create in this silence of God and man their little tender life, intimate and domesticated. But what were a dozen houses here, and their few children – whom the country had in any case quickly claimed as its own?

How could Marta, at twenty, have been expected to understand her heart's longing for those enormous distances, those wide horizons – she who now knew their frightful boredom! She looked again at the icons. In their first days at Volhyn, when they were young and enterprising and thought they could tame the prairie, they had built this little chapel far from their cabins, leaving room around it for the village they liked to think would take life and shape in these vast, empty fields. When they had their chapel, a priest would surely come: that was their simple reckoning, their naïve conviction. But no priest ever came, except the one from Codessa to bless the grave of someone out here; and as soon as the rites were accomplished he fled from the place, for it inclined men to see themselves as transients of a single day, here in this world.

Then Marta grew attentive to a breath of air trembling on the threshold; it was the wind, seemingly astonished to find this long-locked door standing open. You'd think it was shy about coming in, though filled with curiosity. "What's going on today?" the wind seemed to whisper.

And Marta smiled as if a friendly soul had made a little sign to her. Nothing could be more caressing and enchanting than the wind, so often furious in this country. All the moods of the spirit, the sterile revolt of man that disturbs the mind almost to madness; the great waves of boredom that wash in from all sides; but also the relaxation, the gentleness and calm – it seemed as if the wind contained all these and tried to express them, one after the other. It must know our souls or something of what goes on there, Marta thought to herself at times. How else could it be so changeable, so impetuous, sometimes submissive, but always searching, searching. "What are we searching for, will you tell me?" she asked, as if she and the wind were trying to solve the same riddle. Then in a lively voice she invited it: "Well, come in, won't you?"

And as if the sound of that human voice had really called the wind, it crossed the threshold. Light and singing, sweet smelling from its journey across the plains, timid and joyful at once, a breeze invaded the narrow chapel. She heard it leap from one side to the other, bounce gently off the walls, lift a scrap of paper from the floor, then freeze in some corner like a playing child who pretends he is unseen.

"You're feeling young today," she told the wind. "You've forgotten the troubles of the world."

It was amazing how much in creation made her think of childhood: flowers, the wind sometimes and birds. For her, what was old was winter, anger, boredom. Summer and tenderness were unalterably young.

Suddenly her three little ones were before her eyes – had she ever really had them to herself except when they were very small? Just long enough to teach them the speech of the

144

Ukraine, a few songs, a few dances from Volhynia, and the government had taken them away, teaching them English, shaping them in its own way for a life quite different from the one she could have offered. What should she have done? Follow the path of the younger generation? Go to school herself? Perhaps, but it would have been too hard; she and Stepan were already too stupefied by drudgery, too worn ou. for that new, desperate effort. And now they were irrevocably separated, she in Volhyn and her children somewhere far away, leading the life of the times. Could she blame them? Marta tried to imagine how it might have been if she'd appeared at home in her own mother's lifetime, seeing that old woman, so stubborn, so ignorant that she'd predicted to the young couple about to leave for Canada: "You'll never get there. There's a great abyss somewhere, you'll fall into it."

Marta trembled. She realized that her children, if they were now with her and old Stepan, would feel as estranged as she herself would under the thatched roof where she was born. She caught herself weeping softly. She saw herself, as it were, without parents and without children. What was the reason for such loneliness? Too much progress, and too fast? Or not enough? All she could seem to glimpse was that one day descendants of hers far enough from their origins to feel sure of themselves in this country would perhaps not be ashamed of their old immigrant grandmother. She smiled in her heart at these strangers, one of whom she could hear asking, "Our little old grandmother Yaramko, what was she really like?"

At last she left off crying and said, as if excusing herself for a fault, "It's the sickness does that." And as she looked again at the icons she was suddenly resentful of them. They were Ukrainian saints. What did they know about the life of immigrants in Canada? Or about life, for that matter!

But she was afraid that with such ideas she might irritate

them more. What was the good of thinking anyway? That wasn't why she had come here. She just wanted to tidy the place a little, that was all she seemed good for anymore.

She arose, fetched a pail from behind the altar and crossed a corner of prairie to fill it at the creek. The whole meadowland was covered with high grasses of many kinds, unified and mixed together by their rustling sound and their tireless waving to and fro. When her pail was filled she went back along the path she had trodden on the way. In the high heavens the wind was passing, leaving among the clouds the same quiet waves as down below among the grasses. The breathing of this immense and – today at least – placid solitude soothed her mind and its torment of identity. The whole world was lonely, after all, and blessed in spite of it. Besides, it was such a relief not to hear old Stepan grumbling. It was he who had cursed and rejected their children for following their own destinies. Ah, that's no way to act, she reproached him in her thoughts (the only way she ever reached him now: what was the use?).

She looked around her at the waving grass. The slim ears of wood millet, the hairy fescue grass, this great sea of wild grain swept in an unending swell. And this, which she had seen a thousand times, caught her attention again and lightened her heart. Once again the thought crossed her mind that the plain was deep in a great dream of things to come, and was singing of patience, with the promise that all things, in their time and place, would yet be accomplished.

Kneeling on the floor, she attempted to make it shine as it once had. What for? Not for the Lord, at any rate. Supposing he was alive and present, she imagined he would feel more at home outside, on the wind's wings in the cool air, than in this little chapel where the smell of must would outlast all her efforts. Not for the future either did she scrub this floor.

Without its children, Volhyn had no more than a few years, months perhaps, to live. Maybe Volhyn would die for all time on the day she herself disappeared. Perhaps in the last analysis she was washing here only to ensure Volhyn an end that was clean and worthy. So that no one could say, "Volhyn died before Marta."

Her task at an end, she cast a final glance at the icons, whose eyes, dusted clean, could now see how little help they had brought.

She withdrew a step or two, gave them a nod, not quite a friendly one, just polite, then closed the door behind her as she left. And the wind, which had scurried after her along the ground, followed her off, as if today it went everywhere with Marta.

VI

But the Volhyn wind does not long remain the friend of grasses or flowers or the soul that loves and nurtures life. From the side of the distant Rockies it came down in searing gusts one day. Under a darkened sky it stirred and whirled the flying earth reduced to finest dust.

Marta, grieved by the mistreatment her flowers would suffer, tried to come to their rescue. With bits of string she forced the gladioli to submit to their supporting sticks. She herself could barely withstand the attack of the wind and the lumps of earth it tossed in her face; how would the flowers fare on their tender stalks? Her pain, rebelling against the effort she was making, rose against her, rapping at her side with tiny, hard, well-placed blows. "Will you stop!" she said, vexed. "Have I time for you just now?"

No more than two steps from her house, battling against the wind, she resembled some blurred human form caught in a desert dust storm; and the flowers around her, all bent in the same direction, were like lopsided butterflies.

When she had safely anchored her gladioli it seemed unfair

not to do the dahlias. Having gone to the rescue of a few of her creatures, how could she ignore the others? They might notice! Not until she had given the whole garden what protection she could did Marta herself take shelter. Standing at her little window which was almost obscured by the storm, her face against the pane, she watched her flowers' tormented dance in the gloomy, thickened air until at last they too turned grey under their coat of dust, like the sky and air around them. Occasionally one, torn loose, would rise in a whirl as if in an invisible spiral.

Then, waiting for the storm to end, Marta sat down, crossed her hands and remembered how this little garden was born and grew, for in a sense it told the real history of her life.

At that time they had not been long in Volhyn. Everything was still to be done. They had nothing but a shelter, camping in a shanty that barely kept out the rain, with a few chickens, a cow and their babies. They were short of everything, and Stepan that day was about to set off on the stiff forty-mile trip to buy the things they needed most urgently. On the point of leaving he had asked, "Do you want anything else now, besides the sugar and salt and bread?" In those days he was a fairly good husband, asking about her wants in a tone that was still well-meaning.

It was spring, an immense springtime of mud, of almost liquid earth, with a lofty sky that was reflected in a thousand unsewed patches. "What else do you need?" With this memory a smile came to Marta's face, a smile of compassion and friendship for what she had been in those hard times. Wouldn't it have been simpler to ask what she could do without? The list of indispensable things had grown so long! Discouraged at having to choose, she had looked around at the mud and the endless unfurling of the desolate naked plain

149

that surrounded and laid siege to their shanty. As soon as you stepped outside you sank into sticky clay that clung to your soles in heavy clumps. That was when she had the idea of bringing her first garden flowers to this lonely land: sunflowers, maybe poppies too.

Surprisingly, Stepan had no objection, and brought back what garden seeds he could, seven or eight little envelopes that produced a fine harvest and plenty of new seeds to plant. The following summer these formed a harmony of colours that immediately seemed at home, as much so as the horizon or the clouds. A house in its own place, a flower where it belongs, a tree where one is needed – what was the meaning of all that? Marta had often wondered, without ever finding an answer that satisfied her.

But do wonders not bring other wonders? One evening, a few years later, a stranger – they never found out anything about him or what chance brought him so far into that country – a stranger came along the bumpy road in a little car that sat high on its wheels. At the sight of her giant sunflowers and shining poppies he stopped and got out of the car. He approached the flowers and greeted them with an astonishment that his hasty movements betrayed. He bent down, plucked a gillyflower, examined it closely and smiled. Finally he turned toward the wretched hut a gaze that called for an answer.

Marta, who was spying through the little window, felt that she had to go out. At once the stranger began speaking volubly to her. She did not understand his language. In her turn she spoke in Ukrainian, but he too failed to understand. They looked at each other in embarrassment. But Marta would have sworn that this man felt indebted to her for a sudden buoyancy of spirit. Was it the flowers? But how could ne take them as a personal offering? Could it be that for

150

certain souls confidence in life, wherever found, came as a precious gift? If so, they themselves must be generous and noble, Marta had said to herself.

Well, about six months later they received – from the stranger, beyond a doubt, but with no letter or explanation – a little package of bulbs that had sat for a long time in the Codessa post office.

Marta looked up, searching in the whirling dust outside for the countless purple dahlias that had come from those dozen bulbs, and the gladioli too, whose shining white still showed in glimpses through the opaque light.

"And what about the story of the rose I had from Lubka!" she said.

From that dear old friend in Codessa, whom she had not been able to visit, alas, for so long, she had received a rose of India taken from her garden. It was pressed between two blank pages as a kind of letter – for Lubka, poor soul, had never learned to write. From this one flower, hung from her ceiling to dry – head down, as it should be – Marta had been able to recover some three hundred seeds, which had given Volhyn almost as many roses, and each of these in turn had produced its hundreds.

Marta lost herself in her calculation of the infinite descendants of a single flower. She entered into the contemplation of such munificence as into a dream, beautiful and absurd. One hand on her ailing side, her eyes fixed in a deep reverie, she listened, no longer discouraged, to the howling, hot wind from the west. Neither wind nor tempest nor any winter could ever prevail against the gentle will to live of these lovely things she saw on earth!

Now drought descended on the tortured country. With so many grievous sights in the world, how can we find in ourselves room for regrets or compassion for mere flowers? Sitting in the oppressive heat on the bench beside the house, almost as crushed as the few flowers that had survived the storm, time and again Marta was on the point of fetching some water for them. But the only water was in the dug-out, a kind of pond hollowed to hold the rainfall for the animals during torrid summers. It was far away, on the only sandy spot of their farm, about a quarter of a mile off. There were moments when Marta dreamt sweetly that the thing was done: she had dragged herself thither, brought back two pailfuls and distributed the water as fairly as she could. But then her eyes opened on the drooping leaves and corollas and she felt almost bitter against these creatures, always calling on her for this or that. Weren't they all going to die in any case, with the autumn's first frost? What was so important about keeping them alive an extra day?

But finally off she went. Which will go first, she wondered, me or the garden? And in spite of everything, her heart hoped it would be the garden, so that when she herself went she would have no worries over it.

Far away in the fields Stepan looked up. He saw this spectacle: the old woman – and there was no doubt she had suddenly grown very old – with her two pails, struggling with all her body as if to pass through an invisible wall. What madness was this? When everything was perishing with heat, thirst and despair, and life was an immense, dust-ridden exile, how could anybody still worry about a few wretched flowers? Now it was flowers, in the old days it had been songs and music. He was slowly grasping, and had been for some time, the way in which Marta had always been his enemy, loving life as she did despite the bitter blows it had rained upon them. He was seized by a kind of jealousy and fury, seeing only evil intentions around him. He would show this old woman what he could do when pushed to it. Either she would declare herself for him and against life, or he would have his vengeance. Indeed, on days like this, with the wind always from the same quarter and always whining, plaintive and exasperated, on days like this, filled from morning to night with a raging discontent, Stepan Yaramko went almost mad. And he looked like a madman, the way he suddenly grasped his tousled head to squeeze out of it the boredom and the wind's howling and his sickly thoughts. A few minutes later he ran to hitch Ivan, the black horse, to the buggy. Formerly high-spirited, Ivan was now almost as brutish as his master.

Marta saw the rig go by adding its own cloud of dust. Stepan, standing up, was lashing with the reins. With raucous cries, like a cossack on his mount, he sent Ivan at a gallop on the road to Codessa.

He's dying of drought as well, she thought, and he's going to what his demon tells him is salvation and well-being. But alcohol will never do more than consume still further his poor, half-burnt-out soul.

VII

When he was well on his way, Stepan, who had shouted his lungs out at his horse, at himself and at the wind, finally sat down and collapsed into a shapeless mass, his eyes reddened, his eyelids and whole face coated with dust. He seemed dazed. After his rages he often fell into a state of gloom and stupor. At such times he might remain for hours only half conscious of what he did or said or even thought – for he followed his thoughts from afar, disinterested, as if they barely belonged to him. Even the certainty of having lived escaped him, or his life appeared to him at best like a long, monotonous day, a day some thirty years long and without milestones, without events, except perhaps for the distant scene which he now recaptured with some clarity: famine was raging in Volhynia; his kin had begun to show the hideous symptoms of chronic hunger, their features hollowed, their ribs protruding, their bellies swollen, and an expression in their eyes which had never left him, despite the dull uniformity of so many unchanging days.

Then a great blur of space and time panned before him. He was suddenly in the midst of fields of tall, ripe wheat. A threshing machine was rumbling. The grain trickled out in an inexhaustible stream; it filled carts and granaries and more granaries until it had to be left running out on the ground, exposed to the coming winter. No one knew what to do with it. The same frightful abundance was everywhere. The incredible harvest of that year was baffling; they had talked of burning the surplus. And about that time a letter arrived from Volhynia. It told him of his mother's death, which came as an end result of the famine. To keep his wheat from moulding and complete loss, Stepan fed it to his pigs. Thus two things were strangely connected in his memory: the letter from Volhynia along with the distraught look of hungry faces; and then the brimming trough and the avid guzzling of the swine, their little eyes shining with pleasure.

What more did he remember of the long, dry, windy day that was his life? A harsh, brilliant sunlight; then sudden, furious storms, brutal cold and so much snow that everyone in Volhyn was prisoner in his house for weeks at a time, with no news even of his nearest neighbour. Again the contrasts, again their unreality: it was enough to make a man doubt his own common sense, his very existence. And it was at the end of a life like that, as if to give thanks, that Marta was still watering her flowers.

Stepan trembled and came back to the present under the shock of his resentment. He whipped his horse a few times, shifted in his seat and suddenly wailed aloud. He grudged the joy of others in a life that he himself would have liked to see accursed.

You passed a few houses, then for a long time you rode through a marshy zone, low-lying land and damp, with rotting reeds and a smell of slime, where the frightened cries of birds went crossing at intervals. Stepan sank deeper into his mood, lost in a somnolence of the mind where scarcely anything could reach him.

But suddenly a child's face moved in the mist of his reflections, appearing as much alive as if it had emerged that moment from the grasses of the marsh. Little bare feet were dancing on the beaten earth in front of a poor shanty; the little girl's braids, too, danced around her head. Stepan almost called out "Irina!" Stalked by tenderness, he put a hand to his moustache, which he twirled, then he drove the memory off with a flood of rancorous reproaches. Children! They were no children of his, he wanted no part of them – the girl with her conceited airs and the others stuck up as young lords. They had shown up at Volhyn only to give advice: "You should do it this way, that's not the way to farm, this is how you go about it. . . ." Or there'd be messages scribbled in English on a postcard, with "Best regards, happy memories," and even from time to time a real letter addressed only to Mrs. Yaramko. Stepan had intercepted the last one, thrown it in the fire. That would teach them to take sides against him with Mrs. Yaramko.

But what if she were really sick, sick enough to leave this world! How could he find out? Life is a mystery and illness a greater one. Everything is mystery. A touch of anxiety crossed Stepan's mind in rapid flight. It was not quite grief, nor yet regret, but closer to fear, a vague feeling which he could not grasp.

At last he was out of the hateful marshland, with the hissing of its whip-like grass and its fetid odour. The air grew cleaner, the landscape changed. Stepan was entering a fertile region. Farmhouses appeared, well-kept ones, surrounded by havens of green that kept them sheltered from the wind, houses and barns properly placed, with metal-winged windmills to pump water from the ground or even generate electricity.

Bitter resentment seized Stepan. He saw fences that outlined the groups of farm buildings with perfect neatness. In front of some houses, more like city than farm dwellings, a tractor would stand or a big red truck, sometimes even a new car, its body glinting in the sun.

That won't last, he was going to say, as he often did to console himself. But he quickly saw that this prosperity was there to stay, this fine easy life Ukrainians led nowadays; and they owed it largely to the frantic efforts of the pioneer era, this generation reaping in joy what had been sowed in bitterness by the one before. Rolling his eyes in stupefaction, Stepan felt himself a victim of the greatest possible injustice.

Sounds of voices and human activity pierced through his musings. He was coming into Codessa. As he looked up he was disconcerted. . .as if he were arriving in a village for the first time in his life and had never seen anything like it. Not that the village was very lively on such a hot, windy afternoon. The infinite silence and wildness of the plain still crept too close for that. But its pathetic reminder only emphasized the sight – between two glimpses of the infinite – of a wide commercial street that, in two blocks, concentrated almost all the business section of Codessa. The sign of a little printer's shop, a shoemaker's, a movie house, two banks side by side, the window of one of those self-service stores where you saw the stock laid out in long rows. Then the town offices set up in a kind of barn, and those of the Department of Agriculture right beside it, not much better housed. Farther on, the cleaners and dyers, a garage with gas pumps, an auto junk yard and finally, back there a little, the elongated dome of the curling rink. This was the heart of Codessa. Stepan blinked, astounded. He couldn't get over it.

157

Yet, no doubt because of the violent heat, most people were holed up in their houses. With its banks, its store, its garage almost empty for the moment, Codessa seemed to have risen from the earth for one brief instant to a life with no reality.

Stepan climbed down in front of the beer parlour, tied his horse to a hitching post and disappeared into the dark interior.

A few old faces invaded by whiskers, their gaze perpetually lost, looked lazily up at him, in questioning rather than in greeting.

"Good day, Yaramko of Volhyn," he heard from this one, from that one.

He mumbled some vague, churlish reply, sat down and began to drink.

A little later, with the help of alcohol, words came back to him. And there it was he'd let it slip out: Marta was sick. At first he might have thought it was a trick for getting out of hard work and doing what she pleased. That's what he had thought. Now he wasn't so sure. Maybe she was really sick. She'd changed her ways. Almost good-natured these days. And everybody knew how she used to be, eh? Jealous and hot tempered as they come.

Then he fell silent again and began to see the possible truth in what he had just said. He should have held his tongue. As long as a thing was left unsaid you could pretend you didn't know it, pretend it wasn't there.

His suspicious eyes spied at the faces around him, strayed to the rectangle of light at the doorway. He made signs to himself as if swearing to hold his tongue. Who could a person talk to, anyway? Was there a listener on earth that you could trust? Despite himself he risked his luck with words again. His tongue was thick now, his eyes vague.

"Maybe," he said, "maybe Marta's going to die."

And he sat stunned as he realized that he'd known this all along.

"She just wants first chance at laying complaints," he said. "I know her. She always wanted to be the first to go. Get a head start on me. So she could blab all the things she has against me. That's how Marta is."

He stared at one drinker, then another. They'd begun to show some interest. His stare was watchful, sly and imploring at the same time.

"Hey you, Fedor," he said, addressing one of the old men who had come from Volhynia at the same time as himself. "Do you believe old women who die before us find anybody there to listen to them whine? Is anybody there at all?"

And Stepan began laughing aloud, wiping off his moustache wet with beer. He thought, Marta's leaving her precious garden now and going to milk the cows. That'll teach her. That'll teach her.

"Well, Fedor?"

In silence Fedor seemed to be searching the bottom of his glass for an answer to this embarrassing question. He was a frail old man of the first group to arrive, those who were forced almost without tools to invent a shelter and a few daily tasks, something measurable, vulnerable and human within the wide spaces, the unchanging horizons. He had been left with a feeling of bewilderment, an idea of the futility of human undertakings. Now he drank his old-age pension in three days and lived the rest of the time off a bitter little wine he made from wild berries. He slept beneath a tin roof at the edge of the village, in a kind of shack put together from odds and ends. It kept him more or less sheltered from the winds. Within hearing distance of the eternal silence, he had retained a taste for dangerous speculation. What should these poor people seek if not what lay at the bottom of that silence?

"Does anybody listen to the women there?" Fedor repeated at last. "Do you mean God? Could be, yes, it could be, Stepan Yaramko."

Everyone was listening carefully now to hear what the old man would say.

"God has to listen to somebody," Fedor began tentatively. "That's all right. He doesn't listen to the living. Not that I know of, anyway. When we're dead he has to listen. That's what I think. You see," he went on, noting that the others were looking on approvingly, "the Lord needs to know more about us men. And where could he find out if not from the dead souls when they come before him?"

"Tattlers, are they?" someone asked.

"Witnesses, I'd call them," said Fedor. "To my notion that's where our Lord gets his information. It's true information he gets that way. Perhaps the only truth. For where," he demanded, growing more animated, "is the Judge going to get the exact truth? Not from the living! They all lie more or less, we know that. Where did you ever see," he asked, turning to Stepan, "a live man that wasn't some kind of a liar? As long as we live, we lie."

Stepan hunched down in his chair. Ah, it was true: one lived and lied. But did we lie for pleasure or because we were uncertain about things? And now Marta was going to testify against him. Patient, quiet, busy with her flowers? Oho! She was acting exactly like someone who's sure of having the Judge's ear before too long.

Suddenly he struck the table violently. He couldn't let that happen! Was there no way to shut her mouth? He'd managed to shut her up around the house for years now.

Ah yes, it may be possible on earth, said Fedor. Afterward it's not so easy.

Almost completely drunk by now, Stepan was making a

tremendous effort to follow the flight of a maddened fly by listening to its buzzing. Suddenly the vague outline of an idea tempted him, like a revenge. What if he had her looked after, his poor old woman? What if he took her to Edmonton, to the surgeons if need be? It would take every cent he had, and he saw himself reduced to beggary, his savings sacrificed in vain, for Marta would surely never get well enough to help again with the heavy chores. Did an old woman grow young after the hospital? Did a wasted woman grow robust and alert once more? Tears came to his eyes. Held back at the edge of his lashes, they revealed better than his gaze where his eyes were hidden, deep in the grass-like growth of his face. He sniffled once more, his head nodded. Soon he was half asleep, his elbows on the table, his forehead hidden in his hands.

VIII

Twilight had come long ago. A grave and touching illumination spread over the western slope of the sky. The very horizon seemed unable to tear itself away from the contemplation of its own enchantment. At this hour – Marta's favourite – she remained sitting with her face to the red sky, wondering over the meaning of this incandescence against which everything on earth shows black and seems more than ever transitory, more than ever magnificent. The prairie at this time of day appeared to grow wider, if that were possible, yet the human soul was perhaps more confident for all that.

But little by little Marta became conscious of the long complaint of the animals penned in the corral. Stepan had gone off without thinking of them, and the cows were suffering from their swollen udders. Poor things! Wasn't it enough that they had to live just to serve the needs of men? Did we have to let them suffer too, and them without the power of reason?

She went off to get her pails and crossed the grassy prairie to where the animals stood lowing in their pen, their heads

162

turned toward the house. At night when the window was lit by the flame of the lamp, you would have said their call had a different tone, perhaps that of confidence.

In other times milking had been one of the more agreeable chores for Marta. She would sit on a low stool, her forehead against the animal's warm flank and feel beneath it the rumblings of inner rumination. The milk spurting at the side of the pail at first made a clear, high-pitched sound that afterwards grew thicker. True, she'd be pestered by flies and insects of all kinds and often cruelly stung; but the work gave you time to gaze around at the countryside, and it was then that Marta had most intensely felt its beauty. She remembered curious and unexpected surges of happiness, like gusts of perfume carried across the fields, all the more memorable because they were unexpected. For a long time during her life of ceaseless labour those moments had been her only ones of relaxation. She still remembered a cow that had been particularly gentle and obedient. She had only to tell her, "Stop that, keep your tail still!" and the little red cow would protest only with her ears, constantly waggling, even in the worst of fly-time.

When she was ready to carry back the brimming pails, Marta stopped, finding it absurd to use her last reserve of strength to retain a drop of milk or anything that she could not take with her forever. Her life had been made of the need to do just that. Yet she would not be able to take her flowers along. What then had made her sacrifice herself for them? she wondered, but found no good answer. No doubt it would take another to answer all the questions she had to ask.

She let the cows drink the milk she had just taken from them, keeping a little at the bottom of the pail for the cat and also for the "old bear." Sick from his binge, he might be glad to find a small jar of milk set to cool.

She bent down to get through the barbed wire. After the stubbly grass of the corral, the prairie was soft underfoot. At one time they'd planted timothy hay, but the ancient grasses had regained the upper hand: the meadow cat's tail, the purplish bent grass, twitch grass, lyme grass with its stiff ears, and foxtail – a great herbaceous mass pervaded by a constant breath of life. Even on a calm evening like this the whole plain was gently waving and a long, slow swell left for the far-off horizon. At this late hour of summer, of her life, Marta marvelled again at the face so delicate yet impenetrable that Volhyn's solitude had taken on for her.

Back at the house, she dropped heavily to the bench by the wall, suddenly feeling all the fatigue of the effort she had made. Her exhaustion was so great she feared she would never get her thoughts together again. She could barely perceive them; they were still too far, and they took on the form of dreams rather than reflections: vague, friendly shadows seeming to deal one way or another with their deep astonishment at this strange human life.

She went inside and drank a mouthful of cooled-off tea. Then, a little bowl of curds in her hand, she came out to the threshold to eat a few spoonfuls and look pensively at the lovely side of the sky, still pink, while the rest was already dipped in the deepest black. Under her white kerchief not much could be seen of her face except her eyes fixed with strange insistence on that lively tint in the sky, a last pulsing of red and gold melted together like a sleep embellished with dreams.

Marta went in again, rinsed out her bowl and tidied the small kitchen. It was a pleasant room, a little anxious, for it seemed to remember that a soul at grips with loneliness had tried humbly to beautify everything around her in her wish to escape. In other years Marta had painted it delphinium blue, with a narrow border in pale yellow halfway up the wall. From the low ceiling with its heavy beams hung braids of onions, bundles of drying poppyheads and ears of corn tied in sheaves, giving off a light smell of autumn. The old peasant cupboards, formerly painted blue like the walls, were decorated with designs she had done from a pattern. The table was covered with an oilcloth with big red flowers on a blue-and-yellow background. All these colours were slowly dying but sometimes, such as now, the lamplight ephemerally brought them back to life in a last, feeble effort at revival.

Marta returned to the doorway. It occurred to her to look far out across the plain to a lonely tree that she had always known. The night was now dark blue. Against this background everything turned to a silhouette, and she easily spied the little tree, far as it was. With its foliage pulled over it like a cape and its lower branches like striding legs, it had always seemed to her to be walking, perhaps a monk, perhaps a pilgrim, but someone who had trudged a great distance. Time and again Marta had come to the doorway just to descry in the distance that walking silhouette, always bowed under its tireless efforts. Had anyone else ever had such a strange companion? In her mind she had turned it into everything imaginable: a peddler with a few rare flower seeds in his pack, or perhaps someone who had seen her children and was bringing news of them.

Then she turned to see the frail aspen grove. Tonight it was making a gentle noise, like the voices of a group of people speaking softly, cordially, in the dark.

With no instrument but these trees, the air had invented so many sounds that gladdened your heart! Marta tried to remember all of them but it was impossible. Often the trees had imitated rain so skilfully you were completely fooled; and

165

then they'd make their leaves rattle like the castanets of some distant, youthful feast; sometimes their soft rustling had made her think of sympathy for human suffering.

Nor did Marta forget to greet the giant sky which dipped so low tonight and lit its stars so close you could have taken them for window lights on the endless Volhyn plain. Was this an image of the future that Marta saw? Could the world's loneliness at last be filled?

She pushed the heavy door shut with her knee to make sure it was home in its ill-fitting frame. She started up the steep stairway with its sharp turn at the landing. There she caught her breath for a moment and thought about great, strange things; for above this narrow staircase she saw as never before the immensity of the sky. She climbed the remaining steps. She changed the linen, lay down on the bed and, her eyes on the ceiling, experienced again the feel of the vast, living sky she had just seen.

"Why, oh why, did I have my life?" asked Marta.

IX

Coming in the house on some pretext or other around eleven that morning, Stepan cocked his head, listened, but heard no sound from the room beneath the roof. What could she be doing? Wasn't she going to come down and look after him as well as herself? What was the meaning of this immobility? Was she going to stay in bed for good?

He went out again and pretended to busy himself with one of the innumerable chores awaiting him, though they had all been neglected so long that perhaps it wasn't worth starting. Could he even save a bit of his harvest, dried out where it stood? Things had gone to the dogs here for too long. What could one man do alone with no help against such a load of work? Might as well let the work pile up and bury you right away, up to your neck, and never lift a finger. But what about Marta? Was she hungry? Would it be fitting for him to bring her something? A man serving a woman! The world upside-down, eh?

He came back toward the house, went inside and over to the foot of the stairs to listen for any sign of life upstairs, holding his breath. Still nothing. Should he go and look? That was an unpleasant thought. Once upstairs, what would he say? He'd have to mumble something or other, ask a question at least. He thought it over, his mouth under the thick moustache forming grimaces of objection. Fedor had maintained there was only one way to buy the silence of those about to leave this world: that was to speak as freely to them as if speaking were no concession. But Fedor was a widower and could say what he pleased. Who could be sure?

Finally Stepan put water to boil, threw in a handful of oatmeal. When the brew began to thicken he poured it into a bowl, stuck a spoon in it, added a little milk and started upstairs, clearing his throat to announce his coming. He hoped things would go well, that he wouldn't have to say a word. For what could he say? What name would he use? Just "Marta"? Impossible! He'd lost that habit too long ago. It would be as embarrassing as if he turned up shaved in front of her.

He arrived at the top of the stairs, looked sideways at Marta in her bed, put the bowl of oatmeal in her hands. He had thought of saying, Eat a little something, but even that was beyond his power. She looked up at him perplexed and seemed to be on the point of speaking. But speech was difficult for her too. She took the spoon, tasted the gruel, took another spoonful.

Well, it was eatable, maybe it tasted good, and she'd likely finish it off as soon as his back was turned. Then she'd get her strength again. Perhaps he could even save her now that he'd set his hand to it. So there wasn't such a hurry about committing himself with words.

He went downstairs and was about to head out to the fields again, perhaps to harness himself to this chore or that – one would do as well as the next and none would get him very far. Then he saw the chickens having a fine time in the garden! Scratch here, scratch there, get that root up, no, that one! Tear off that stem. . . . A hundred times a day until now he had seen Marta running, waving her apron to chase the intruders with cries that rose almost to a wail. Suddenly, without realizing it, he began to do the same, charging the fowl head down, waving his arms. When he had them back in their pen he saw that it was full of holes. He straightened a picket, tried to bend it to cover another breach left by another crooked picket. The whole place here, the fields, the buildings, matched the state of this wretched coop. Was it worth patching? As he tried to block a gaping escape hole he raised his head, suddenly suspicious again, and saw Marta's white face at the window. So she still placed some hope in him. He abandoned the chicken pen and went off with rapid strides, under the sky lowering with a coming storm, grumbling aloud in great waves of discontent. Where could he start? What was best? Could he still mow a patch of wheat? Why not? But a broken part from the mower had not come back from the repair shop, and he'd forgotten to ask in Codessa if he could still count on it. For that matter, thinking of his feuds with everyone in Volhyn, would he find anyone to come and thresh it for him?

A little later Marta heard again beneath her window the familiar grumbling voice accompanied by a great sound of straining and bumping. She pulled the curtain back and saw Stepan clearing up the little grove – their grove, just as in Poland. Surprise made her face turn paler than before. Grunting to encourage himself, Stepan was hauling out and piling up for a bonfire all the broken boxes, the buggy seat with its torn leather, the rubber boots in shreds, and heaven knew what else – broken cans, rusted gratings, in short, the whole junk heap! And the grove was beginning to breathe. It reappeared slowly as it had been in the first years of its life, pure, young and open, so that you could see through beneath its branches to the luminous prairie in the distance. And Marta drew a deep and easy breath, as if, with the aspen grove cleared, she finally saw accomplished one of the last commands of her own fate.

X

The summer in Volhyn seemed to have been no more than a dream. From her bed, Marta would pull back the curtains in the mornings and look out at the ravages of autumn. Only her strongest flowers were still alive – the zinnias, a gladiola spared through some unknown privilege and a few roses among those rarest kinds that dared to flower just before the frost.

She thought of summer and all she had done in her lifetime in favour of that short season, to hold it back, to embellish it, to see it flourish. How she had cherished it! As if only for the summer was it worthwhile to raise hope. Summer is a great mystery, she thought, and hope itself, and youth. Old, broken, almost dead as she was, Marta was turning back now, as if in search of herself, back to the distant regions of her own youth. She saw that her robust health and her vital energy, her love and ardour for life, had been the real part of her. Thinking of that young, almost lost being, she said, "Only then was I myself!" And she felt surprised and hurt by this, as if she had been confronted with the basic injustice inflicted on human life.

From that she came to thinking of her children. Despite the slackness of her bond with them, just to be sure they existed she would repeat their names and the names of the places where they lived.

Would it soon be time to have them come or was it too early to bother them? How would she do it anyway? If she watched out for Michael Stroulikov who came by every Thursday to pick up the cream, could she give him some message to send on? But if their father gave them a bad reception.... Even in this extremity, Stepan was quite capable of slamming the door in their faces. Marta's thoughts wandered off in conjectures. The telephone wires took words along them. Could she not use these to speak directly to her children? She indulged in tender thoughts of them, dreaming that the wires picked them up and bore them off to Irina in Prince Albert, to Taras in Moose Jaw, to Stanley in Rorketon. For her the names of these cities where she had never been had a melancholy and captivating attraction.

Just the same, thought Stepan, this may be the time to speak to her. That would be the hardest part. The rest had been nothing by comparison. The thing was, once you'd stopped it was almost impossible to start again. Stepan brooded about it day and night. What was the right moment to speak again? For this reason or that he would always put it off a few days longer. Then, with the silence piled still higher, it came to be such a serious thing – such a concession – to break the wall at last.

How long had it lasted anyway? Two years, or three, or more than that? When was it they'd had that last quarrel over the children, after which Stepan and the old woman had almost ceased to speak? And where could he start again? At the point where language had been interrupted between them? Or anywhere at all, about the weather, for example? In the dark Stepan cleared his throat, coughed a little, tried for words that refused to come out. Was it really so hard to say, It's cold outside.... You know, old woman, I think the frost's coming this time. That'll be the end of the flowers and the garden. And the summer...but in a way, it's a relief...just the same.

That night the cold was indeed so bitter that Marta shivered under the warm eiderdown. It was one of those October nights that in a few hours devastate what is left of the patient and incomparably delicate work of summer. In the morning the sky was of that clear, unmistakable blue that presages winter.

Marta hesitated to look over toward the garden. What would she see but wilted flowers, the very death of summer? Yet she pulled the curtain back and glanced down at the little square of earth. It was her own soul she had tended there perhaps as much as her flowers. Among grasses stiff with frost she glimpsed, intact for one more day, her golden asters, mauve chrysanthemums and a few of those roses of India that reminded her of Lubka, with the consoling thought that at least Lubka had led a happy life, with her children beside her, and a good husband who had spoken to her every day.

Then, as she pulled the curtain farther back she saw close by the house a big, calloused hand lifting the little paper cones with which the plants had been capped the night before to help them resist the cold. The whole pile of Codessa newspapers must have gone that way. Now the poor old fellow would have nothing to read in the chill, lonely November days.

At the same time Stepan's grumbling voice was heard, and Marta pulled back quickly so that he wouldn't see her face at the window or feel that he was being watched.

But what she had done for her flowers at the time of their worst ordeal, the old man had done for her in return, never suspecting that he was causing the bitter cup to overflow with tenderness. But she would never be able to show it. That would frighten her old bear too badly.

That night she thought about immortality. Could it be that souls survived in some unknown region? Perhaps it was possible for certain ones: the great souls, the noble and profound minds, whose loss people would never cease to mourn. But Marta! An ignorant old woman who lagged so far behind even her own children – how could she deserve to be rescued somewhere beyond this world? No, she could not imagine herself living forever, surviving herself. Yet it was a sorrow to her, after all, that she would not continue in the spirit and sound of the wind, in the soft protest of the grasses, in the murmur of the little grove, their "grove in Poland."

The hours were running out. She had no other relief from pain than the aspirins Stepan had bought in Codessa. She doubled the dose that night, mysteriously warned that she need no longer ration her supply. Was she in great suffering? Even of this she was not sure. She would first have had to know how much others suffered, and you could have only a faint inkling of that. In any case, the aspirin helped a little. In this margin of comfort her thoughts, as if already released, rose and flew off to the past to find a distant melody. A song that spoke of summer – always summer, season of life, season of the heart – celebrating warmth and cherry trees in bloom and telling as well of young men and girls who met on a meadow to dance in the grass around a solitary tree. And through these few snatches of melody that came to her memory, these few words that floated in her mind, she felt herself mysteriously reunited with a soul unknown to her, whose nostalgic tenderness was still quite alive in this old song of the Ukraine. Was immortality then not just a dream?

What was it now that the old bearded priest had mumbled

about it when he came to bury another of them, and spoke to the handful of survivors around the earthen trench where they in turn would soon descend? It was almost always fall when there was a funeral, and the wild wind had carried off half his words of consolation. Nonetheless, Marta fancied that on those days of separation the priest had talked of space, space without end, immeasurable in distance and time. But she'd had enough of infinite majesty and space; what she wanted was mercy, what she wanted was forgetfulness. She dreamed of the prairie grasses that bend so docilely at the least breath of air.

An impetuous gust of wind passed over the little house, shaking it as if to carry it off, then was lost in the high places of the sky. She had listened so long to the wind, and with such patience, that even in this night she could tell apart all its varied elements: its sighing voice in the aspen grove; its frantic bounds over the naked plain; a short knocking summons at the window; and in the endless environs of the sky a kind of immense and despairing interrogation. Could this, after all, be eternity – that Marta herself had been wished for, and thought and decided by a Creator? All these things were too enormous for her, and too hard. Rather listen to the wind. If he remembered her sometimes, for she had loved him so much; if as he crossed the land he said something of her life – that would be enough for her: the wind in his loneliness consoling himself in her, and she in his errant spirit. . . . Suddenly voices, some of them deep, some high and shrill, burst into chorus, as if outside a city full of souls were singing in the night.

Marta crossed her hands. She sighed. To this humble immortality of air and wind and grasses she would entrust her soul.

ENCHANTED SUMMER

Gabrielle Roy

Translated by Joyce Marshall

CONTENTS

Monsieur Toong

I

The bullfrog lived on the edge of the inhabited world. You went to the end of the village, which is already somewhat remote, and now there was just enough room between the wooded mountain and the wild shore for the railway line. Only its single track could manage to insinuate itself between the rubble of rock on one side and the piled-up boulders on the other.

Nowhere else in the world have I encountered such a tranquil railroad.

Right beside it lies the river, which has all the room it needs to extend its great tide-racked body for a breadth of twenty-two miles. At flood tide, waves splash against the embankment; at times you can hear the sound high on the rocky hillside as if the waves were breaking within the stone. On the crest are some ancient, rarely silent pines. One, flung out on the slant, mourns with a curious insistence just before the fading of the light.

Another surprise too; all along the track wildflowers grow in profusion as if, once accustomed to the exhalations of the engines and the poverty of the soil, they

9

find certain rare advantages here. They are never browsed and, furthermore, seldom picked. There is no one to speak of but Berthe and me to pick them. And we are always reasonable, Berthe and I. We are careful not to pull them up by the roots and we never take more than enough for a bunch apiece.

At the end of fifteen or twenty minutes' walk far from all habitation, after a sharp bend where everything threatens to tip into the river, you come to a very desolate spot. In the shadow of a rock-face rising sheer as a chimney lies a pool of perfectly black water. At daybreak it may be gay and sparkling but this cannot last for long since the space is restricted, the mountain high, and the sun has soon circled the cape. This rock chimney is undoubtedly compelled to live the greater part of its life in shadow—even more so the pool at its foot. Yet it was here that the bullfrog lived, in this cold sad water. However, as you will see very soon by the way we made his acquaintance, it was not out of misanthropy that he lived so far from others.

Perhaps like the flowers on the track—the evening primroses, the columbines and the bluebells—or even the tall isolated pine on the cliff, he had weighed the pros and cons of solitude and discovered that it offered more benefits than drawbacks.

Berthe and I were coming along the railway track one evening, talking cheerfully, for we always feel gay and light-hearted when we are leaving people and houses behind to rejoin nature, just as we are always happy on the way back, to be returning to people and houses.

Doubtless, in the semi-obscurity of the twilight, that moment of complete attention when nothing could be heard but the sounds of the water and the pine, the unwonted explosion of human voices in laughing and noisy exchange must have aroused the bullfrog's curiosity. And clearly this curiosity became unabashed interest for we had just reached the sharp bend near the pool

10

when out sprang a most cordial greeting, "Toong!"

You would have thought that somewhere under the water a playful musician had plucked a submerged guitar.

In this deserted spot amid the swiftly advancing evening shadows, the friendly salutation was so unexpected we were left speechless for a moment. Standing two steps from the inky water, so lifeless and without a wrinkle on its surface, I finally replied quite at random, "Toong!"

The reply was immediate, "Toong! Toong!"

Berthe and I exchanged glances. Were we dealing with a prankster? Or with some poor hermit so delighted to have someone to talk to that he scarcely knew what he was saying? We determined to find out.

"Toong! Toong! Toong!" said Berthe.

At once the reply emerged from the pool, "Toong! Toong! Toong! Toong!"

The syllables were quite detached; there was no question about it, we were being answered each time by an additional toong. Was this how bullfrogs conversed? Or might this one be a bit simple-minded? It was all rather puzzling. I tried again.

"Toong! Toong! Toong! Toong!"

From the pool came curtly, "Toong! Toong!"

The tone was a shade impatient also as if, without losing his good humour, the bullfrog was trying to point out, "You must be brief. Your long human sentences drag out so."

This gave us something to think about. Without insisting further, we left our conversation with the bullfrog there and hurried on to the trout stream, which we like to visit once each summer. Under a screen of broad damp foliage, it gurgles loudly, like a bottle being emptied.

In the gathering dusk we didn't linger. Just long enough to make sure the bottle was still being joyfully emptied. And then we retraced our steps.

It was almost night when we passed by the pool

again. No sound indicated life. The birds had suspended all movement. Even the quivering pines scarcely murmured now, as if to trouble us as little as possible with the tale of their persistent loneliness. It was hard to believe in our lively conversation only an hour before with the invisible occupant of the pool.

Disappointed, I called loudly, "Monsieur Toong!"

The place, so solitary, seemed astonished by the noise and did not deign to answer by as much as the faintest ruffling of leaves.

"Monsieur Toong!" Berthe called in her turn.

Nothing.

"Monsieur Toong, are you asleep?" I asked. "You're asleep now, Monsieur Toong?"

Then from the depths of a profound slumber, as if from the bottom of the sea, a faint sound emerged—sluggish and drawn out, friendly still but with undertones of "Just when I was sleeping so soundly"—"To-o-ong!"

We hadn't the heart to persist but stole away on tiptoe.

"With frogs," said Berthe, "who knows, it may be as it is with people, the first sleep is crucial. Sometimes when I'm wakened out of my first sleep, I can't drop off again."

We felt rather regretful at having perhaps disturbed the bullfrog's repose.

"I daresay he begins his day very early, with the sun," I said. "It must touch his pool first."

"In any case," said Berthe, "playing the guitar under water, and in perpetual dimness, must be exhausting. At night Monsieur Toong must be dead tired."

II

One calm cool evening the following summer, we were hurrying to reach Monsieur Toong's hideaway before nightfall. The hour of our walk coincided, as we had

12

intended, with that of the high tide. The river sings then, full to the brim. Its song quickens our pace. Yet on the railway track our steps cannot help but be unequal from tie to tie—one short, two long, two short, one long, rather like Morse code adapted for feet. Walking quickly becomes tiring but no matter; a difficulty we impose upon ourselves for enjoyment is a pleasure in the end.

The waves broke with a quiet sound, very gently and without haste, on the boulders the railway workers pile along the roadbed each year to keep it from sliding into the water. Even so, it is slipping in by degrees and will finally be engulfed completely, I suppose, for it is only by constant petitions that our little railway line is kept alive.

Far away on the rippled water of the channel an ancient black freighter drifted without leaving any wake, just as solitary as the railway and seemingly as lacking in destination.

From some distance away we heard the grieving pine. High on the rock it complained gently. Yet there was almost no moving air that evening. Where then had the pine found enough to make its grieving song? Perhaps in the dense woods behind the rocks, from which it had detached itself one day to come and live alone on this sentinel post.

Everywhere, like acquaintances, we found the little flowers of the previous summer: the evening primroses, whose delicate faces open only towards the closing of the day; bluebells drawing from the grudging soil their blooms of clearest azure; the tall Easter candles of mullein; vetch too, that ancient companion of almost deserted railway tracks; and wild roses. Apparently everything that does not die from the harshness of its life acquires more sturdiness and health than it would in gentler places.

Even before we had reached that sharp bend where telephone pole, rails and rock threatened to capsize, impatient to renew relations with the bullfrog, I called, "Hi there, Monsieur Toong! Are you still of this world?"

I hadn't even finished when the answer rang out, joyful and clear, "Toong!"

I can't deny that my heart turned over.

"Is it really you?"

"Toong! Toong!"

"And me? Do you recognize me?"

"Toong! Toong! Toong! As if there could be more than two people who'd come and talk to an old hermit in the lonesome twilight."

"And me?" Berthe asked.

"Toong! Toong! Toong! Toong!" Monsieur Toong assured her affably.

It was the same as last year. Our friend never went beyond four toongs; he then invariably returned to two. It was all a bit baffling and the bullfrog seemed to enjoy his little game.

One thing was new, though; this time Monsieur Toong came to the edge of the pool to talk to us. He climbed as high as he could without slipping on the wet bank and here found a purchase for his two front feet. From beneath a very shallow film of water he studied us with a sort of anxious friendliness. He was of good size and of jovial mien, making at least four of an ordinary frog. He spoke to us in music from close at hand and so we were able to see just how a bullfrog plays the guitar.

He swelled, swelled, swelled his throat, the flabby skin stretching like a leather bottle filling with water. His huge eyes bulged with the effort. The pockets of his cheeks seemed ready to burst. Now we had seen how much effort it cost the musician to produce a single note. Finally he released all the air that had puffed him up like a balloon and we heard the incomparable sound, "Toong!"

"Bravo!" we congratulated but did not ask any more of him.

We understood at last why you must not try to engage in lengthy conversations with a creature like Monsieur Toong, for whom every sound is exhausting.

With regret just the same we said, "Good night, Monsieur Toong. Keep well ... till next time ... Monsieur Toong," all the while hurrying off to outstrip the night, which advances very quickly in the almost perpetual shadow of these rocks.

A few pleasant, drawn-out toongs accompanied us— a little sad too perhaps as if from the dark water we were being reminded, "Come back. Don't let too much time go by. Life is short."

III

Once again we returned on an evening of calm weather to the black secret pool at the base of the sheer chimney of rock. This time too we had both the high tide and coolness to chase away insects and, I suppose, the mood to appreciate such things.

The water splashed against the embankment, the solitary pine transformed into a mild complaint a bit of air that came to it from far away, bluebells chimed without sound. But our pool, when we reached it in the last glimmers of the twilight, was silent. Terribly silent. Suddenly it made one think of the shadowy depthless water under the trapdoor of an oubliette.

On its banks we called in turn, "Monsieur Toong? Have you gone? Or are you just playing dead?"

Nothing replied but the song sparrow, who suddenly broke off his roundelay as if it had occurred to him, at hearings news asked of Monsieur Toong, "That's true, what indeed has become of Monsieur Toong? We haven't heard of him around here, if I'm not mistaken, for many months."

But too heartless to concern himself for long with the fate of the bullfrog, he hopped from one branch to another, shaking the elder-bush in which he was hidden,

15

and without further ado resumed his endless refrain.

From whom else could we ask news?

I picked up a stone and flung it into the middle of the pool. Water gushed upwards. Circles spread, widening, over the surface. At the same moment a shape appeared among the rushes at the base of the mountain, a long-legged bird that at once withdrew a little farther into its hiding place.

Berthe's quick eye had recognized a little heron.

"Maybe it was the heron," she said thoughtfully, "that did away with Monsieur Toong."

"Quite so, quite so," an aged crow, a familiar of these parts, informed us in passing.

Then she circled the cape, and the silence that enclosed us was like the silence that falls when the story has been told, the outcome divulged and the words "the end" inserted at the foot of a page.

We returned haltingly, our steps now lengthened to reach a more widely spaced tie, now shortened so as not to trip over its neighbour. We had no more inclination for talk. The old pine, high on the rock, still hummed softly in snatches, between silences when it seemed to be drifting off to sleep. Water splashed as merrily as ever against the boulders of the embankment. From far away, at certain turnings, borne on a brisk current of air, came a few last echoes of the joyous drunkard under the broad leaves, drinking right out of the bottle.

But to us now it was rather as if this corner of the world had been emptied.

Monsieur Emile's Gatte

The word must have been invented by Monsieur Emile, one of many he invented in the course of his life. He was a man with a bent for creating expressions to his own taste for objects that seemed to him poorly named or whose dictionary appellation he didn't know. He was equally ingenious at eking out a living from a parsimonious soil, for this was still the time when one could manage to subsist from the fruit of a multiplicity of small activities: maple sugar in the spring, a bit of hay in summer, eel fishing in the fall, and in winter chopping wood.

Monsieur Emile's farm stood off to one side, against the base of the mountain. It was composed of a number of little fields of various shapes scattered here and there around the road and sundry natural objects: a diamond below the dirt road; a square near the house; farther along, beside the brook, a sort of deeply curved arc; even a circle around a huge stone no one had ever been able to move. Of all this Monsieur Emile made good use; from the square he obtained potatoes, from the bent arc fine

17

clover, from the circle around the stone millet in abundance. And from all sorts of other bits and pieces hay that he cut with a scythe.

Towards the end of the summer there was no trimmer sight than Monsieur Emile's farm as, pipe in mouth, his great scythe in his hand and a whetstone in the pocket of his trousers, he tidied up the borders of his innumerable enclosures. Soon not a blade of grass escaped from fields that were now as smooth as the ancient rock in their midst. Only his gatte defeated him.

A patch of spongy ground, uneven, always damp, it was pitiable beside the other well-kept fields. It couldn't be drained. Nothing grew in it but a sort of coarse couch grass. Nevertheless, in the interests of neatness, Monsieur Emile fenced in his gatte. He did it in the old-fashioned way with roughly split rails set one upon the other snaking around the wretched bit of ground. Thus tidily set apart, the poor gatte looked at least a little less abandoned. But for a long time still it was to remain unproductive, a disgrace to Monsieur Emile, who could not hide it from view, exposed as it was right beside the road for all to see.

Came the day when, unable to put a refractory cow with the others, Monsieur Emile had the idea of confining her for a few days' penitence in the gatte, never suspecting that the action would be rich in consequence. For in no time the cow, Rouquette by name, had uprooted the couch grass that was stifling all other vegetation. Then, bored in her solitude, she took to turning and turning on the spot, a hundred times, a thousand. She dug the hollows in the soil even deeper with her hooves and everywhere she spread her dung.

Thus all was made ready for the miracle of next spring.

For in the desolate gatte, pitted all over like an old sieve, there appeared a plant unknown in these parts till

18

now. On each of the driest hummocks in the muddy ground it bloomed in great clusters of that marvellous rosy pink of certain sunsets in the country. You might have thought it the modest ancestor of the glorious oleander. It was kalmia, discovered by the Swedish botanist, Peter Kalm, and dedicated to him by his master, Linnaeus. Covered in old rose, the gatte looked young and gay.

But where had the graceful flower come from? Far away in its dense colonies in Baie-des-Rochers had it heard that Monsieur Emile's gatte was more hospitable to its species now that Rouquette had turned and turned about and enriched the soil? Was it carried there on the wind? Or by the birds? Or perhaps the seed had been present already, so deeply embedded in the ground there was no chance of its climbing to the light on its own. And Rouquette, frenzied with boredom, by trampling the soil, finally brought it to the surface. I for one incline to this version and I also believe that, having exhumed the seed, she then nourished it with her dung.

The kalmia blossom only lasts for a month or so. But the shrub had gained a firm foothold in the ancient gatte. And next spring the rosy clusters on each dry hummock were twice as thick as the previous year. The folk of the region now knew where to find the pretty flowers that to some recalled the azalea and to others the oleander. As you passed along the dirt road you could see in many windows, amid geraniums and fuchsias, bunches of kalmia in old mustard or peanut butter jars.

But plants are like people. The moment a group is happily settled somewhere, everyone wants to move in. Scarcely was the kalmia installed than all around it were blue flags. The two did not harm one another though, for while the kalmia sought out the driest spots, the flags delighed in the oozy hollows. Buttercups crowded in between them. The old gatte, all rosy pink the year before,

19

was this year of varied colours. In autumn goldenrod and long-leafed asters circled the stagnant water that glimmered faintly in all the little hollows of the gatte. And these minuscule holes, each scarcely bigger than an eye, managed to reflect the long gilded plumage of the goldenrod, the delicate muted lilac of the asters, a bit of sky, passing clouds and even, on occasion, the flight of some bird of land or sea.

So because Monsieur Emile, a careful man, enclosed this bit of a field and put a balky cow to graze there one day, the untilled soil was in a fair way to becoming the most inviting spot in the region. Right until freeze-up there were flowers, colours, and a sort of life that seemed more tender and more gentle than elsewhere.

But you will say, in the winter, covered with snow in the bitter cold, especially at the desolate hour of nightfall, the gatte must look precisely what it is—an old, saturated sponge.

Well, no. Quite the reverse. For, you remember, the gatte is at the edge of our settlement, right at the foot of the mountain. So that before it circles behind the cape, the sun always stops momentarily on this field. For that instant it is completely illuminated, as if by a strange searchlight; the pallid lifeless snow becomes at the centre pink like the kalmia, along the edges blue like the flags, and here and there it lights up with the glowing hue of the dead goldenrod. For three or four minutes each day the gatte is radiant with the most marvellous colours of the summer. Then it sinks into the night.

Aimé's Cows

I always cut across the fields when I go to my neighbour's. Aimé's cows, at my passage, stop grazing. They raise their heads and look at me, following me with their eyes as if to place me once for all. I don't know why cows are called stupid. The expression of these three, as they examine me closely and note details, clearly shows a sort of reflection.

"Ah good. It's the lady from the summer cottage, on her way again to our master's. The one who comes from the city. Who spends the summers here."

And back they go to their quiet grazing. Proof that their minds must work in much this way is that if I go by again ten minutes later, they consider me briefly without bothering to stop grazing or raise their heads, as if they were concluding, "The same as before."

But if I don't pass by for two or three hours, the whole performance begins over; they follow me with their eyes with renewed curiosity. And then finally, "Why, yes. It's the lady of this morning. The one from the cottage. The one who comes from the city. The one who goes to our master's a hundred times a day."

It's as if they lacked memory rather than sense.

Or as if they were as absent-minded as certain people who "can't quite place" their acquaintances.

My theory no longer holds. Today I walked twice through the pasture at intervals of an hour. The second time like the first the cows stopped grazing. Examined me at length. Stared at me, you might say. Showed the same curiosity as two hours earlier. As the day before.

I spoke of it to Aimé.

"Do they recognize me, do you think? Are they able to recognize people?"

"Ah yes."

"Then?"

. . .

"So? They find me so astonishing?"

Aimé politely, "That may be . . . at times."

Jeannot the Crow

Nothing in this world is more difficult than to distinguish one crow from another. If I was finally able to recognize Jeannot, this was because he came without fail on days when the wind sang from the southwest, to perch in the delicate tip of my wild red cherry tree and let himself be rocked for a long time, the tree in this summer wind being simply a swing in the sky.

None of our other trees can be compared to this wild red cherry. We began to shape it when it was still a sapling, pruning here, straightening there, rectifying this; and just as with human beings when you apply yourself to them in time and gently, we obtained astonishing results. The tree is so striking now that it is always compared to something other than a tree. In repose, with the wind playing on it with muted strings, it is a lyre. Viewed from below and a slight distance, it looks like a vase overflowing with flowers on a shelf above the ocean. When the wild wind flings its leaves forward as if over a face, it suggests a young woman shaking and shaking her outspread hair with joyful movements of the head. However,

23

it is in the southwest wind with Jeannot at its tip that our wild red cherry tree is most graceful.

Many of our friends exclaim when they visit us for the first time, "What a beautiful tree! Where did it come from? From what country?"

At first we used to reply that it was an ordinary little tree of a sort that grows all along the cliff, native to these parts, nothing more. That we'd only had to prune it a trifle, encourage it, give it water and fertilizer. Now we feel compassion for the bewilderment these simple remarks always awaken on people's faces, as if they can't bear the idea that they might do as much. Perhaps it's having to do as much that appals them. Now when our guests exclaim, "What a tree! You must have had it brought from far away," we say nothing to make them think otherwise. And in one sense it's true that our wild red cherry tree comes from far away.

As you might expect, the birds are very much attached to it. With most of them, it must be admitted, from self-interest. A few years ago I noticed that cedar waxwings, beguiling birds with crew cuts, arrived almost every day in July, seven or eight of them together, to perch here and there in the tree. After a while I realized that they had come to see whether the little fruit, which were just beginning to take colour, would soon be good to eat. At last one day they were ready and in an instant the tree was stripped. For the rest of that summer I never saw another cedar waxwing.

But the following summer they were outwitted. Six big blue jays in company discovered that there were some of these exquisite fruit in our yard. Through the red clusters one morning I glimpsed their brilliant uniforms of cobalt blue. The shriek of a soul in agony rose a short distance away where a seventh jay stood sentinel, and nothing is less appropriate to these splendid uhlans than this truly terrible shriek. Seated in the tree, the six jays feasted. The berries, however, weren't quite ripe. The cedar waxwings had dropped by the previous day to taste them and had decided to give them one more day. Much good it did them. When they returned on the morrow, the cupboard was bare.

But the next summer the blue jays were forestalled in turn. Evening grosbeaks, seemingly less finicky than the greedy jays, arrived early one July morning and cleaned the cherry tree of its small fruit while they were still green. Perhaps it gave them indigestion. Served them right.

But let me come at last to my subject, for if I've mentioned these successive raids, it was to show the difference between Jeannot and other birds. He at least came to the tree neither to eat nor even to sleep but only, as far as I could tell, from affection.

I daresay he pilfered elsewhere. A bit to the right, a bit to the left, so that it was not too apparent in any one garden: for instance, a leaf of red lettuce from Lucienne, my third neighbour—and how could a crow fail to appreciate the tasty lettuce that we were all constantly begging for ourselves?; perhaps a few sweet juicy cherries from Berthe; and here and there, from people who still had the heart to grow them, that delicacy of all crows, the seeds of those giant sunflowers that used to bloom everywhere of old. But from me Jeannot took nothing.

Besides, he came only when the rocking wind blew, bowing our little tree endlessly against the background of sea. Days without wind and without music, "dead" days when I myself grow lonely—perhaps for eternity—there was no sign of Jeannot. But as soon as the song of the rustling leaves resumed, I could be sure I'd see my crow again. Shortly afterwards, in fact, I would discern in the intensely blue sky an approaching speck of black.

Sometimes he'd have trouble navigating so as to land precisely in the middle of the cherry tree. He'd be obliged to repeat his approach again and again, carried each time into the distance. He'd then glide on motionless wings, and to recover his speed and momentum, he'd turn at the base of the mountain where the air is always calm. At last he would manage to make a perfect landing on his little perch. This was a tiny fork formed by two supple twigs high in the tree. Once settled and sure of his equilibrium, Jeannot would relax and let himself be carried fearlessly from one side of the horizon to the other.

In this way, by certain infallible signs, I learned a few years ago to recognize a friendly crow.

Jeannot never slept in the tree. With the field glasses I would see his eyes glinting in his black shiny face. Nor did he give any of those caws that grate so on the nerves. He was quite silent. He seemed to be there only to dream while contemplating the mountains, the whitecaps on the river and, far in the distance, the line of the south shore, always somewhat hazy on warm days. Like a small black lookout in the crow's-nest of a ship, he swung back and forth in the sky.

By other characteristics too—a way of holding his head to one side, a stiffness in his right wing as if it had once been slightly injured—I became better and better able to recognize my gentle crow. I could finally follow most of the activities and movements of his life.

First of all, where he spent the night. In a tree but this as different from our little wild red cherry as day is from night. A tall melancholy tree, shaggy, dead on one side and with numerous long branches, some dry, others leafy, a very old maple with room, storey upon storey, for the whole tribe to settle at nightfall, in families. At the end of a wild field, on a desolate plateau in a remote spot and with sombre woods in the background, it had been known for as long as anyone remembered as the Tree of

Crows. When they gathered there at dusk, the tree, already dark by nature, looked truly fearsome with those little pitch-black shapes pressed against one another along all the branches, even the skeletal ones. What did it look like then? Well, what else but a scarecrow made of crows?

To those of the species who didn't lack humour or a comic sense, it was perhaps amusing to inhabit a tree that seemed designed to scare them away.

At sunrise, however, nothing was gayer for a brief moment than that ancient tree with all its tenants in a great commotion of departure, giving voice to resounding caws. The new light awoke iridescences in the lustrous plumage that the vainest among them were still polishing with their beaks. Then they rose together into the sky and the old maple fell back into its mournful solitude.

The crows then broke ranks. Some, the more sociable, proceeded to the charming town of Baie-Saint-Paul where there were well-tended gardens to pillage. Others chose the uninhabited wild region of the abandoned pool of Monsieur Toong, the bullfrog. Still others remained in Petite-Rivière-Saint-François and spent their days flying round the mountain and along the shore of the river.

My Jeannot was rather solitary; by day he seldom rejoined his kin. He was even less inclined to fraternize with the gulls gathered in compact groups on the rocks uncovered by the receding tide. A few crows risked it, however, and there was no more curious sight in the empty immensity of the river than this close companionship on the crests of breakers of black birds and white birds. When I examined them with field glasses, however, I never caught them conversing with one another. They were together, it's true, but apparently without any sort of communication. And from afar, thus assembled and yet not acquainted, they resembled human beings

What did Jeannot do all day? Unquestionably, if the wind was favourable, not much else but rock in the tree. He also pilfered a bit from the gardens to right and left. As his territory was so restricted, he finally drew attention to himself and in the course of the summer I began to hear threatening remarks directed at Jeannot.

"That dratted crow!" grumbled Monsieur Simon, my neighbour. "I'll settle his hash!"

As excuse for Monsieur Simon and several other enemies of the crows, I should mention the trouble they'd had that year rescuing their fruit and vegetables from caterpillars, slugs and potato bugs. And now it looked as if the crows would snatch what remained from under their noses. Yet it seemed unjust to me that all the blame should fall on the head of poor Jeannot, who was perhaps less prompt than other crows to make off when Monsieur Simon approached, sweeping the air with his arms and shouting, "Dratted crow! Dratted crow!"

Besides, how could Monsieur Simon imagine that he was always dealing with the same crow, since he had never learned to distinguish one from another with the eyes of affection?

However, while believing that he was speaking each day to the same crow, Monsieur Simon managed to offend a good many birds—from the most scatterbrained to the oldest and most dignified. The tribe finally banded together to harass this man of such little perspicacity. From then on there was always one looting his garden while another drew his attention elsewhere.

He took to lying in ambush in his lilac hedge, loaded rifle in hand. One afternoon I thought I heard through the rustling of the leaves the sound of a shot from the garden next door. I was very anxious for a few minutes.

But soon, a black speck in the radiant immensity, Jeannot appeared. He came, moreover, from the opposite direction to the dangerous garden. For that day at least he had not joined in the foray against Monsieur Simon.

He sank to his perch as gently as a flower drops from its stem. He remained for a good twenty minutes that day, I believe, huddled in his little niche, journeying across the sky.

II

The next month was one of the most pleasant I can remember. The southwest wind filled the air almost continually with the roaring of a river that must have flowed for days and days. All living creatures were lulled by this strange and mysterious river, Jeannot in the cherry tree, I in my wooden swing, Aimé's cows motionless at my fence, delivered for one more day from gnats and horse-flies. From moment to moment, borne on the moving air as if on a high and sonorous wave, sounded the melodious tinkle of the bell the Rover set in motion each time she craned her neck to reach over the hedge for a cool leaf.

This blessed wind I imagine as having been born in a distant happy country where beings never hunt one another but live quietly side by side. Furthermore, I noticed that it was only on such days that the black birds on the exposed rocks far away in the murmuring water joined with the white birds.

My Jeannot arrived almost every day now at a regular hour. He came to rest between two thefts. Mere trifles: a leaf of Lucienne's fine lettuce, a strawberry at Berthe's and, more serious, three pecks from a tomato that might never heal.

"That cursed black devil!" I thought I heard in the distance.

Completely safe with me, wings pressed to his body and head tucked in, Jeannot travelled through the sky.

There were calm periods. Then the wind stilled and, the music of the foliage abruptly silent, we were back feet first in what is called "reality," and it seemed insufficient, confining, intolerable. But soon the atmosphere would resound again with the stereophonic music of those summer days in the country.

Truly it is a complex music and requires the participation of many players. To my left, the house of my closest neighbour is enclosed by a group of old willow trees with heavy branches. It is here the wind attacks. As it forces a passage through the low and often deformed branches, it acquires that deep voice of a powerful river. You can hear the abundant water, at once free and confined, discharging no one knows where. This is the bass that supports the voices of the more subtle instruments. Suddenly the wind has crossed the road and given the signal to my pines. Nothing is silkier than their masses of fine needles and here the wind stirs eddy after eddy. In these eddies you can hear the most curious sound ever to come from a tree; it's like the passing of a little country train, very far in the distance, perhaps only in memory. Next the music is communicated to my wood of aspens and silver birches, about thirty of them together on the edge of a ravine. In this grove of young trees the wind suggests the trickling of a cool brook. Trickle, trickle, a young brook trickles steadily in my wood of birch and aspen.

Finally the instruments combine to take up the theme of triumphant summer. All is peace on such days, even though every form of plant life shakes, bows and dances about like a musician under the baton of an orchestra leader, even the grasses at the foot of the trees gone mad, running and running in place, without ever finding time to straighten up. The river in the misshapen willows, the faraway train among the pines, the swift brook on the edge of the ravine, all speak of a mysterious and secret accord.

On these days of full-throated music, my wild red

cherry tree, a quivering silhouette against the backdrop of the river, can scarcely make its muted song be heard.

So without contributing much to the symphony of the world, it sways at least to its own rhythm, all sails unfurled. With the black bird aboard and me in my garden chair, we spent many hours travelling together on the same wave of time.

III

But alas, Jeannot was growing old. He was becoming less prompt at extracting himself from scrapes. More than once I had heard a bullet whistle perilously close to him when he stopped off in passing to have a bite at Monsieur Simon's. I had told him to be careful, that misfortune would come from that side. But he was never one to take advice willingly from humans. Or from his own tribe either. He was a loner.

I was waiting for him one day in my place in the garden. The air stirred the leaves, the pine needles, the grasses. It was a day fashioned in every respect to delight Jeannot. Then through the vocal ensemble that at times so closely imitates the wind high in the sky, I thought I heard the dull sound of a shot. How anxious I felt as I scanned the unbroken blue of the sky. But then, what a relief, the familiar little shape appeared. I was about to laugh once more at the fruitless efforts of Monsieur Simon when—misfortune—the bird plunged towards the ground like a plane in distress. Oh little friend, I thought, at least don't fall on the road where car after car will run over your crushed body.

Jeannot exerted a surprising effort. Steadying himself more or less, he reached a current of air that carried him almost to my yard. Just before he managed it, however, he almost fell again, climbed clumsily, dragged himself, you might say, on his wings to a point just over the cherry tree. At that moment the air ceased almost all movement, as if to aid the wounded bird. His perch received him. Once again he dug in his claws. The gentle wind resumed and wafted him through the sky.

Then the little form at the heart of the tree collapsed, suddenly soft. Jeannot's attire of such beautiful black caught fire as a ray of sun pierced the foliage, making it shine between the branches like a polished coal.

At once the gulls announced high in the sky that Jeannot was dead. Though he had never stood with them in strange companionship on the exposed rocks when the tide rose or fell, nevertheless they were the first to mourn him.

"Jeannot is dead! Jeannot is dead!"

Thus the news reached a huge detachment of crows just returning from Baie-Saint-Paul. As one they continued their flight straight to Monsieur Simon's, crying, "He's the culprit! He's the one!"

Never have I seen so many birds rise up in so little time and from all sides at once. They came from the high fields between the village and the mountain ridge. They came from the more distant hollows behind that first ridge. They came from the fields below. And all converged upon Monsieur Simon's garden.

The poor man must have believed that the birds had gone mad and his last hour was at hand. Beating at the air with his hands, he ran here and there, shouting till he was breathless, "Go away! Go away!"

Far from going away, the birds inscribed great circles in the air, descending lower and lower to brush against Monsieur Simon. And they shouted at him in turn, "Caw caw! Shame and pity! To have killed Jeannot for a tomato!"

Finally they left a place now forever detestable in their sight. They flew to my house and circled round the small black shape in the branches, chanting the funeral service of Jeannot. At last the wind swept him to the ground. I asked Aimé to come then and together we dug a grave at the foot of the wild red cherry tree. Here Jeannot reposes.

And since that day the crows have never failed to call to me as they pass, "Caw, caw, caw!"

The Rover

Today Aimé's three cows are standing with their feet in the bit of a pond near my house. They are grazing on the flowers that encircle this speck of water—mostly swamp candles at this season. From time to time one leans down to taste the sun-warmed water, savouring it rather than drinking. Around her neck the Rover wears the bell Aimé rushed off to buy for her in Baie-Saint-Paul the day she stayed hidden for hours in the alders, refusing to show herself at his call.

"At least now I'll know where she is, the bitch."

Since then the bell has jingled at each of the bitch's movements and you always know where she is. Furthermore, the urge to hide seems to have left her now that the bell at her neck announces her presence wherever she goes.

Its tone is melodious, sweet and charming to hear.

If we're in one of our heavy calms, there is no other noise and the thin chime delights us. If there is wind, the sound can just be heard over the stirring of the leaves.

Sometimes it reaches us from so far away we feel that it comes from another time, another country.

Today the three cows are together. Feet in the water, they muse for long moments, their eyes scarcely raised from the ground, staring ahead without expression like many of the people I know when, without being quite aware of it, they follow some vague idea.

For, curiously, ever since the Rover has scattered music around her, the other two cows never leave her side. So when Aimé finds the Rover, he finds them also.

An instant ago all three came over to my fence, as if stirred by a sudden curiosity to know what I was doing.

The bell pealed loudly, very close. And why did it suddenly waken a memory—that I had believed dead—of the time in my childhood when I used to spend summer holidays with my uncles on their farms in Manitoba? The moment I left the train, I'd be greeted by the tinkling of the handbell with which the hotel keeper on his doorstep announced that a hot meal was ready ... and the sound would make me mysteriously happy as if we were being summoned, all of us strangers on the platform, to a splendid meal of festivity and friendship.

Because Aimé became exasperated with his cow and put a bell around her neck, I was given back this curious joy of my life, though even now I am not quite sure what it is made of or why it enchants me still.

Souls in Torment

O ur killdeer is certainly the most nervous and appre-
hensive of living creatures. That is to say, he and his
wife. For these two are as one. Just let Madame Killdeer
weep and Monsieur Killdeer also weeps.

They chanced that summer to live not far from me
near a bit of water beside the road. It wasn't a pond or
even a pool, really no more than a puddle of rain and
melted snow. Alders, a hundred times cut down, a hundred times grown up again, enclosed it with a low but
bushy wall, it was this that retained the moisture.

Curiously enough, before it was a hollow, this puddle was a small pebbly elevation. A few years ago my
neighbour Aimé began to remove gravel from it for the
road or his own use. The result was this hole that is filled
up each spring by the thawing snow and heavy rains. In
summer the level falls but never sufficiently to uncover
the bottom completely. There is always at least enough
water to hold a mirror to the placid countryside around.
And as the bottom is sandy and the water clean, the mirror offered to the serene sky and the new shoots of the al-

ders remains limpid and reflects everything with perfect fidelity. The modest little spot, pretty in fact, is as pretty in its mirror.

And it became even prettier as all around the water there formed a border of flowers.

The first to appear, I believe, were the swamp candles. The wind helped their rather difficult migration from the damp meadow at the base of the hill to our narrow dry plateau, which till then held little attraction for them. But the appearance of this bit of water among the alders apparently changed everything. Swamp candles, for so long abundant in the lowlands, migrated in force so that there were soon enough of them to encircle the water with a fringe of delicate flowers of the most exquisite yellow. Or rather with two fringes, one erect and the other reversed in the water; and which was the most lifelike it would be difficult to say.

The next year came the flags. Some planted themselves squarely in the puddle; a good number remained timidly on shore, mingling their dreamy blue with the soft yellow of the swamp candles. But the reeds must have arrived even earlier for there were already a good hundred of them, a little sparse in places, in others tangled together.

Things had reached this point and the clear surface of the water with its double girdle of flowers and young reeds already looked like a sort of lake when one fine morning along came Madame Dragonfly, arrayed in tender blue, to revolve silently and continually in this tiny corner of the vast country.

More creatures than one might imagine like to live in peace around a lazy stretch of water that never flows. Frogs were present already with their tadpoles; also skater bugs, leaving momentarily on the surface the marks of their zig-zags; a spider too—all of them peaceable folk, good neighbours, whose natures were marvellously in tune with the tranquillity of the surroundings.

But one day in May two travellers from Minnesota, Monsieur and Madame Killdeer, descended upon us, and the place lost forever the peace and harmony that had already won it renown in far-off corners of the land.

Scarcely had they arranged a sort of nest right on the ground in the alder thicket, and scarcely had Madame Killdeer laid four eggs, than she and Monsieur Killdeer became frantic with apprehension.

"Don't come over here!" they screamed to all comers. "Not over here! For pity's sake, keep your distance! Good heavens, our poor eggs!"

Now the spot, despite its touch of wildness, was much frequented. To the left lay the dirt road to the village. To the right was the private path, faintly traced among the alders, that I used as a short cut to go a hundred times a day to visit my good neighbour Aimé.

Almost hourly someone passed this little corner that the travellers from Minnesota must have staked out on a calm day and expected to be just as calm from one end of the year to the other.

Invariably the killdeers flew into a senseless panic. Madame Killdeer rose above the cropped alders, sobbing heartbrokenly.

"Kill-dee! Kill-dee! Go away! Go away, all of you!"

Monsieur Killdeer raced about madly on his long thin legs, now to the right, now to the left, to make us believe the nest was anywhere but where it was.

"It's over here!" he lied. "It's over here!"

Meanwhile, not hearing what her husband was saying, Madame Killdeer shrieked just as loudly, "It's over here! It's over here!"

And off she went in the opposite direction.

Of course no one believed either one of them. In any event, there wasn't a human being among us who would have dreamed for a moment of taking their eggs or, later, their poor little nestlings. Yet what a summer of misery we spent! Always on the alert. Always on the watch.

First there was the milkman, stopping as usual at the house near the puddle beside the road. Immediately out burst wild lamentations.

"It's over here ... over here ... !"

"No, not here ... not here ..."

"Here ... here ..."

There was an interval of silence. And since the fat green frog and her children, Madame Dragonfly and the spider never make a commotion, everyone rested for an instant.

Then the baker's van arrived.

Monsieur and Madame Killdeer ran senselessly, each to his own side, shrieking as if to drown out one another's voices.

"Over here! Over here!"

"Not true! It's over here! Over here!"

Our cheerful baker, who likes to chat from house to house, came out of Madame Maria's and stood for a good five minutes on the stoop, giving the news, his arms full of bread.

Insane with nervous tension, the killdeers cried in turn, then together, "That's enough! Enough! Quite enough talk!"

Our baker, who's as wholesome looking as his bread, finally stopped talking and departed. Madame Maria went back into her house. There was peace for ten minutes perhaps.

But soon up the hill streamed a band of village children, pails tinkling joyfully in their hands, on their way to pick raspberries. The pleasant metallic sound and the clear childish voices were lost in the eternal complaint.

"What are you going to do here? Here? Here?"

"Not here! Not here!"

It was enough to make you lose your mind.

40

When I myself ventured along my path a while later, I took great pains not to alarm the birds, which had just calmed down. I walked warily, not cracking any branches. No use, the small delicate ears of the killdeers caught my approach. They rose from a clump of alders, fluttering here and there as if this was the first time they'd seen a human being.

"Kill-dee!" one informed me almost intelligibly although I've never known what this could mean in kill-deer language.

"Kill-dee," repeated the other firmly, then they took up their usual shrieks of "Over here!" and "Not here!"

I had time to examine them as they flew low around me. They were very handsome birds, as gifted for flight as for racing about on their long fragile legs. Clearly on their breasts they wore double collars of rich velvet-like black. But such incorrigibly anxious natures!

"With this disposition," I asked them one day, "why oh why did you come to live in such a travelled spot? Couldn't you find a better hiding place? Why here?"

"Kill-dee, kill-dee!" one replied. "It was this restful water that attracted us."

"There must be plenty elsewhere ... better hidden," I said.

"Kill-dee ... kill-dee ... There's no water anywhere as pure as this or as pretty. ... Now take yourself far from here ... here ..."

I couldn't get another word from them.

"At least," I said, "do try to profit from your mistake and next year seek elsewhere."

"Kill-dee," they said. "We won't come back here. Not here."

But a moment later I believe I caught, "Perhaps again here! Again here! Again here!"

The big emerald-green frog finally had enough of these comings and goings and the endless complaining. Of a cheerful nature herself, she was unable to under-

41

stand how anyone could spend his whole life fearing the worst and seeing enemies on every hand. With forty of her children who were now old enough to hop after her from hollow to hollow, she emigrated to a rather dark and far less attractive pond that had at least the advantage of being wrapped in silence. And there she aged gently in a very short time, without losing any of her inclination to look on the bright side of things.

Meanwhile on our plateau the killdeers had reached a high pitch of nervous excitement. For it was now July and scouts had come to camp in the district. At all hours of the day they paraded past, singing at the top of their voices. In the evening, seated around their campfire, they sang again. As well, there was a constant stream of visitors at my neighbour's. Almost all the aunts came, then the nieces, then cousins and more cousins. I too had my share of company. To make matters worse, the village children raced tirelessly along our little road on their bicycles, all the dogs of the plateau at their heels, barking non-stop. This excited Aimé's cows, which began to run like mad creatures in their pasture adjoining the water. To describe the panic of the killdeers those days is almost impossible. Scarcely had they descended into the alder brush to comfort and reassure their children than they would take to the air again or dash across country. And they contradicted one another more than ever, so jittery now they no longer knew what they were saying.

"Kill-dee! Our nest isn't here! . . . Not here!"

"Kill-dee! It's over here! . . . Over here!"

And they ran hither and yon, one to the right, the other to the left, each denying what the other had said.

Surely they've finally learned their lesson, I told myself, and we'll never see them here again.

Monsieur Killdeer agreed, "Oh no! Never here! . . . Never here!"

But Madame Killdeer, perhaps not catching what he had said or just contrary, insisted, "Well, yes! It will be here! For where would you suggest that we go?"

"No, I said not here!" I heard in the distance from poor Monsieur Killdeer, hoping to have the final word for once.

Then at last, having raised their children as best they could, Monsieur and Madame rose from their wretched hiding place one day with their four little killdeers. To fly directly to the South, with a brief stopover perhaps in Minnesota.

"Kill-dee!" they flung back, for once both saying the same thing. "It's all over ... all over ... all over ..."

And a silence such as we had not known for many months settled around the dreaming water.

Then, though we were on the brink of autumn, who do you think returned? Our emerald-green frog, delighted to be back in her original home now that it was peaceful again. She knew all its advantages, having tried another that was much less desirable. At one side of the water there was mud and here she dug herself a deep shelter for the winter, disappearing into it completely after one final look from her big bulging eyes at the world around.

The swamp candles and the flags died but they had entrusted their survival to the sodden earth, which preserved it. Likewise the reeds. Then the little pond seemed lifeless. From day to day the sky darkened. Would you believe me if I tell you that in the grey desolation that marks the approach of the harsh season, Berthe and I came to feel regret at no longer hearing the lamentation of the killdeers? Because it is akin to the anxiety of the human heart? That may be. But certainly something was missing.

In any event, it's well over, I told myself. We won't

see Monsieur and Madame Killdeer again. They've suffered so much misery amongst us, they'll never forget it.

Winter took hold. Our simple-minded frog slept without dreaming, deep under the ice. How the spider hibernated I don't quite know. Soon snow accumulated in the hollow beside the road. What had been, you remember, a pleasant semblance of a lake, almost oval in shape, became an insurmountable snow bank which the wind piled higher with each new storm.

Under the mild spring sun the snow yielded a great deal of water. The soil appeared, rejuvenated. Then, clear yellow, the family of swamp candles, twice as numerous as last year. Also the flags, perhaps the most pensive of all flowers. The alders, cut down in the fall, sprang up afresh, as determined to live as ever. In the centre the new water reflected sky, some small white clouds and from time to time the flight of a duck as with wings outstretched and harried expression he headed only he knew where.

But we mustn't forget to mention Madame Dragonfly, who had arrived a while ago. Just as the summer before, she kept circling about in the perfect little spot to which, I may say, she added the final graceful touch as she brushed the clumps of flags with her wings.

And then, believe it or not, in the midst of all this peace and harmony, as I was coming along my path through the alders one lovely June day, what did I hear?

"Don't come here! We have eggs! Keep your distance! Go away!"

"Over here! ... It's over here!"

"No! ... Not here! ... Not here!"

"Are you crazy?" I asked. "When you had the whole mountain to hide in. And the wild shore of the river beyond Cap Maillard. And the entire old seigneury of Monseigneur Laval. What came over you? Oh what came over you to return?"

Between two anxious cries, I thought I heard, "It was this lovely little bit of water, so calm ... the yellow flowers all around ... the sky in the water ..."

"And the blue flowers ... and the peace ..."

"... that drew us back ... kill-dee ... And even the people, who no longer frighten us very much ..."

"Almost not at all ..."

"Just a little still ..."

And in the sky I heard fear and happiness, dread and trust; and I said to myself, "These birds with the wavering hearts—they're you, they're me, they're all of us, children of this Earth."

A Mobile

Marcel found a family of daisies—about twenty—set at long intervals on a single supple stalk. Quite ordinary field daisies, white with clear yellow centres. What gave them their beauty was the graceful way they were scattered though still attached to the same source. He put them in a narrow-necked vase on a low table from which they projected far into the room. They were so slender and so delicate that a faint current of air set them quivering.

"A mobile of flowers," I congratulated my husband.

Mouffette, my little cat, jumped on the table. She tapped one of the flowers as she might have struck a note on a keyboard; all the flowers trembled. She reached for another higher up; the same result. Then Mouffette turned her head as if to say, "What a lovely toy!"

"Mouffette, no, stop," we protested. "In the whole summer we may never find another such keyboard of daisies."

One paw in the air, she was enjoying herself immensely. The game of the little black-and-white cat

47

juggling with the quivering flowers was so graceful that we finally let her be.

I set this daisy a-shaking; nineteen other daisies vibrate. I try to stop the game; off they go wilder than ever.

Suspended from the tender daisies, paw now on one, now on another, Mouffette looked like a little carillonneur.

Long Skinny Minny

As everyone knows, cats are not very fond of going for walks with their masters. They prefer to wait for them to return, sitting on the stoop. Or perhaps on a window ledge, where they are in a good position to see within and without. It is said that they are more attached to places than to people though this is far from being proved. What is certain, however, is that they love their houses dearly. For proof you need only see them on the first brisk fall days, huddled shivering on the doorstep, fur standing on end, paws tucked in, waiting perhaps a whole day for their folks to get back from visiting in some distant concession. The icy wind may be blowing from that side. No matter. They want to wait as close to the doorstep as they can.

However, there are cats that do follow their masters, very few, but there are some. Like Grisou, a little blue-grey cat that spent its entire short life trying to accompany Aimé, my neighbour, when he went each day to the mountain to chop down trees.

In the still shimmering dawn Aimé would set out

49

along the rough path on foot. Regretfully leaving his cosy nook behind the stove, Grisou would once again manage to leave at his heels without being observed. Confronted with the huge frigid outdoors, he would hesitate for a moment, meowing with fear and shock, yet still not losing sight of Aimé striding ahead. The freshly fallen snow often engulfed the little cat to his eyes. He would extricate himself with an effort and catch up with his master, then rub against Aimé's leg in contentment, wasting his energy trying to purr. So that once again he was left behind. He would try to find short cuts, plunge into the soft snow once more, call for help, mewing desperately, overtake his master again and lose him again and finally sit down, very small and frightened, wailing among the great dark tree trunks. At this Aimé, who'd hoped to exhaust the patience of the little cat and force him to return home, would retrace his steps, take poor cold-stiffened Grisou and set him on his shoulder. Together the two would continue the ascent, Aimé's breath in a white cloud, the little cat clinging with all his claws to his master's woollen jacket. Even so he would appear to be dancing on Aimé's shoulder as it rose and fell with the rhythm of the walk. And as soon as the terrain became smoother and the cat's equilibrium more secure, he would begin to purr in his master's ear.

"Crazy little fool," Aimé would say. "When will you learn to stay home?"

This was quite an exceptional case among cats and, if I've described it, that was only to show the difference between Grisou and, for instance, his own mother, who was as stay-at-home a beast as you could find.

Called Long Skinny Minny, she was not in the least handsome. A scrawny attenuated cat with a crooked tail, she had irregular splotches of bluish grey scattered haphazardly over her white fur, which I must in fairness say she kept scrupulously clean.

By nature she was sullen, morose, stubborn and always fidgety.

Either she was about to have kittens and was turning over her old hiding places in her mind, those that had succeeded and those that had been discovered, with an air of complete distraction as she asked herself, "Are the oldest ones now sufficiently old to be safe to use again? Or would it be better to find one that was brand new?" But she had already had almost sixty offspring. The farm was running out of secure places for the first days of the kittens. Once their eyes were open, they were safe: too cute to be disposed of.

Or if she wasn't about to produce a litter, she'd just had one. But she'd be as distrustful as ever, taking a new complicated way to her hiding place each time. So that she sometimes became completely muddled and lost her way.

However—how strange was the nature of that cat— the moment her kittens were able to fend for themselves, she again took her place firmly among the humans. Henceforth the single thought in her head was to live in the house with the people, installed among them in the best chair, lending an ear to all conversations. And she was constantly at one door or another, begging to be let in.

Now Berthe and her brother Aimé have a strict rule: in summer cats are best outdoors. So they are not readily admitted to the house.

Scarcely had Long Skinny Minny contrived to sneak into the kitchen on someone's heels than she would find herself unceremoniously back outside. No matter. She would hear Aimé coming from the barn with the milk pails. Immediately she was at the back door and had managed to get in, Aimé having no free hand to prevent her. If he tried to bar her way with his foot, she vaulted it easily.

"The cat's in again, put her out," Berthe would say,

51

busy frying a pan of salmon trout or slices of bread soaked in maple syrup.

Naturally it was at the most enticing hour that Long Skinny Minny always deployed all her efforts to reach the kitchen. In the bustle of supper hour with everyone occupied, she more than once succeeded in leaping onto the table and devouring an entire trout right under our noses before we could recover from our surprise enough to shout, "Shoo! Thief!" which didn't disconcert her in the least.

"That cat has no pride," Berthe decided one day.

Seated rocking while everything was being made ready, I went somewhat mildly to the defence of the cat.

"She may be hungry."

"I've just fed her the heads and guts of the fish," said Berthe. "Scat! Out!"

And she dispatched the cat outdoors.

As we were on the point of sitting down to eat, in came the baker and Long Skinny Minny entered triumphantly behind him since he hadn't thought to slam the door in her face.

He sat down. She also.

Two minutes later Berthe accompanied the baker to his van to choose some cakes and took the opportunity to put the cat back out, and the cat took the opportunity of Berthe's return with loaded arms to enter anew.

She eventually wore people down. Aime's house is lively with many visitors. In the course of a single evening I've seen the cat put to the door twenty or even thirty times. Towards eleven o'clock it was not unusual to see her ensconced in the best chair, pretending to be asleep. From time to time she would open her eyes and bestow upon the company a strange glance in which there was less friendliness than a stubborn need, I think, to establish her importance and her place among us.

Nowhere in the world, I imagine, was there a more

stay-at-home-and-sit-by-the-fire cat than this. Unlike Tontine, the little dog of the household, who went into a frenzy of joy whenever she was invited to go for a walk, Long Skinny Minny on her cushion always seemed eager to see us depart. Stretching indolently from head to toes, she would toss us a queer look, at once detached and a shade impatient, as if she were saying, "Why can't you be off then? It's never so nice as when the masters are out and you have the house to yourself."

No doubt it must also have been pleasant for her to be free for an hour or so from the perpetual humiliations and insults of that detestable Tontine.

Be that as it may, this cat, hitherto so set in her ways, finally did something one day that she had never done before and thus dumbfounded us completely.

Berthe and I were getting ready that day to go down to the river to fish for tommycod and Tontine was dancing around, beside herself with joy, giving piercing cries, "Yes! Yes! Let's go down to the river! Let's hurry!"

The small dog with the long reddish fur, half mongrel, half Pekinese, was so passionately fond of going down to the river that she'd learned to recognize the word. If we as much as uttered it in conversation, even though Tontine seemed to be sound asleep, she would immediately open her eyes, lift her head and half rise, already excited by the hope of going with us.

But why she so doted upon going down to the river remained puzzling. For once she'd reached its banks, she didn't even look at the water. Nor did she listen to what was for Berthe and me an inexhaustible joy: the infinite sound of the waves, forever dispersing, forever gathering themselves together again. And she certainly never went swimming but was careful to recoil sharply when, some time after the passage of a ship, a long wave broke unexpectedly on the shore. Moreover, she never went down there on her own as she might have done a hundred times a day. I decided finally that it was seeing us, human beings, made happy by this surprising expanse of water that in the end won over the little dog. "Since they like it so much," she perhaps said to herself, "let's give it a try too." For she had a warm heart, though dreadfully jealous.

So as we had been on our way for several minutes, we suddenly observed Long Skinny Minny trying to follow us and already entangled in the long grass. She must have managed to sneak out behind us without being noticed as she'd managed to sneak in a thousand times.

"This is a surprise," I said. "What's come over her?"

"She's getting old," said Berthe. "And when she's expecting kittens now, you'd think she no longer knows what she wants—to stay or follow, be with people or alone."

And she called over her shoulder to the cat, "You'd better go back to the house. It's too far for you."

That was a mistake, for Tontine had also turned and had seen the cat, who at once flattened herself in the grass, trying to disappear. Tontine raced up the hill like a meteor and repeated the advice in her own way, eyes furious, lip drawn back. For once Long Skinny Minny seemed about to turn on her old enemy. She spat three or four times in Tontine's face. Caught for a moment between these deplorable manners and Berthe's remonstrances, "Ah, bad girl! Come here, bad girl!" Tontine eventually obeyed and returned to our side.

But snarling still, she threatened in an undertone, "Just as long as she doesn't come any closer, for then I promise nothing."

After a moment we saw that Long Skinny Minny was still following us but at a distance, ready to flatten herself in the grass as soon as Tontine glanced in her direction.

54

"Between the slinking cat and the growls of the dog, we're going to have a cheerful walk," I said.

Berthe also seemed disappointed. But she said with a sort of compassion, "It's pitiful just the same."

And she tried again, gently, to send the cat back.

"You'd be much better off at home. Go on. Go home."

Halfway up the hill the head of the cat, scarcely higher than the grass, shook in negation, rather sadly.

We found it inexplicable that Long Skinny Minny should apparently be every bit as attached to us today as she had previously been to the house.

"You'd think she was afraid to be alone these days," said Berthe. "And as for getting her to change her mind, if she's taken a notion to follow us, you might as well try to move the mountain."

So we went on, more or less together, a drawn-out line with Long Skinny Minny far at the rear.

But matters became even worse. For to reach the river you have to go down a steep hill. Great rocks pierce the surface, which is rough and uneven at best. In spots the path is dry, in others always wet. You need to be appropriately shod. Long Skinny Minny kept cutting her paws on the sharp edges of the rock. She got them wet in the damp places, which seemed to displease her even more for she kept drawing one or other of them from the water and shaking it vigorously. At intervals the poor creature sat down to lick the tender cushions of her injured paws. With a helpless look she inquired of us, whimpering, "Couldn't you at least slow down? You know perfectly well I'm not wearing good heavy shoes like you."

Tontine, still nursing her rancour, raced up at once to laugh in her face.

"What came over you to decide to follow us to the river? The river isn't for you. Now put up with it."

Berthe and I finally sat down to enable Long Skinny

Minny to rest for a while. Clearly the harder the way became, the less she would consent to give up. It was as if she were trying to tell us with her big eyes, so full of fatigue and stubbornness, "Do you folks think now that I've managed all this difficult bit I have any intention of returning?"

Tontine made a detour and sat down some distance from the cat, ostentatiously turning her back. And she gave a great sigh of repressed ill-temper.

The place where we were sitting is leafy and shadowy: a narrow clearing between the tangled alders and a few birch trees whose white bark relieves this slightly too sombre wood. We had seated ourselves on a smooth rock and in some connection that escapes me now began to talk about life, how it changes as we advance, as we ourselves change, how hard it is at times to find ourselves again.

Already we could hear, rather faintly, the beating of the water against the shore and the sound became linked with what we were saying. The river and life, both in motion, seemed very close to one another, though the movement of the river soothes us and life often gives us pain as we try to follow it.

"When I was a child," Berthe told me, "my mother used to send me to the spring in this wood with butter, milk and cream. Now we have a refrigerator to keep things cool. It's a thousand times more convenient but we've lost the pleasure of the spring."

"Where is it?" I asked.

She showed me. We uncovered it under some tall dark-green ferns. It made only a tiny sound, scarcely louder than that of the hand of a clock marking the time. It was gentle and enigmatic, as mysterious as at the beginning of its life.

"It's years since I've seen it," said Berthe. "Now that we don't need it any more."

Leaning over the water, we could see very dimly our own darkened faces.

"You can only wonder," I said, "whether what we gain in living is worth what is lost."

At this Tontine, her muzzle flat on the ground but her eyes wide open and her ears impatient, barked briefly as if trying to say, "Do stop talking about life. What's the use? What can you change? Come on, let's get down to the river."

But Long Skinny Minny appeared happy to hear us speaking about the difficulties of living with ourselves and with others. She was lying on her side, still panting slightly, and from time to time she half opened her eyes to give us a golden look that was beginning to grow peaceful.

"That's it," she seemed to be saying. "Talk about life, which is hard to understand and hard to live."

And she turned to Tontine a face of stone.

When we had all four rested, we resumed our descent. The cat lamented less. Doubtless she thought the roughest part of the journey was over and she had a chance of seeing the end. But as if to taunt her by showing how easy the path was for anyone who had the hang of it, Tontine had taken to a cruel game. She raced up the hill and down just as quickly, then raced up again, each time circling the cat, yapping. With more dignity than one would have believed possible, Long Skinny Minny no longer spat or even answered this provocation but simply withdrew a single step from the brazen Tontine.

Then we came out onto the beach with its scattering of great rocks. Beyond lay the accustomed splendour of the river—to which, however, one never grows accustomed. For the thousandth time it gripped our hearts. At the same time the murmuring of the water, the most ancient song of Earth, welcomed and enfolded us. Tontine gave us a knowing look, assuring herself that it was the same as on all the other occasions, we were already so-laced. Then she found herself a nice dry spot behind one of the boulders, turned in a circle and lay down with another sigh, this time of relief.

"At last you'll be quiet for a moment. I'll avail myself of the opportunity to have a rest myself," she told us with a look in which all her concern for us was gradually borne away by a need for sleep.

A little higher up the cat stretched to her full length, scrawny everywhere except for her almost constantly swollen belly. She cast a vague, somewhat bored look at all that water stretching into infinity. What a detestable element! And to think there are people who'll go right to the edge of it—or into it even! She panted gently, composing herself after the emotions of the journey, then she too closed her eyes.

For Berthe and for me, time was of little account, we scarcely see it pass when we are beside the river. It drifts into the song of the tide, which rises and falls, almost the same always. The eternal has seemingly no need to change. To our animal friends also time doesn't seem long near the water, provided we are with them. While we dream, released and marvellously free, they sleep, their minds finally reassured on our account.

Why then did I suddenly break the spell that day by suggesting, "Berthe, suppose we walk along the track?"

Tontine rose to go with us, resigned to follow because she must, but with a rather cross expression.

"What a notion, when we're so comfortable here in the cool, to seek misery elsewhere! How like that curious friend of my mistress who's never happy anywhere for long."

As for Long Skinny Minny, she looked utterly horror-stricken. "What sort of surface will I find there for my already sorely tried paws? And what's the track? Why are they now talking about such an unheard-of place?"

To tell the truth, with her crooked tail, her frantic expression, the amazement in her eyes at wakening here beside the water, she looked crazier than ever.

Yet—what else could she do once launched upon such a foolhardy escapade—she went a little way back with us. There, on a narrow bit of level ground parallel to the river, lies the railroad track.

Berthe and I moved haltingly over the ties, which are set irregularly, as if to discourage people from walking there. The body quickly becomes weary. However, the spirit rejoices, as if it imagined itself freer here than on the road of everyone else.

We had covered a fair bit of ground before we noticed that our animals were—as the saying goes—dragging their feet. Even for Tontine the rough ballast was painful. She was walking like an arthritic with short steps, head down, but without complaint. You have to give Tontine her due, she's not a whiner. But Long Skinny Minny, seated between the rails, eyes bewildered, looked as if she were on the point of giving up but, perhaps not remembering the way or simply too tired to go in either direction, she lamented at the top of her lungs.

"Where have we got to now? Where are we going? Where can it lead, a road like this? Oh why didn't anyone tell me we were going to the back of beyond?"

Tontine gave her a brief glance and a brief growl.

"We did tell you. If you don't like it here, go back. It's hard enough on this road as it is without having to listen to your doleful wails as well."

Poor Long Skinny Minny. To think that she was about to demonstrate a rare and unsuspected talent just when we, in our ignorance, thinking her too stupid, were ready to turn back. But happily I became a child again and had an impulse to try to walk on a single rail, as I used to do when I was seven or eight.

Arms extended to either side for balance, I at first

managed only six or seven steps. I got back and did a little better. Still nothing brilliant. Berthe passed me on the other rail. I began to feel jealous. We then joined hands across the roadbed, trying to support one another. In a moment we were laughing. Life suddenly seemed tender, comic, amusing. Were two slim little girls who had run nimbly along the rail looking at us across the years with a touch of pity? The dog and cat were astonished, in any case. Tontine, who had never seen her mistress give way to such whimsy, was dumbfounded. And as always when she can no longer understand the actions of those she loves, she was whimpering. However, Long Skinny Minny, seated again between the rails but not wailing any more, was watching us, her small narrow face now all attention, all shrewdness, all intelligence.

And suddenly she took off. She passed us easily, tail held high. That perfectly erect tail gave her an entirely new personality. Never would I have thought that the mere angle of a tail could make such a difference.

A short distance ahead of us she jumped onto the rail and continued along at the same speed, tail still high and straight. She didn't even waver but proceeded as if it were nothing. Then, without slowing down, she tossed us a look over her shoulder.

"So this is what you find so difficult! But it's perfectly simple!"

We were thunderstruck. She went on at her ease. A nice firm little trot that never varied. And all this time her head assured, ears erect, tail high.

"That's marvellous!" we congratulated her. "No one on earth is better at running the rail."

Modestly, as if not to claim more than her due, she granted us a brief glance that said, "Ah, that's because you have such wide feet and, poor souls, you only have two."

Despite her unassuming air, we could see that she was rather proud of herself.

The one who looked small at this moment was Tontine.

One ear drooping, tail brushing the ground, an expression of complete incredulity on her face, she watched her bitter enemy continue on her way with such sovereign ease. She gave sighs of envy and grief that reached their height when, without thought for Tontine's feelings, we once more congratulated the cat, "Bravo! Bravo!"

Then Tontine committed the folly of follies. She pulled herself onto the rail and immediately fell off. Obstinately she tried again and with great difficulty achieved four heavy hesitant steps.

The polished steel provided no purchase for her clumsy claws. The poor stubborn creature teetered and landed on her back.

The sole comment of the cat, which had all the cards in hand for a magnificent revenge, was a sort of shrug. She was still running along ahead of us, with an occasional look behind that said mockingly, "Are you still hale and hearty? Shall we go as far as the eel fishing at l'Abatis? To Sault-au-Cochon?"

She seemed suddenly to know the whole region, its peculiarities, its geography.

"Or even to Petit Cap at the bottom of the old seigneury? How long is it now that I've heard you say you'd go there on foot one of these days?"

We had to call her back. Drunk with her success, she was capable of leading us right to Quebec. At first she played deaf and wouldn't even hear of leaving the rail. But when she saw us already halfway up the hill, she decided to return.

No doubt it was not so much running on the rail that intoxicated her as the fact that she'd astonished us. For she had further prowess to display.

In three bounds she ascended the steep hill, stomach on the ground, tail in a straight line with her nose.

At the top, however, she had the good grace to wait for us. There she sat with her tail wrapped around her paws, gazing at the river, the clouds and, far away, between blinks of her eyes, our little procession laboriously climbing.

And on her features was that vaguely amiable expression that comes to people as to animals when for once in their lives they have been admired.

The Tree Brothers

I t was a mild summer day. Three crows on their way to Grande-Pointe settled in the branches of the two aspens beside the road near our house. I call them the twins for never have two little trees growing side by side resembled one another so closely: same height, same slimness of body, same distribution of foliage, same slightly timid way of holding themselves, so character-istic of aspens—the least haughty of trees—yet perfectly straight and enveloped in their own subdued music. All day long they can be heard. If one is silent, it is only to permit the other to speak. But usually they murmur to-gether, both saying the same thing. Seeing the two of them, issues apparently of the same stock, their foliage intermingled, so close to one another that only a thread of light can pass between them, you might believe they had come into the world with the sole aim of mutual support.

They stand at the edge of the road, just this side of the old snake fence that Aimé patches up spring after spring. A little farther and they would be right on the road. So you cannot miss them, singing together, growing in the same proportion every year, touching in their similarity. Yet no one ever spoke of them. No one as much as hinted that he'd noticed them. Except the crows. For this wasn't the first time I'd seen some of them stop in the branches of the young aspens. And though at first I might have believed this a matter of convenience, I came to realize that they simply liked to perch in the little trees.

Two side by side on the same branch, the third facing them on a branch of the twin, the three crows began to converse beak to beak.

In my swing behind the cedar hedge I cannot be seen from the road but I have a fairly good view through its gaps of everything that passes by. Furthermore, I am in the best possible position to listen.

My three crows, who believed themselves completely alone, were chatting familiarly together. It was apparently the oldest that did most of the talking, the other two confining themselves to an occasional "Aah, Aah." And nothing could more resemble a peaceful conversation.

Even their "Caw caw" was not noisy and irritating today as it is when they themselves are irritated—if, for instance, one of their kind is being pursued or insults are hurled from earth into the sky, "Thieves! Robbers!"

Up from the village came a troop of little boys—not bad children usually but suddenly one of them picked up a stone from the gravel beside the road and flung it at the birds, shouting, "Ugly old things! Ugly old things!"

Two others followed suit.

Surprised, the crows were silent. As if slow to understand, they looked down at their feet without stirring. Then they rose from the branches and flew towards the wooded mountain, trailing their wings regretfully, three small black shapes that in the unfurled blue of today's sky suddenly struck a note of reproach.

The children mocked them, "Caw! Caw!" then went on their way.

In the renewed silence I heard the sighing of the two little trees just this side of the old rail fence.

Then half an hour later, all being calm again, the three crows returned and took up their former positions in the aspens, two on the same branch, their comrade opposite. And back they went to their conversation without the slightest hint in their stance or tone of voice that they were holding a grudge.

Yet crows are far from stupid. And they have memory to burn.

Then, announced by what you might call a mechanical shriek of agony, a truck with belly full of oil toiled slowly up the hill that leads to our peaceful plateau. The scents among which we live without always being aware of them—the smell, at once healthy and slightly rotten, of the tide; that of the sweet vernal-grass hidden by the brook; of clover too; and, when the wind is favourable, of old-fashioned roses around the roadside cross—all these delicate scents were drowned in the strong sickening reek of heating oil.

The crows didn't need to be told twice. If there is anything that will persuade them to take wing it is surely what we used to call impure air and now refer to as pollution.

The B.O. oil truck had scarcely reached the top of the slope when my three crows flew swiftly across the little meadow at the foot of the mountain, protesting with all their might, "Faugh! Faugh!"

And in the distance I seemed to hear them lament, "What shall we do? Will lack of air finally separate us from each other, the people and the birds? They in their village? We in the mountain? It will be sad. Heartbreaking."

"Heartbreaking," the little trees replied with a single voice.

"Heartbreaking," a robin seemed to agree with nods of the head as he busied himself searching for food in the grass nearby, and he gave me an incisive sidelong look.

The three crows must have been just as fond as I am of the two slender aspens, which are so united always that no one has ever heard them contradict one another. Or perhaps what they liked was their place in the branches, so convenient for seeing everything that comes along the road where, in their opinion, the good may outweigh the bad.

At any rate, they were soon back but now all lined up on a single branch, as if in a box at the opera, and not uttering a word.

Then from the direction of Grande-Pointe floated another pungent smell, this time not wholly disagreeable. It was the smell of the strong coarse tobacco smoked of old in the country districts. In an enclosed room it might be trying but mingled with the sea breeze it is not unpleasant. Soon I could see Wilbrod the Simple, the only one in the neighbourhood who still smokes this coarse tobacco of former times. He approached, wearing his checked bush shirt and lumberman's boots, his wide-bowled pipe in his mouth, his big scythe over his shoulder and a whetstone protruding from the back pocket of his trousers. He had been hired to hand-scythe the little bits of fields where the machine cannot pass—the specialty as it were of Wilbrod the Simple, he having also acquired one since everyone around him is now mechanized.

With his usual habit of announcing to himself out loud what he has to do, I heard him telling himself pleasantly, "You're going to clean up the apple orchard at Aimé's. Then you'll go home and milk the cow. Then you'll wash yourself all over ..."

Through a hole in the hedge I saw him stop short at sight of the three crows, immobile, listening. At once his ancient face lit up with delight. He set his scythe blade-down on the ground and leaned on it as if on a cane. Despite the cloud of tobacco smoke that struck them full in the faces, the birds didn't even move. Wilbrod, head raised to look at them, began to address them very gently.

"Pretty little ladies. Pretty little crows. Sweet young ladies."

Immediately you would have said that the birds came as close to the road as they could with a sort of sliding of their bodies. The brilliant eyes of all three were fixed upon Wilbrod.

"My, they're smart," he said. "They see everything. Understand everything."

The crows inclined their heads slightly to the side for a better view through the leaves of this curious man who seemed to know whereof he spoke. The aspens quivered with the passage of a light breeze.

Wilbrod, arm resting on his scythe, asked the birds, "What do they think? Yes, what can they think? Of us? Of our world?"

When his young ladies made no reply, he said in farewell, "Smart little things. Smart as paint."

Then he departed, his scythe over his shoulder, puffing from his pipe almost as much smoke as rises in spring from maple-sugar shacks.

On the branch, imperceptibly, the three little black shapes had moved again to follow Wilbrod the Simple with their eyes. And they listened, beaks pointed, in the most attentive silence, as he informed himself, "Then you'll wash all over. Then you'll change your underwear. Then you'll say your prayers . . ."

And the tree brothers replied in the same breath, "So be it."

The Festival
of the Cows

Today the cows are resting. All three lying down, their calves too. With nothing to do but let the warm wind rid them of flies, horseflies and gadflies. It was the first time I'd seen such a thing: in broad daylight, hooves tucked under them, all turned to receive this blessed wind between their horns, letting themselves live. Until now I'd never seen them when they weren't scratching themselves, first with one foot, then another, tails revolving, ears twitching, always in a state of defence against the torturing insects. I'd come to the conclusion that it was natural for them to sleep two minutes here, ten minutes there, and to live and die, as it were, on their feet.

As I cut through the field where they lay so perfectly at ease, I took care not to disturb them or force them to get up.

None of them rose as I passed but each one greeted me vaguely from somewhere deep within her eyes. They appeared to recognize me at first glance today. Because the dry wind had cleared their brains? Perhaps. But perhaps also because of my little white hat. I've noticed that

69

they seem to recognize me more quickly when they see it appear through the alders. Always, however, with a certain stupefaction, as if they were asking themselves, "When on earth is she going to buy herself another hat?"

Now what they do not know is that I buy a new hat every summer, identical always to the old one.

I zig-zagged between them, then, so as to disturb them as little as possible. I could hear their quiet breathing. Perhaps to savour this day that was unparalleled in their lives, they weren't even ruminating. With their big pleasant eyes they were saying, "We're at ease. What more do you want us to say? We're at ease. Today is the festival of the cows."

If they were still moving their tails gently, it was, one would say, as dogs do, simply to show their contentment.

One, two, at most three days of well-being in the whole summer, I told myself, and see how happy they are!

In fact, with their huge placid eyes, faces in the wind, backs to the river, they seemed to be thanking heaven that they'd come into the world as cows.

Not in the least stupid, moreover, they were lying on the highest point of the field where the air circulates most freely. Then, to enjoy the wind even more, they dug their noses into it and closed their eyes.

I arrived at Berthe's almost in a state of jubilation.

"Berthe! Berthe! Berthe!"

She was coming down the steep stairs from the attic. I didn't notice at first that she looked a little tired.

"Berthe, the cows are lying down. All resting. It's the festival of the cows!"

I saw then that she seemed concerned.

"What is it, Berthe?" But full of my subject, I didn't wait for her reply. "Cows happy to be cows, Berthe! Have you ever seen such a thing?"

"Oh, if all our friends were as happy," she said in a tone of slight reproach.

And she led me to the flower garden, which in my haste I hadn't stopped off to admire first thing as I usually do.

Everything had suffered here. The poppies hung down, their faces faded; many of the lupines were broken; the roses were shrivelled, the delphiniums shattered. Only a few of the strong dahlias held their ground though barely.

"It's this wind," Berthe said. "It's broken them all. I put up wind-breaks but you'd need a separate one for each flower."

I helped her erect others. From time to time I glanced towards the cows. On their hummock at the end of the field, in relief against the sky, they presented a rare picture of contentment. Or perhaps, now that the wind was in their favour, of egotism. They were certainly indifference itself as they watched us trying to rescue the flower garden.

"Well, what would you? For so long, every day has been the festival of the flowers. Today it's our turn." And they thrust their noses back into the wind. "Oh, how delicious!"

The Pair

Everything alive wants to live as one of a pair. Needs his counterpart. Or lacking a counterpart, some other creature.

Aimé's horse was obliged to live much of his life alone of his species. That is why he joined forces with the cows.

He spent the winters with them in the same little stable and the summers in the same pasture.

In summer he wasn't entirely with them. The cows formed their own compact small group and he stood some distance away—but never very far.

When the cows took a notion to descend the steep hill and seek cover in the alder brush, Prince went down also. (Between ourselves, this Prince led a rather menial life: bringing in the hay, transporting maple sap, hauling wood from the mountain.) The animals sometimes spent part of a week below, most of the time invisible. The day the cows returned, up came Prince at their heels.

Prince's attachment to the cows didn't become fully apparent to us, however, till the day Aimé decided to put

73

him by himself for a while in a field across the road. He'd be much better off there, with grass that hadn't been browsed all summer, fine trees for shade, even a brook.

Yet he stood unmoving at the fence, gazing across the road at the cows. He called to them, whinnying. Or perhaps he was calling for his master to release him, who knows? All that day he neither ate nor drank. And there is every indication that he didn't sleep either.

Then the next day this horse, hitherto so gentle, began to lash out at the fence with his hooves and to fling himself against it so violently that he was considerably injured after a few hours. That night he managed to smash the fence down and at daybreak he was in his customary place near the cows on the knoll overlooking the river. And he was browsing with pleasure on the scanty grass of this wretched field that had already been browsed a hundred times.

Days when the cows suffered cruelly from the stings of no-see-ums and black flies, he suffered patiently at their side.

Days of rest, he rested with them.

After some time Aimé made another attempt to put Prince by himself. This time the horse leaped the fence almost at once and was back with the cows the same day.

Here and there, the animals still had a few days' relief. Then all four stood in the wind, the cows in the lead, the old horse bringing up the rear.

In these periods of respite the cows seemed more than ever to lose themselves in indolent daydreams that were reflected in their placid gaze.

But in the great agitated eyes of the horse there was still a shadow, a distant sorrow, perhaps the vague recollection of a lost happiness.

The horse was for so long a wild animal and may remember his freedom still.

* * *

But before the onset of the bad weather, Prince experienced a joy such as he had never known in all his life. A certain Adélard Dufour of the village was obliged to be away for a few weeks and brought his horse to board at Aimé's.

Aimé led it into the cow pasture.

Prince approached to meet the newcomer. The newcomer greeted him. Immediately they were friends.

Yet they had nothing in common except being horses. Flick was a pretty little white beast of very mild disposition that had almost never worked except to bring in a bit of hay each summer for his own cow, which was deeply attached to him and must miss him a great deal these days. Prince was an old roan, worn out by the hard transport of wood in winter on a steep snow-covered mountain road.

No matter, for as long as they were in the same pasture, they never left one another. They formed their own group. They were a pair. They stood together, heads crossed over the fence along the road. Here Flick had stationed himself as soon as he arrived, as if already watching for his master's return.

Prince joined him there, laying his neck on the neck of the little horse in consolation.

Since then they had spent hours, the neck of one on the neck of the other, silhouetted against the sky. If there were flies, they defended themselves with the same movement of tail and ears.

Their manes undulated similarly in the wind.

And shadow, sorrow, perhaps even memory too, had almost disappeared from their huge eyes.

Dance, Mouffette!

For three days my mischievous little cat hadn't thought of any new tricks to make me laugh or scold. Her hiding places had all been discovered, to Mouffette's considerable vexation.

First there was the one on top of the buffet. This is a mastodon of a piece, which almost touches the ceiling. Came the time to put Mouffette to bed in her basket in the kitchen. I called her; no answer. Of course it is always just before bedtime that she looks for a place to hide, as though she were saying, "If I have to be shut up, at least let me choose where."

I searched under the beds, in the cupboards, behind the chairs and the sofa. Without being very big, Mouffette at four months is quite easily spotted even at night, thanks to her white costume with black stripes.

Finally there was nowhere left to look except on top of the buffet. What gave me the idea was that I'd noticed a possible way to get up there: several book shelves first, then a catalogne rug on the wall, finally a bit of bare wall —a mere nothing to one who has good claws!

I placed a chair on the table and climbed up. There, squeezed against the ceiling, stretched out rather absurdly the better to escape unobserved, lay Mouffette, not in the least annoyed at being caught. Quite the contrary, she gave me a sort of wink that seemed to signify, "Ha ha! Fooled you that time, eh?"

Then she yawned, rose and seated herself at the extreme end of the buffet, which overlooks a bay window facing the sea. The little cat gazed into the distant water and assumed a look of contemplation as if to indicate that she'd climbed so high expressly to have a good overall view. And there is little doubt that, far above people and furniture, she must have enjoyed a unique panorama. At any rate, she was so content there that only hunger could bring her down.

The very next night Mouffette found another hiding place. Never the same one twice! This time she managed to slide under the tightly drawn bedspread without making a single wrinkle. In other words, lie invisibly in a made-up bed. She was so flat that I passed that way a good twenty times and didn't notice even the tiniest bulge or the least pucker. The twenty-first time a slight movement of breathing that barely lifted the bedspread caught my eye. I whipped off the spread. Discovered, Mouffette looked enchanted. She spends her time hunting for hiding places and yet she'd be bitterly disappointed if I didn't find her.

But hiding places were running out. There are limits to those you can be sure of in a small country house when, in addition, you have a mistress well versed in the trickery of young cats.

So after the bedspread caper, Mouffette became bored. There was no use my offering her favourite toys: a spool of thread, the balls of newspaper with which she plays hockey, even the big grocery bags she promenades about the room, hidden inside so that they seem to be walking across the floor on their own; I presented all these to no avail. Mouffette just complained with a sad meow, "It was much more fun when you used to hunt for me for hours, turning the house upside down while I played dead."

And the little demon, so full of tricks, yawned in my face. I have never ceased to be amazed that such a small creature can yawn so enormously. For several minutes, ideas failing her, she looked as if she didn't find life at all amusing.

Until yesterday evening. Yesterday evening there were no-see-ums. These are nasty insects, invisible to the naked eye, that sting ferociously. If there is light in the room, they go right through the screens and harass you in your bed. So I didn't put on the lights. Just an old oil lamp that I keep in case of power failure. Also a few citronella candles. So in the night infested with no-see-ums, I was as if in a fortress, protected by my counter-fires.

I sat in the gentle glimmering that seemed to make me even more aware than usual of the old wardrobe, the ancient chest that looks as if it came from a pirate ship, the tall well-waxed buffet, the prints on the walls. Mouffette too must have felt pacified. She jumped on my knees and examined my eyes at length by the flame of a candle. And I myself believed that I could see her great semi-phosphorescent eyes more clearly than ever before.

Then some friends arrived. I wanted to put on the lights.

They begged me not to.

"It's so much more pleasant to sit by candlelight."

"We haven't had the opportunity for such ages."

We discovered once more that sitting by candlelight, the door open to let the faint sounds of the night unobtrusively enter, is one of the wonders of life in the country.

Voices at once become softer, melting, as it were,

into the half-light. No one tries to drown out anyone else or talks non-stop, as if the chance to speak once lost would be gone forever. Each voice comes in its turn, measured and slow, broken by silences that are full of meaning. Coming from the heart, each voice seeks the heart.

And in the gentle glimmering, eyes often take on the quality of a dream. You might think they were tiny lakes, enclosed in darkness, illuminated by the far-off rays of some invisible light.

Fascinated, Mouffette went from one to the other of us, jumped onto the knees of this one, then that one, looked into our eyes in turn and suddenly tried to capture the glow with her paw.

Everyone flattered her, telling her she was the prettiest cat in the world, which Mouffette never tires of hearing. This little animal heart has just as much need as any human heart to know that it is loved.

Suddenly as she passed through the flickering of a candle, Mouffette caught sight of her misshapen shadow. Was she afraid? Or had she already grasped the comic possibilities of the situation?

Whichever it was, she played the broncho. Head down, neck twisted to look at us askance, back arched, tail likewise, she leaped high into the air in a series of bounds to the side, always presenting that menacing profile.

We laughed heartily to see this amicable little beast transformed into a dangerous animal.

No doubt our gaiety intoxicated Mouffette. The little fool was now playing at frightening herself.

"Dance, Mouffette!" we begged.

Sidelong glance, ears flattened, back raised, she sprang into the air, landed on all four paws.

"How lovely! Dance!"

Mouffette leaped higher still, took another bound, threatening us with that terrible profile.

"Dance, Mouffette!"

She jumped, came down on all four paws, rose again, cast us a wicked look.

She was prepared to dance all night now that she'd found the game of scaring us to death.

Dance the brief flames of the candles in their glasses! Dance the amused glimmer in the eyes of the humans all around! And dance in the middle of our circle the little black-and-white form dizzy with its success!

The Mass
of the Swallows

Adjacent to the cow-pasture, behind a clipped cedar hedge and near the pond, stands a chapel with room for about fifteen people. A rustic cottage close by that I call "the little presbytery" is used as retreat house by My Uncle the Curé, Aimé's brother, when he comes home to rest. On these occasions he celebrates Mass in the chapel. To announce Mass he pulls a cord that rings a bell with a very thin sound. On days of high wind it can just be heard. At once people set out from all corners of the plateau: several of Lucienne's children; little Claude in his best suit and a cap; Berthe without fail; some of Monsieur Simon's family; strangers if there are any; I myself from time to time.

I went by way of the pasture that day. Roused by the tiny sound that recalled the tinkling of the bell worn one summer by the late lamented Rover, the cows trailed after me to the fence and tried to gain admittance on my heels into the sacred enclosure. Did they believe that the light tinkling would lead them to some vestige of the deceased, who has left such pleasant memories behind? Or were they simply consumed with curiosity to learn at last why so many of their acquaintances gathered like this in broad daylight, seemingly to do nothing? Whatever their reason, they remained at the fence all through Mass, standing devoutly.

As My Uncle the Curé always leaves the door of the chapel open—otherwise we'd stifle—the cows in their places could follow the Mass quite well out of the corner of their eyes.

My Uncle the Curé, who might have been seen an instant before relaxing in his old corduroy trousers and turtleneck sweater, now appeared in a chasuble embroidered with gold thread. Little Claude's eyes almost popped out of his head in wonder. My Uncle the Curé greeted us with a few friendly words, we being his neighbours, then absorbed himself in the Mass.

We all had our noses more or less touching the altar. Standing so close to one another, we should have felt cramped. Yet it was quite otherwise because of the open door, which admitted the pool with its limpid surface, the endless blue folds of the hills, and a bit of river and sky near the point of Ile aux Coudres. Sometimes a freighter drifted into our field of vision, enveloped in its smoke. Thus into this insignificant little chapel the distance penetrated.

When Mass had begun, the swallows arrived in a tremendous flurry as if to make us overlook their tardiness. They skimmed the surface of the pond with their breasts, sprinkling us from afar as if with holy water.

"Nobis-nobis," we heard them say with their little mouse cries.

They apparently were not aware that the Mass is no longer said in Latin.

"Oh Christ, have mercy," said My Uncle the Curé.

"Nobis-nobis," replied the tiny voices of the swallows.

"Have mercy," intoned little Claude in his clear singing voice.

"Mercy," breathed the cows at the fence in a great sigh.

They pushed against one another, but not roughly, trying to get a better view of the inside of the chapel. Then up trotted Miquette, little Claude's German shepherd. With a severe look the boy riveted the dog to the door-sill. She lay there, her body outside, only her muzzle in the church. And, eyes raised to us and to the officiant, paws together, she had an air of such piety that only the most stony-hearted could have sent her away.

"The Lord be with you," said the priest.

"And also with you."

The atmosphere, which had been charged with electricity all day, crackled. Thunder sounded in the distance. The hills rolled with its growling. And suddenly the storm was upon us. You would have thought the rain was doing its best to drive nails through the flimsy roof that protected us. It jostled the bell in its tiny belfry. The entire chapel seemed about to be carried off by the wind. The hills were drowned. Of the vast expanse of river and sky of a moment ago nothing remained but a vague sallow tint. The swallows had found shelter. With cautious movements of her folded paws, Miquette wriggled forward till she was entirely under cover, except for her tail, which she had not the audacity to draw into the church.

The cows by the fence could scarcely be distinguished in the deluge though they did not stir. For a moment I thought I could glimpse Prince behind them, trying with his great mournful eyes to see into the chapel. Then he withdrew. Or the mist absorbed him.

"On the night he was betrayed," said the priest, "he

took bread and gave you thanks and praise. He broke the bread, gave it to his disciples and said: 'Take this, all of you, and eat it: this is my body which will be given up for you.'"

We had forgotten that he was My Uncle the Curé. Now he was only the priest. Just as we for this instant at least were only children of the Father.

As abruptly as it had broken, the storm subsided. A luminous hole appeared, as if a small window were being opened in the high wall of the sky.

The swallows took to the air again and, as they passed the doorway, we heard their almost imperceptible response, "Nobis-nobis."

"When supper was ended, he took the cup. Again he gave you thanks and praise, gave the cup to his disciples and said: 'Take this, all of you, and drink from it.'"

The marvellous story unfolded once again and once again held us enthralled.

At a single look from little Claude, Miquette slithered out of the chapel. Now she was only half inside, her head almost dry, her back damp, her tail so saturated you could have wrung a stoupful from it.

Little Claude was first to go forward to receive the host in his hand, which he extended as if expecting a treasure. His face shone like the freshly washed countryside around. Miquette gave him a look we had never seen before, humble and proud at once, as if she had a king for master.

The young took communion in the new way, the rest of us in the old.

Suddenly, rubbing their wings together, the crickets decided to play an accompaniment to the communion. The cows by the fence almost dislocated their necks in their efforts to see what we were eating. Prince reappeared for a moment, head towering over the cows, then he vanished again. Mass has never held much charm for him, dull-witted as he is.

"May almighty God bless you," said the priest.

"Nobis-nobis," entreated the tiny voices of the swallows, for once putting their response just right.

The priest opened wide his arms.

"Go in the peace of Christ."

On the doorstep we were dazzled by the brightness of the landscape. All its dust had been carried away by the downpour. Each leaf now held a bubble of water. The sky was a gleaming matter. One by one the hills were reborn to our sight with the contours we have always known and yet seeming to be revealed to us afresh. Then a rainbow appeared, stretching from one side of the pond to the other like a suspended bridge. Part of it crumbled away and now, like the bridge at Avignon, it stopped in mid-span.

"Nobis-nobis," the scatterbrained swallows resumed. Having served Mass all askew, they seemed not to know that it was over.

Then Berthe's grey cat came hurrying along the path through the high grass, bitterly disappointed at having missed Mass, which she dearly loves to attend, seated on her tail.

Miquette rubbed against little Claude and looked up at him with profound respect. The boy stroked her forehead gently. The cows scattered quickly to let us pass, still staring at us fixedly.

It was as if our domestic animals felt for us today something very close to adoration.

Or perhaps a humble and confused jealousy.

"What do they know that we don't know? What have they seen today? Received? That touches their faces for a moment with such beauty?"

The Day
Martine Went Down
to the River

I

Tontine is getting on in years. When we gather in the evening in Aimé's kitchen, she dozes. She has no interest in our talk of the cost of living, inflation and the Vietnam War. Her slumber is broken by nightmares that must be violent for occasionally she whines and we see her tremble all over. For a long time now she hasn't danced with joy when she hears us mention the river. Out of consideration for her aged bones we avoid pronouncing the word in her presence. We use evasions. We say, for instance, "Shall we go down ... to ... to the edge of the water?" We have finally stricken even this word from our vocabulary for she has come to associate it with the river, or rather with the sea, as we usually call the St. Lawrence in these parts.

Sometimes as we fumble around the subject, she opens her eyes and gives us a look marked with the distrust that comes to very old people when a sort of protective conspiracy is woven around them. And the aggrieved expression in the eyes of the little dog reproaches us for no longer speaking openly in front of her.

But still very shrewd, she has caught onto the fact that when Berthe puts on her rubber boots, it's almost always to go down to the river. And the other evening when Berthe opened the boot and broom cupboard beneath the angle of the stairway, Tontine bounded to her feet. She tried, in the middle of the kitchen, to give one of those lively performances of former times, all laughing, frisking and supplications. Blind in one eye, her haunches and neck stiff, she succeeded in showing something of the joy that used to fill her in the days of her youth. For just as it is with human beings, the chief happiness of Tontine's old age comes from the memory that she was once young and full of life.

She makes me think of old cousin Martine when she came home after fifty years' exile in a lodging without air or vista to see the river once again before she died.

II

Her children brought her by car. It took four of them to help her out and half-carry her up the front steps and over to the nearest chair.

For a few days she sat rocking in the kitchen right beside the window that overlooks the sea, gazing at it with each forward movement of the chair.

"It's coming in," she kept saying. "It's still coming in. ..." Then, "It's beginning to go out. ... It's going out. ..."

At first this was all she could find to say about what had been perhaps the deepest attachment of her life, "It's coming in. ... It's going out. ..."

She had been given a room with a view of the river so that just before she slept and as soon as she wakened she had time to look at it again. Finally this was no longer sufficient.

One day we heard the mild little woman lamenting, "Isn't it a shame! Isn't it a pity! To come from so far away and not even go down to the river."

90

"Ho ho ho!" her eldest son Edgar replied with some severity. "Go down to the river! Put that idea right out of your head, Mother. You have to hang onto a chair even to get around the house. And yet you want to go down that big hill. Do try to be sensible, Mother."

"I'm much stronger now," said Martine defensively.

This was true; she could now manage on her own the seven or eight steps from her bed to the window to have one last look before she slept at the sea as it rose or fell.

Her other son, Déodat, though less impatient, also tried to reason with her.

"It's pretty nice anyway, isn't it, Mother, that we've brought you to spend two good weeks at home? Remember all the trouble we had getting you down those steep steps from the third floor. You musn't demand too much."

And so, having set their mother to rights, they went off to spend the day fishing for trout in the mountain brook.

Martine was silent for a few minutes, staring into the distance, then, unaware that she was speaking out loud, began again, "If just once before I die, I could go down to the river!"

"The river! The river! You can see it from here, Mother!"

Startled out of her reverie, Martine looked with astonishment at whoever it was who was speaking with such lack of comprehension; she sighed, then gave up trying to give an explanation. There are so many things the old give up trying to explain to the young, which the young will not understand till the day when they in turn give up trying to explain them to others younger still. And so the muffled circle of the generations closes.

But Berthe, though far from old herself, understood the keen desire that was tormenting the small arthritic body of Cousin Martine.

"Build up your strength a little more, Cousin," she said one day. "Then you and I will go down to the sea together."

"You'd do that! You'd bother with me?"

Deep in the wrinkled face, her eyes shone so brightly that we glimpsed a little of the young Martine we had never known.

I joined in. "I'll come too. It will be better with three."

"My children! How sweet you are! What a lovely day we'll have!"

"We'll help you over the roughest spots," said Berthe. "We'll even carry you a bit."

"As far as that goes," Aimé suggested, full of good will, "why couldn't I take you down in the tractor?"

Martine gave him an indignant look.

"In a tractor to the river!"

She burst into fresh clear laughter.

"In a tractor to the river! At my age! Just think of that! In a tractor!"

And it was as if she were saying, "To church in a tractor!"

Aimé, a little disconcerted, said defensively, "I was just trying to be helpful ... really."

In fact, there were four of us to go down to the river. For Tontine was of the party. At the sudden confusion in the house, she had suspected that an event of some importance was afoot. When just as we were about to leave, Martine in a black satinette dress asked for her city hat as well, Tontine was overcome with excitement and cried heartbreakingly, "I want to go! I want to go too!"

"She may as well come," said Berthe finally. "At the speed we'll be travelling, it won't be any harder on her than wearing herself out trying to get through the screen door. Come along then, my little idiot."

Enlivened by the keen air of the summer morning

and the intoxication of the departure, Martine went a good bit of the way alone. Her movements were trembling and uncertain but her face was as exalted as that of a child taking its first steps.

When we reached the fence, we grasped the tiny old woman under the arms, hoisted her over the wire and deposited her on the other side. Martine was still laughing when we joined her, we two also over the wire and Tontine beneath.

Then as she was a little tired, as much from laughing as from walking, Berthe and I made a sort of chair out of our crossed hands and here Martine took her place, steadying herself with an arm around our shoulders. When I used to play as a child at crossing the jungle, I was sometimes the potentate who permitted herself to be carried in this manner but usually one of the slave porters of the potentate. Martine was choking with laughter at finding herself borne aloft above the uncut hay. From time to time she gave one of us a light tap of encouragement on the shoulder. Tontine brought up the rear, lips drawn back as if she too were laughing—or perhaps simply amazed. For never before in our region had she witnessed the spectacle of a person being carried on a chair made of hands through the high grass. She was not jealous, however, and when Martine let one of her hands trail, she licked it gently.

At the edge of the birch and alder thicket where the hill begins, we halted and seated Cousin Martine on a smooth rock. Though she was incredibly tiny, weighing scarcely more than eighty pounds, we were breathless. So we sat down beside her.

"Poor children," she said, out of breath herself. "I'm almost killing you."

We said no, not in the least, we were ready to go on, and we began to suck at tender grass, which we gathered around us.

It was a dim leafy spot with no view of the river.

Conversation became melancholy. We discovered that Cousin Martine was not very different from the birds of the shore, almost light-hearted one moment, sad the next.

"In Hochelaga," she said, "I wasn't really so far from the river. I could have walked down there more often. But the few times I did, I scarcely recognized it. Along the shore you couldn't even see the water. Just banana peel, orange rinds and dirty papers thrown from boats. And you could breathe nothing but oil. Just once I closed my eyes and caught, coming from far away, the faint, faint scent of the tide. Then I lost it."

She fell silent, hands folded across her hollow stomach.

It was difficult to accept the idea that from this thin small body had come great heavy Edgar, weighing in at almost two hundred pounds, and Maurice who was nearly six feet tall. Even the daughters looked like big solidly planted trees beside their reedlike little mother.

"I had fourteen altogether," Martine told us, "fourteen children. Nowadays women with two or three to raise complain, 'It's too expensive. It's too much work.' I had fourteen to raise," she repeated proudly.

Then sadness overcame the joy in the cracked voice.

"I lost more than are left to me. There was Geraldine ... so tiny and finely made, my Geraldine. After her, Marie-Ange, perhaps my prettiest one."

A herring gull lamented in the distance as he passed again and again across the patch of sky we could see from our shelter beneath the trees.

In just as doleful a voice Martine told of her dead children.

"Horace who was so sweet. ... Never saw such a sweet little child. Then my Solange. ..."

Tontine, who still possessed her wonderful gift for sensing the grief of human beings, approached Martine and looked deeply and with compassion into her eyes.

And the little old human mother looked back just as deeply at the little old animal and stroked Tontine's forehead with a sympathetic hand.

Then we hoisted Martine onto the seat made of our crossed hands and off we went again.

"Come, Cousin," said Berthe. "This is no day for sorrow. The river's awaiting you. You mustn't show it a sad face."

"That's very true," said Martine, beginning to smile again under the brim of her hat.

Suddenly she decided, "What use is this?" She took off the hat and hung it on the branch of a tree where it could easily be retrieved on the way back.

The wind stirring her thin hair, she laughed again with her light mocking laughter.

"What an idea of Aimé's to take me down by tractor!"

She turned to measure with approval the distance we'd already covered. "It's much better to go on foot like us three."

"Yes, indeed," we agreed, "it's very much better to go on foot like us three."

A little later, unable to walk another step, we set Martine down on the slope of the wooded path.

"Poor children," she said, though perhaps without quite as much compassion as before. "I'm tiring you. It's hard going, eh? But at your age one recovers quickly."

Curiously, Berthe and I, who just the evening before had been telling each other we were no longer good for anything much, felt brisk and energetic today beside Martine. Perhaps the most miraculous gift of the very old is that they make those who are not really young feel youthful again.

We picked Martine up, put her down, picked her up once more. At the end of the wooded path where the river appears in all its immensity, we set her down finally for, suddenly imperious and independent, she wanted to approach it "on my own two feet."

However, she had to accept a little more help from us to cross the railway track, then a field, and to navigate a final rough passage between huge rocks.

And now we were right beside the river. With a sort of impatience she pushed us away with both hands at once and went on alone, over the pebbles, through the coarse sand. She did not waver. Her entire being carried her forward, a soul straining towards God.

Leaving her alone with the river, we withdrew a short distance, first warning her, "Watch out for the big waves after the passage of a ship."

She flung a look over her shoulder that informed us: "There's no need for such as you to tell me about *my* river."

Tontine also appeared anxious. She fussed around Martine for a moment, asking us with a worried look, "Isn't it dangerous to leave her all by herself?" Then she went to sit in the place that had been hers for years, well sheltered behind the boulders.

Martine stood motionless. At her feet waves broke with a tender whisper. Around the small figure in the black skirt all was blue today: the water right into the farthest distance, the tiered line of hills over towards Les Eboulements, the faint shadow of Ile aux Coudres barely visible above the water.

She stood there on the threshold of immensity, with her regret for her dead children and the recollection of the troubles she had endured, with her bereavements and her sorrows, with the memory of her endless waiting for this return to the river. And it was all being weighed in a mysterious balance: the cruel waiting and this radiant instant today. And who can say that the instant did not tip the scales?

The teasing wind blew up the old-fashioned skirt that hung long on her calves and dishevelled her hair. Patiently as she had lived, she smoothed down her skirt, then her hair, tucking in the loose strands. Then she turned to us a face on which lost youth shone for a moment like the reflection of a distant sun.

"I almost think I'll take off my shoes. Put my feet in the water. Seems to me it might do me good."

We went down to help her. She had seated herself on one of the stones. We removed the heavy shoes that had been resoled and mended several times.

"They're the only ones in which I'm reasonably comfortable," she said in excuse.

We drew off the thick black stockings. Her feet appeared, as small and white as a child's but incredibly twisted. And it was on these poor insignificant feet that Martine had got through her hard life. She looked at them as if surprised herself at all they'd been able to bear.

"They've held me up at times long enough to iron twenty-five men's shirts at a stretch."

We rubbed them gently, then accompanied her to the edge of the water. She went in valiantly, hitching up her skirt. Tontine had come down too and asked us with a troubled look, "Do you really think you should let her do it?" And she sat down to keep a close watch on this old cousin who was behaving so oddly.

Daringly Martine advanced a step farther. The water encircled her pale ankles. The sea breeze bathed her worn face.

In the vast unfurlment of water and sky she made a stain scarcely larger than the black bird beating its wings on the shore. Did one of the oldest crows think it had found its counterpart? It circled several times above Cousin Martine, then gave a sort of cry of surprise, "Can it be little Martine come back? The little girl who loved nothing as much as paddling in the water?"

"Not possible, not possible," croaked another ancient crow which was also renowned for its memory of former times. "Today little Martine would be seventy-eight ... seventy-nine years old. It couldn't be little Martine."

"It is so little Martine. See. She's still paddling in the water."

Martine followed the conversation with a wondering expression as if she grasped something of what was being said in the sky.

For my part, the more I looked at her the more I was reminded of those pilgrims of the Ganges in Benares, whom one sees with loincloths tucked up, frighteningly thin but their faces illuminated with fervour.

We finally removed our own shoes and joined her. I think she was pleased to have us at her side in case she stumbled. But she didn't want anyone to take her hand or, for the moment, speak to her. She had suddenly become aware of the invisible as if behind this day that she had waited for all her life, she glimpsed another more radiant still. And she needed to be alone and all attention to recognize intimations of the unknown.

Suddenly, barefoot on the rim of the summer sky, she began to ask questions—doubtless the only ones that matter.

"Why do we live? What are we sent to do on this earth? Why do we suffer so and feel lonely? What are we waiting for? What is at the end of it all? Eh? Eh?"

Her tone was not sorrowful. Troubled perhaps at the beginning. But gradually it became confident. As if, though she didn't quite know the answer, she already sensed that it was good. And she was content at last that she had lived.

Then almost at once she drooped with weariness, with emotion and from touching the mysterious goal.

It was for them both the last journey down to the river.

Tontine was found dead one morning in her place behind the stove.

As for Martine, scarcely had she returned to the cramped little flat with no outlook and no light than she departed for those open spaces she had longed for all her life.

The Day's Visitors

Today a number of my friends dropped by to pay me a visit.

Some came that I didn't even see but merely heard. Among others the catbird.

My transistor radio beside me, I was in my swing, listening to a Bach cantata broadcast from Sainte-Anne-de-la-Pocatière.

Wonder of wonders! In some capital of the world, musicians interpreted the cantata, a tape fixed the music and now it was being transmitted across the river by La Pocatière to blend with the choir of my pines as they sang in full voice, "Hallelujah! The day is magnificent!"

Then the catbird joined in. He played a sort of accompaniment on the beak-flute. A tiny air of great delicacy, scarcely standing out above the instrumental ensemble.

The music from Sainte-Anne-de-la-Pocatière concluded and the flautist, carried by his own momentum, went on alone for a moment and stopped in the middle of a trill, abashed at having drawn attention to himself.

Then from a clump of cedars came a bird so modest looking in his slate-grey garb that I would never have taken him for the brilliant soloist of a minute ago. I had barely caught a glimpse of him when he left for a concert tour among my neighbours. And their gain was my loss.

Next seven cedar waxwings arranged themselves on various levels of the same tree, as if to be seen in all their beauty from every side at once.

Thereupon some of my human friends arrived. They saw the splendid birds in the tree and, as they are city folk and not spoiled by such sights, they exclaimed, "Ah! What magnificent creatures!"

Now that they had produced their effect, the cedar waxwings could depart. Which they did without further ado.

For a few minutes there were no more bird arrivals. My human guests were talking too loudly.

Except for the familiar crows that call to me every day as they pass, "How do you do?"

Ever since they surprised me one day, seated in my swing with a notebook on my knees, writing stories, they've been very careful not to disturb me. But even so, they can't bring themselves to pass over my house without at least saying, "Good day. Work well."

Later some herring gulls came to fly above our tedious earthly life. Sometimes in the course of the summer, no one quite knows why, they leave the river and their usual existence to venture quite far inland. On these occasions they soar over fields, hedges and houses. Do they feel a sudden urge to exchange lives with the land birds? Is it this or something else? We hear their cry, so similar to a squeaking gate, from close at hand. Yet the curious sound is beautiful to hear and so mysterious no one has ever learned to grasp its meaning.

But the herring gull is admirable above all for its flight.

We watched them glide, bank steeply on the edge of

one wing, lean back, you might think, into the wind and then right themselves—all their subtleties.

Their performance completed, the gulls too left the stage.

Next came a flock of swallows, also to be admired for their flight, all darts and spurts.

"Ah, swallows!" cried my friends.

It is a fact, this bird need only appear to be applauded. Never, to my knowledge, is any other bird made so much fuss over. True, the others in their modesty don't care in the least. So for about ten minutes nothing existed but the swallows.

Then a quarter of an hour later, as we were chatting loudly in the garden, into our conversation burst a bit of a phrase of neither rhyme nor reason, "Hast thou seen Fred-er-ic, Fred-er-ic, Fred-er-ic?"

It was the white-throated sparrow.

He sings when he pleases—whether there are guests with me or not, whether the day is fair or cloudy. He has his hour to sing and sing he will.

He has his hiding place too but you mustn't tell; it's just below the third branch from the bottom of the huge dark-green spruce next to my twisted birch.

My friends had begun to discuss the latest novels and current literary trends and the little fool kept on trilling "Hast thou seen . . ."

"What is that tiresome refrain?" asked Edmonde de Saint-Martin, the friend who talked the most.

I told her it was one of my very punctual and friendly visitors and added that each of us, either by the tone of voice or the nose or one of our other characteristics, is akin to some bird.

"Just listen to her!" said Edmonde de Saint-Martin mockingly and in a tone so reminiscent of "Hast thou seen . . ." that we all smiled—except Edmonde de Saint-Martin, who hadn't caught the resemblance.

Next there was a general rushing about. Someone—

Alice? Adrienne?—had caught sight of a hummingbird.

"It's here."

"No, it's there."

We were like mad things, running this way and that, trying to distinguish the hummingbird among the flowers.

"Do you see him?"

"No, do you?"

Finally we all spied the tiny helicopter at the same instant, rising and falling as it fed on flower after flower.

We saw its long beak burrow into the calix of a lily, withdraw, then prick the heart of a bluebell.

But the body of the bird we could scarcely glimpse, it's so small and swift, so similar in colour to the flowers it haunts.

Moving from one to the other, it appears to give each a peck and to love them all but only in passing.

"What a marvel!" cried Alice.

I put an arm around her neck. With us Alice is in a sense our hummingbird.

"Ah," she says to one of us, "there's no one quite like you," then turns and says to another, "Precious, you have no equal," and to still another, "Angel of my heart, you're absolutely unique."

And even though we know Alice repeats herself, we would rather have her refrain than that of the long-faced-who-dole-out-their-tidbits.

"Dear hummingbird," I said.

And the astonishing thing is that she didn't seem any too delighted with the compliment.

Soon afterwards my friends said they must leave if they were to be home before dark. We embraced in the house. Then on the steps. Then at the gate. (It is a fact that in the country people embrace more often than in the city.) Then they all waved as the car drew away. I was alone.

104

At this hour, which is always a little sad, when friends have just left and evening is about to fall, the world seems empty. I find myself circling aimlessly, not quite knowing what to do with myself, something is missing. I feel alone and finally I go and sit in the swing.

Then the robin appears. The robin is a bird with no great talent for flight or song, some say, though I myself enjoy his cheerful whistling like that of a man walking along with his hands in his pockets.

He is clad in perfectly plain grey-brown, his one adornment his pleasant close-fitting rusty-coloured vest. He arrives on foot. By day he can be seen perching on a branch or, on occasion, on one of the telephone wires. But in the evening he is just a little pedestrian like you and me. And his roundabout begins. I take four dancing steps. At the fifth, stop, thrust out my chest. Spy you out of the corner of my eye. And go back to the beginning: four dancing steps, chest out, quick sidelong glance.

Thus for hours, never losing patience, the robin keeps me company, inscribing a hundred times, a thousand, his wide circle around the swing.

I could probably get him to eat out of my hand, as the saying goes. But to what purpose? He comes as soon as I am alone, as soon as there is no more sound in me or around me. He was nowhere an instant ago. Now he never leaves me.

And I take my four dancing steps. And I thrust out my chest. And I glance at you out of the corner of my eye. And find that you look a bit sad this evening. Yet you needn't feel badly. It's true, there's always a painful moment when the day is about to end. I know something about that. One has more need than ever of a friend.

We sat up late that night, the robin and I. When it was almost dark, he was still there making his trip around the swing, after every fourth step giving me a lightning glance.

In the dark blue of the twilight I could just discern my companion, who was perhaps waiting for me to move before he retired.

So I played a trick on him. I gathered up my things and went into the house, acting as if I were going in for good. I closed the door, put on the lights. I let a moment pass.

Then I went back out very quietly and returned to the swing. There was no one there. The robin was perhaps already asleep, head tucked under his wing. But I no longer felt lonely. I was waiting for the first shooting stars.

The Night
of the Fireflies

Night had come. By now my friend the robin must be fast asleep in the hollow I know, in the thickest part of the hedge. God watch over his little ephemeral life! Shooting stars plummeted through the sky. I made a wish. I wished that the children of these regions would never tire of listening to their planet Earth. Even though in our day we receive news from the moon.

The stars shone brilliantly, then paled. Now they were half effaced, like tarnished nails in the ceiling of a chapel long abandoned to its memories. And I knew suddenly why the stars had dimmed. It was to give the fireflies their turn to shine. For now they appeared in their hundreds in the mild and tranquil night.

There was still a trace of music clinging to the tops of the trees. You might have thought they were quivering in their dreams. I could not resign myself to going in. On some rare nights one feels that it would be a crime not to wait up with them a little longer. Not this time because of the weight of the world's anguish but because the darkness was permeated with the most mysterious joy. And now came the bearers of the flame.

On the freshly mown grass they shone in brief bursts, like the intermittent beam of the lighthouse that signals to ships the passage round the tip of Ile aux Coudres.

On the dark grass innumerable tiny lighthouses flickered on and off as if to guide invisible travellers of the night. It might be you, it might be me, who often have to seek our way.

Then the little creatures rose into the air and now they were ballet dancers. And spin. And turn on the spot. And pivot, a diadem on the forehead. The sky was full of them. It was impossible to follow all of them at once. Who invented this choreography of such tireless fantasy? Fire above, fire a little farther away, and fire suddenly almost in my hand. Had I been quicker I might have grasped the flying flame. Berthe has told me that as a child she caught more than one firefly. I myself would fear that I might shatter the delicate mechanism that releases the swift blue flame. And I am troubled by the thought that by day I might mistake for a common insect one of these celebrants of fire.

Why do they exist? It is said that they announce hot weather but no doubt they announce very much more.

And now they were a little calmer. No longer dancing in the air, they had become ordinary strollers. They moved back and forth midway between earth and sky, the fire of their little lamps revealed or hidden according to the twists and turns of the mysterious promenade.

The night was indescribably tender. One might have believed oneself on the threshold of the infinite, ready to touch at last the goal to which, unknown to ourselves, our spirits strain. The brief flames continued to flutter through the blurred dark of the night.

Their existence is fugitive. Perhaps fireflies live only long enough to give forth their fleeting light.

Like all of us.

Fortunate are those who at least once before they are extinguished shine with their full light.

Caught in God's fire.

The Dead Child

Why then did the memory of that dead child seek me out in the very midst of the summer that sang? When till then no intimation of sorrow had come to me through the dazzling revelations of that season.

I had just arrived in a very small village in Manitoba to finish the school year as replacement for a teacher who had fallen ill or simply, for all I know, become discouraged.

The principal of the Normal School had called me to his office towards the end of my year's study. "Well," he said, "there's a school available for the month of June. It's not much but it's an opportunity. When the time comes for you to apply for a permanent position, you'll be able to say you've had experience. Believe me, it's a help."

And so I found myself at the beginning of June in that very poor village—just a few shacks built on sand, with nothing around it but spindly spruce trees. "A month," I asked myself, "will that be long enough for me to become attached to the children or for the children to become attached to me? Will a month be worth the effort?''

Perhaps the same calculation was in the minds of the children who presented themselves at school that first day of June—''Is this teacher going to stay long enough to be worth the effort?''—for I had never seen children's faces so dejected, so apathetic, or perhaps sorrowful. I had had so little experience. I myself was hardly more than a child.

Nine o'clock came. The room was hot as an oven. Sometimes in Manitoba, especially in the sandy areas, an incredible heat settles in during the first days of June.

Scarcely knowing where or how to begin, I opened the attendance book and called the roll. The names were for the most part very French and today they still return to my memory, like this, for no reason: Madeleine Bérubé, Josephat Brisset, Emilien Dumont, Cécile Lépine. . . .

But most of the children who rose and answered ''Present, mamzelle,'' when their names were called had the slightly narrowed eyes, warm colouring and jet black hair that told of métis blood.

They were beautiful and exquisitely polite; there was really nothing to reproach them for except the inconceivable distance they maintained between themselves and me. It crushed me. ''Is this what children are like then,'' I asked myself with anguish, ''untouchable, barricaded in some region where you can't reach them?''

I came to the name Yolande Chartrand.

No one answered. It was becoming hotter by the minute. I wiped a bit of perspiration from my forehead. I repeated the name and, when there was still no answer, I looked up at faces that seemed to me completely indifferent.

Then from the back of the classroom, above the buzzing of flies, there arose a voice I at first couldn't place. ''She's dead, mamzelle. She died last night.''

112

Perhaps even more distressing than the news was the calm level tone of the child's voice. As I must have seemed unconvinced, all the children nodded gravely as if to say, "It's true."

Suddenly a sense of impotence greater than any I can remember weighed upon me.

"Ah," I said, lost for words.

"She's already laid out," said a boy with eyes like coals. "They're going to bury her for good tomorrow."

"Ah," I repeated.

The children seemed a little more relaxed now and willing to talk, in snatches and at long intervals.

A boy in the middle of the room offered, "She got worse the last two months."

We looked at one another in silence for a long time, the children and I. I now understood that the expression in their eyes that I had taken for indifference was a heavy sadness. Much like this stupefying heat. And we were only at the beginning of the day.

"Since Yolande ... has been laid out," I suggested, "and she was your schoolmate ... and would have been my pupil ... would you like ... after school at four o'clock ... for us to go and visit her?"

On the small, much too serious faces there appeared the trace of a smile, wary, still very sad but a sort of smile just the same.

"It's agreed then, we'll go to visit her, her whole class."

From that moment, despite the enervating heat and the sense that haunted us all, I feel sure, that human efforts are all ultimately destined to a sort of failure, the children fixed their attention as much as possible on what I was teaching and I did my best to rouse their interest.

At five past four I found most of them waiting for me at the door, a good twenty children but making no more noise than if they were being kept in after school. Several of them went ahead to show me the way. Others pressed around me so closely I could scarcely move. Five or six of the smaller ones took me by the hand or the shoulder and pulled me forward gently as if they were leading a blind person. They did not talk, merely held me enclosed in their circle.

Together, in this way, we followed a track through the sand. Here and there thin spruce trees formed little clumps. The air was now barely moving. In no time the village was behind us—forgotten, as it were.

We came to a wooden cabin standing in isolation among the little trees. Its door was wide open, so we were able to see the dead child from quite far off. She had been laid out on rough boards suspended between two straight chairs set back to back. There was nothing else in the room. Its usual contents must have been crowded into the only other room of the house for, besides a stove and table and a few pots on the floor, I could see a bed and a mattress piled with clothes. But no chairs. Clearly the two used as supports for the boards on which the dead child lay were the only ones in the house.

The parents had undoubtedly done all they could for their child. They had covered her with a clean sheet. They had given her a room to herself. Her mother, probably, had arranged her hair in the two very tight braids that framed the thin face. But some pressing need had sent them away: perhaps the purchase of a coffin in town or a few more boards to make her one themselves. At any rate, the dead child was alone in the room that had been emptied for her—alone, that is to say, with the flies. A faint odour of death must have attracted them. I saw one with a blue body walk over her forehead. I immediately placed myself near her head and began to move my hand back and forth to drive the flies away.

The child had a delicate little face, very wasted, with the serious expression I had seen on the faces of most of the children here, as if the cares of the adults had crushed them all too early. She might have been ten or eleven years old. If she had lived a little longer, I reminded myself, she would have been one of my pupils. She would have learned something from me. I would have given her something to keep. A bond would have been formed between me and this little stranger—who knows, perhaps even for life.

As I contemplated the dead child, those words "for life"—as if they implied a long existence—seemed to me the most rash and foolish of all the expressions we use so lightly.

In death the child looked as if she were regretting some poor little joy she had never known. I continued at least to prevent the flies from settling upon her. The children were watching me. I realized that they now expected everything from me, though I didn't know much more than they and was just as confused. Still I had a sort of inspiration.

"Don't you think Yolande would like to have someone with her always till the time comes to commit her to the ground?"

The faces of the children told me I had struck the right note.

"We'll take turns then, four or five around her every two hours, until the funeral."

They agreed with a glow in their dark eyes.

"We must be careful not to let the flies touch Yolande's face."

They nodded to show they were in agreement. Standing around me, they now felt a trust in me so complete it terrified me.

In a clearing among the spruce trees a short distance away, I noticed a bright pink stain on the ground whose source I didn't yet know. The sun slanted upon it, making it flame, the one moment in this day that had been touched by a certain grace.

"What sort of girl was she?" I asked.

At first the children didn't understand. Then a boy of about the same age said with tender seriousness, "She was smart, Yolande."

The other children looked as if they agreed.

"And did she do well in school?"

"She didn't come very often this year. She was always being absent."

"Our teacher before last this year said Yolande could have done well."

"How many teachers have you had this year?"

"You're the third, mamzelle. I guess the teachers find it too lonesome here."

"What did Yolande die of?"

"T.B., mamzelle," they replied with a single voice, as if this was the customary way for children to die around here.

They were eager to talk about her now. I had succeeded in opening the poor little doors deep within them that no one perhaps had ever much wanted to see opened. They told me moving facts about her brief life. One day on her way home from school—it was in February; no, said another, in March—she had lost her reader and wept inconsolably for weeks. To study her lesson after that, she had to borrow a book from one of the others—and I saw on the faces of some of them that they'd grudged lending their readers and would always regret this. Not having a dress for her first communion, she entreated till her mother finally made her one from the only curtain in the house: "the one from this room ... a beautiful lace curtain, mamzelle."

"And did Yolande look pretty in her lace curtain dress?" I asked.

They all nodded deeply, in their eyes the memory of a pleasant image.

I studied the silent little face. A child who had loved books, solemnity and decorous attire. Then I glanced again at that astonishing splash of pink in the melancholy landscape. I realized suddenly that it was a mass of wild roses. In June they open in great sheets all over Manitoba, growing from the poorest soil. I felt some alleviation.

"Let's go and pick some roses for Yolande."

On the children's faces there appeared the same slow smile of gentle sadness I had seen when I suggested visiting the body.

In no time we were gathering roses. The children were not yet cheerful, far from that, but I could hear them at least talking to one another. A sort of rivalry had gripped them. Each vied to see who could pick the most roses or the brightest, those of a deep shade that was almost red.

From time to time one tugged at my sleeve, "Mamzelle, see the lovely one I've found!"

On our return we pulled them gently apart and scattered petals over the dead child. Soon only her face emerged from the pink drift. Then—how could this be? —it looked a little less forlorn.

The children formed a ring around their schoolmate and said of her without the bitter sadness of the morning, "She must have got to heaven by this time."

Or, "She must be happy now."

I listened to them, already consoling themselves as best they could for being alive.

But why, oh why, did the memory of that dead child seek me out today in the very midst of the summer that sang?

Was it brought to me just now by the wind with the scent of roses?

A scent I have not much liked since the long ago June when I went to that poorest of villages—to acquire, as they say, experience.

The Islands

It is not in clear weather that one can best decipher the distance. Under storm clouds or just before the onset of the bitter cold, we in our part of the world can see some little islands in the open river that are never visible at other times. But when we've had them as companions for only a day or so, they drift away into a sort of dream existence where from time to time we can grasp the vague outline of first one and then another for an instant more.

In the torpid heat of summer the islands vanish completely. For weeks at a time we don't see them even once far across the river near Montmagny. In fact, there is no more open river. On those warm singing days of almost no horizon, we live confined and rocked by the west wind, held in cocoons of faintly whispering water and rustling leaves. And unhappiness seems far away. We find ourselves almost forgetting to think about the islands.

It seems that there are twenty-one in all scattered between Ile d'Orléans and Ile aux Coudres and that only two or three are inhabited. As against those few that are

119

alive with lighted windows at night, visiting back and forth, and the sound of human voices, the greater number are as silent as in the first days of creation. Only foghorns reach them in the splashing immensity of the river. During the summer some sailor on the deck of a freighter that has strayed a little way off course may see one or other of them barely rising above the water and have the impression that he has discovered "his" island.

But all that singing summer we of the north shore had not caught sight of the islands over by the south shore more than once or twice.

Came the sharp days of fall. In the houses animals and people drew closer to the fire. And it was then, strangely, that the south shore drew closer to us so that suddenly, with unusual clarity, we observed churches, roofs and even barns that only the day before we could not see at all. Closer too drew the islands near the south shore. One after the other they came in sight, born, you might say, when everything in nature was dying. Now they were all lined up against the dark blue horizon, twenty-one islands, some of them not much more than circles of land grass surrounded by sea grass.

We began to dream again.

"What are they like?" I asked Berthe for the hundredth time.

She replied that she knew very little about them though she could dimly remember hearing her father say that his own father used to row over to one or other of them in a chaloupe to cut wild hay.

"So they would sleep on one of the islands?"

"Yes, I daresay," said Berthe.

She thought she could recall tales of those days that had been passed down in the family for generations. The men had a tent, at the very least a piece of sail for shelter. Perhaps they used to make a hut out of branches. If there was a sudden storm as happens so frequently on the river at this time of year, they would have to wait two or three days, maybe even longer, for calm weather, huddled in their precarious refuge on one or other of those low tufts of grass. Meanwhile the women in their houses on the north shore would be half dead with anxiety.

The sky remained dark for several days and the uninhabited islands were with us for a while longer. They obsessed us.

"Berthe, I've never wanted to go anywhere as much as to one of those little islands."

She smiled patiently.

"It's not easy. We'd have to go to Quebec. Take the bus to the south shore. Go the long way round by land. At Montmagny find someone to take us to the islands by boat or helicopter. If we went by boat we'd have to have the tide with us."

"In short, to go that little way to those islands we'd need Joliet and Père Marquette."

"Or my grandfather," said Berthe.

While we'd been talking, jet planes had crossed the distant sky. We could not see them, just the trails of smoke that marked their passage. People to whom earth was as invisible as the jet was to us were on their way to London, Paris, Amsterdam.

Almost directly over our quiet little village jets begin their descent for Dorval. Altitude and atmospheric conditions permitting, we see their traces. Otherwise there is nothing to indicate that high above us are travellers returning from London, Paris, Amsterdam.

We grew tired of peering into the sky for signs of voyaging. They are so common now. Have lost their hold upon us. We returned to the islands over by Montmagny. They were all present for a moment more, strung out along the water like a series of points of suspension.

"Are there any animals on those islands?"

"If so, they must be very small. How could they have

121

crossed the water? Unless cats and dogs have been taken there to be abandoned. It would be a sad life for them. There must be plenty of birds, however."

All signs of voyaging had been obliterated from the high sky.

I began to dream again.

"Still we must at least go and discover our little islands, Berthe."

"Yes," she agreed. "We must."

The trouble was, we knew there was only one way: get up at daybreak, row across twenty miles of water, in some places dangerously rough, land in dark of night in a wild cove, make a fire, face what was faced by the people of bygone times.

We looked at one another ruefully. We are well aware that we are not of the stuff of which our ancestors were made. We tell ourselves in consolation that our courage lies elsewhere and I suppose this is true to some extent.

However, those insignificant little islands some sixteen or eighteen miles across the water continued to reproach us for a long time still.

Then the icy fogs enclosed us. The contours of the islands over by Montmagny disappeared. Like the birds that were leaving us for the winter.

What is the appeal of islands to our hearts?

Is it not that we are all lost children who long for a common shore?

Once More
to the Pool
of Monsieur Toong

That summer again Berthe and I walked along the railway track one evening to the pool of Monsieur Toong. Though the cordial greeting of the musician of the water would never again ring out, this was no reason to fail the solitary pine or the bluebells that draw from the rough ballast their colour so similar to the summer sky. Though all that delights us dies a little every day, we must not withdraw our hearts in advance.

And we were well recompensed. Once again the pool was inhabited. By whom? What a surprise it was to find Milord Mallard with his Lady. For there they were, revolving in silence in the ancient pool, which their presence made young again. There was still a hint of brightness at one side of the water and in this brighter patch the beautiful happy birds turned gravely around one another, wing brushing wing. And the water mirrored their gay costumes down to the smallest detail: the narrow forest-green hoods and yellow beaks, even the brilliant, slightly hard little eyes.

We did not try to engage them in conversation since

mallards seem little inclined for talk. Very preoccupied with themselves, they glanced at us rather loftily for a moment and went on circling one another politely.

We resumed our walk, as happy to find the pool alive once more as if we had seen a light suddenly turned on in a house that has long been dark. The beauty of the mallards did not replace the memory of Monsieur Toong. One joined the other.

Slightly farther on, another joyful surprise. All along this stretch of shore, on the banks of silt laid down through the years by tide and current, there are islets of the most pliant grass in the world, for twice a day at high tide the river covers it with vivifying water.

There is nothing abrupt here. Gently the water prevails upon the grasses, gently it withdraws; gently the wet grasses slow and calm the last undulations of the river.

But who was that flying around without fear or haste? Truly it was beyond belief; never before had I seen killdeers so tranquil and content with their lot.

Three of them—father, mother, child—were flying back and forth over the grassy verges whose green was darkening by the minute. They passed between this submerged green and the snowy white of the clouds in a sort of long circular promenade, seemingly with no desire to leave their enchanted circle. And for once I had encountered killdeers who were not contradicting one another. We could hear them quite clearly in the silence and peace of the twilight, talking together in low voices, and what they were saying seemed to be, "How peaceful it is here . . . here . . . here . . ."

"Ah yes," we agreed, "how peaceful it is here . . . here . . . here. . . . And do try not to forget it!"

But we were still full of unsatisfied curiosity.

"Why is it," we asked, "that other killdeers haven't also discovered these grassy verges, these thousands of blessed hiding places? Why didn't they find this refuge?

Why? Why?"

Then it seemed to us that a short distance away in the murmuring peace, the birds were reproaching us for our paltry human questions.

"All are not happy at the same moment," they reminded us. "One day it's one, the next day another ... some never, alas."

They soared out over the river, all three saying much the same thing in the same tone, a little weakened now by the distance so that we could believe we were hearing a single voice, "Here we are happy. ... Over there they are not. ... When everyone is happy together, it will be paradise ... paradise ... paradise. ..."

SELECTED NEW CANADIAN LIBRARY TITLES

Asterisks (*) denote titles of New Canadian Library Classics

McCLELLAND AND STEWART LIMITED
publishers of The New Canadian Library
would like to keep you informed about
new additions to this unique series.

For a complete listing of titles and
current prices – or if you wish to be added
to our mailing list to receive future catalogues
and other new book information – write:

BOOKNEWS
McClelland and Stewart Limited
25 Hollinger Road
Toronto, Canada M4B 3G2

McClelland and Stewart books are
available at all good bookstores.

Booksellers should be happy to order from our catalogues
any titles which they do not regularly stock.